Desert
Cut

Books by Betty Webb

Desert Noir
Desert Wives
Desert Shadows
Desert Run
Desert Cut

Desert
Cut

A Lena Jones Mystery

Betty Webb

Poisoned Pen Press

First Trade Paperback Edition 2008

10 9 8 7 6 5 4 3 2 1

Library of Congress Catalog Card Number: 2007935699

ISBN: 978-1-59058-583-2   Trade Paperback

Poisoned Pen Press
6962 E. First Ave., Ste. 103
Scottsdale, AZ 85251
www.poisonedpenpress.com
info@poisonedpenpress.com

Printed in the United States of America

To Paul, as always

Acknowledgments

Many thanks go out to the Sheridan Street Irregulars, who were generous with their time and suggestions for this project. I am especially grateful to Arizona author Sharon Magee and her excellent *Geronimo! Stories of an American Legend*, for providing some of the information used here. Thanks also to Marge Purcell, Debra McCarthy, and Rod Fenson. Most of all, I owe an enormous debt to the many courageous women and men whose writings—in defiance of belief, tradition, and death threats—brought the central theme of *Desert Cut* to my attention.

Angels wear many faces.

Although inspired in part by true events,
the following story is fictional and does not depict
any actual people, events, or organizations.
For more information,
See the Author's Note and appendices
beginning on page 275.

Chapter One

The morning was perfect. Early October, a clear sky, a symphony of songbirds, and here in the foothills of Southern Arizona's secluded Dragoon Mountains, no sign of the urban pollution we had left behind in Phoenix. But there is always a snake in Eden. A hint of the serpent slithered into view when my horse topped the ridge and I saw a coyote tugging at something white.

Fabric. Protruding from a mound of fresh earth.

"Warren!" I shouted. "Get back!"

Cops—and I had been one, once—know that few people bother to bury yardage. Not out here in the desert, they don't. Perhaps a child's pet lay underneath, a dog, a cat. But I saw no twig cross marker, something grieving children usually insisted upon.

Ignoring me, Warren galloped his horse up the slope and reined it in next to mine. I repeated my command, since the least amount of damage done to a body dump, the better, but, as he had so many times before, he misunderstood me. "Listen, Lena, I'm getting tired of all this, and your behavior isn't help-ing." Then, spotting the coyote, he fell silent.

Interrupted at its meal, the animal pivoted to face us. Fabric dangled from its teeth, one end of the cloth stained with blood.

Warren gasped.

"Do. Not. Move." I told him, then dug my heels into my horse and charged the animal.

Snarling, it ran off, disappearing into a distant creosote thicket. It didn't come out the other side, and I knew why. In the desert, animals took their meals where they found them, and a body dump could provide a two-day banquet, depending on the size of the victim. The coyote was simply waiting for us to move on.

I looked down at the small bundle of rags the animal had unearthed. No, not rags.

A child.

She was wrapped in white and from the condition of her body, not long dead. Her grave had been dug so shallowly that she lay half in, half out, of what was supposed to be her final resting place. An angel smothered in dirt.

At least the coyote hadn't had time to do much damage.

Behind me, Warren called, "Lena? That's not a kid, is it?" His twins were seven, and about this girl's size. Unlike his little blondes, she was black, her fine-boned ebony face sculpted with delicate features. A beauty, even in death.

Keeping an eye on the creosote thicket lest the coyote reemerge, I rode back to him. "I'm afraid so. Give me your cell phone."

With a shaking hand, he passed it to me. I punched in 9-1-1, said what needed to be said, and gave the dispatcher our location. Yes, a child. Yes, we would wait. I rang off, amazed at the steadiness in my voice.

Not yet ready to look down again, I stared up at that hard blue sky and saw vultures riding the thermals. I tried staring at the Dragoons, but that didn't work, either. The mountains simply reminded me of other deaths. Once a sanctuary for Geronimo and Cochise during the Apache Wars of the late 1800s, they now served as a hiding place for the illegals who slipped over the nearby Mexican border on their way to Tucson. Mexican nationals, mostly, with a sprinkling of Central and South Americans. Every now and then the Border Patrol discovered a few Africans and Middle Easterners among them, desperate people seeking easier access to the U.S. than post-9/11 immigration policies allowed.

The illegals who were caught are among the lucky ones. The desert kills the others.

I looked down at the child and willed myself not to cry.

Cochise County Sheriff Bill Avery, accompanied by a deputy and a two-man forensics unit, arrived too long after my call. When I revealed my displeasure at the lag time, Avery, a desert-browned man with startling blue eyes, merely shrugged.

"We get this a lot, Ms. Jones. It's a shame, but short of completing that fence between us and Mexico, there's nothing we can do except collect the bodies when it all goes wrong." His eyes were not devoid of compassion, but the flat line of his mouth revealed a peace officer who found it hard to care when there was so much to care about.

"Still. A child."

Not even a blink. "The crossing's tough on kids. Now tell me again what you two are doing way out here. Camping, did you say?"

Behind me, Warren made an exasperated sound. In his comfortable Hollywood world, law officers treated Oscar-winning film makers with respect. But this wasn't California, it was the badlands of Southern Arizona, where Warren and I were nothing more than two strangers whose discovery had just made the sheriff's job harder.

"Not really camping," I told him. "We're renting a tepee over at the Apache Dream Bed and Breakfast."

One corner of the sheriff's mouth pulled up. "Oh, yeah. I know those things. Tepees, which the Apaches never used. All the amenities, including heat, beds, and champagne breakfasts." He looked Warren up and down, taking in the designer jeans, custom-made ostrich-skin boots, the diamond-sprinkled Rolex. "Not from around here, are you, sir?"

"What's that got to do with anything?" Warren snapped. "You need to get tracking dogs up here, a full forensics team. Undocumented alien or not, that child deserves a full investigation." He started to say something else, then head down, walked away.

The sheriff watched him for a moment, then turned to me, his eyes flickering briefly over the scar on my forehead. "Actually, I did a quick check on you both and found out you're an ex-cop who's set up shop as a private investigator. Mr. Quinn over there's some sort of movie director. I'd think this is a pretty unusual place for you two to be taking a vacation. Especially a sensitive soul like him."

Having been in the sheriff's position many times myself, I understood what he was doing, so I repeated my story. After finishing work on a documentary about a WWII German POW camp near Scottsdale, Warren had taken the raw footage to California for editing. I went along to do some consulting work on *Desert Eagle*, one of those over-glamorized television crime dramas that makes everyone involved obscene amounts of money. Three days ago, after finishing our respective duties, we embarked on a working vacation together, with Warren scouting the area for his new project: a documentary on the Apache Wars.

"You headed back to California after this?" It was hard to tell from Avery's flat tone if he believed me or not.

"If you did all that checking, Sheriff, you know where Desert Investigations is based. The TV thing, I just fly from Sky Harbor to LAX, attend a production meeting, then fly home. When this gets cleared up, I'm returning to Scottsdale."

Avery jerked his head toward Warren. "How about him?"

There was no point in telling him that during the past few months, my relationship with Warren had developed several conflicts. "Beverly Hills. He has a business to run, too."

Then I paused. "Sheriff?"

Avery's eyes were as cold as the day had become. "What?"

"We didn't know her."

A dangerous smile. I'd been wrong. He *did* care.

An angry wind tore down from the Dragoons and whipped at the dead girl's white wrappings. In the distance, a coyote howled. Her finder, lamenting the loss of his meal?

The sheriff winced at the sound. Like me, he had seen the bite marks on the child's hand. "Damn things," he said into the wind. "No wonder the ranchers shoot them." Then he gestured at the tiny body, which the crime scene techs had now completely uncovered. "See how carefully she's wrapped, Ms. Jones? That white stuff, it's probably a shroud. She mattered to the person who buried her."

Yet she had been abandoned in this wilderness.

A beautiful little girl.

Left for the coyotes and vultures.

Jesus.

Chapter Two

Warren and I tried to pick up our vacation where we left off, but I kept seeing the child's face on our ride back to the Apache Dream B&B, during dinner, and even while asleep, where she replaced my usual nightmare. Around three, when I awoke screaming, Warren took me in his arms and traced gentle fingers across the bullet scar on my forehead.

"It happened a long time ago, Lena. You're safe now."

Brushing his fingers away, I buried my face in his chest. I usually hated displaying any kind of vulnerability, but Warren and I were both damaged goods, and so we understood each other. The son of a Hollywood porn king who hadn't known where the screen left off and real life began, he stilled his own nightmares by filming documentaries about society's victims. As for me, I tracked down the victim makers. Sometimes it even helped.

"Better now?" Warren asked, stroking my hair.

"Yes," I lied. But I kept seeing the gun in my mother's hand, kept hearing the shot that ended my childhood.

You can't force yourself to relax, but I tried. I thought clichéd happy thoughts: horses, cactus blooms, the smells of the desert after rain, heavenly choirs…

I stiffened. No. Not choirs.

Warren's baritone penetrated the memory of people singing hymns on a bus. "This is senseless, Lena. Let's pay up and leave."

"But you still have so much to do." I didn't want my night-mares to interfere with his life. It was bad enough they interfered with my own.

When he shook his head, I realized I wasn't the only one having trouble sleeping. "Maybe if I weren't a father it would be different," he said, then added, "We'll leave as soon as it's light."

Relieved, I agreed, thinking that the decision would allow me some rest. The interior of the teepee was dark, but through an opening in the leather-flap doorway, I saw the full moon bathing the main building of the B&B in creamy light. Stars not visible in neon-lit Phoenix spangled the sky. The wind, so strong in the afternoon, had eased to a whispery moan. Lulled, I finally fell asleep.

But the nightmare was waiting. The singing started and my mother raised her gun. This time, though, the child she shot in the face wasn't me.

It was the girl in the desert.

The next morning Warren and I bid farewell to our hosts, two retired real estate brokers from Scottsdale, and promised to return, but I doubted we would. For us, the Dragoon Mountains were ruined forever. As the rented Mercedes wound through low foothills toward I-10, I wondered aloud, "Do you think the autopsy's done yet?"

Warren stared at me, appalled. "I don't want to think about it at all."

"Me neither." *Oh, her beautiful face.* I touched my own scar.

"Lena, a child dies getting across the border, her parents stop to bury her, then continue on their way. It's the sheriff's business, not ours. All we can do is feel terrible about it."

"I need to know how she died."

His hand slammed the steering wheel. "You don't already know? She died from dehydration! That's what gets them all! This damned desert, that damned border!"

Resting my head against his shoulder, I massaged his neck and felt his tension slip away as the saguaro-sprinkled landscape streaked by. We drove silently until we saw the fork in the road. The left would take us to I-10.

"Turn right," I told Warren.

"Right? But that'll take us into Los Perdidos."

"I know."

"You agreed we'd go back to Scottsdale."

I shook my head. "I need to see the sheriff."

His fist hit the steering wheel again with such force that for a fleeting moment I worried the air bag might explode out. "No, you don't *need* to see the sheriff, Lena. You just want to. Why can't you ever leave things alone?"

Averting my head so he couldn't see the tears in my eyes, I answered, "Because I can't." The fact that the girl was now beyond her sufferings made no difference to me. She deserved justice, and to ease my own nightmares, I needed to make sure she got it.

So many children didn't.

Warren pulled the car to the side of the road. After a few seconds, his blue eyes darkened with concern, and he leaned over to touch my cheek. "Lena, let it go."

I said nothing.

"You can't save the world."

"I know that."

He shook his head. "I don't think you do."

"You're a good one to talk."

Sighing, he pulled the car onto the road again. Fifteen minutes later we were in Los Perdidos.

The small city was your typical schizophrenic Arizona town. Named *the lost ones* for a group of cavalrymen who in 1881 had set out in search of Geronimo and never returned, it was an uneasy mixture of New West and Old. The edge of town boasted functional modern structures that housed real estate offices and chiropractors, but leftovers from Territorial days made up the city center, where every other business seemed to be named after Geronimo and his band.

This was the area that drew Los Perdidos' thriving tourist trade, with its raised board sidewalks, authentic saloons, Western store fronts, and the popular Apache Museum. Unfortunately, these charms had been marred by the insertion of an antiseptic steel-and-glass government complex that housed the sheriff's office.

As Warren parked the Mercedes next to an unmarked sedan, obviously a sheriff's vehicle, he made one last attempt to dissuade me. "Lena, we can still salvage this vacation. Let's check into a resort, get a seaweed wrap, and not worry about anything other than ourselves."

"I'm sorry," I said, climbing out of the car. "You're right. I *do* want to save the world, and when I can't, I have to figure out what went wrong. That child…" I couldn't get her face out of my head.

While most sheriffs' offices aren't quite as casual as that of Andy Griffith's fabled Mayberry, they can be cheerful places, with snacks on desks and deputies cracking wise. This was not the case here, where the front office bristled with grim-faced men who stopped talking the moment I walked through the door.

I spoke into the silence. "I'm Lena Jones, the woman who found the body yesterday."

"Wish you hadn't," muttered a rotund man whose uniform stretched tightly over his too-generous stomach. His remark earned him an elbow jab from the lanky deputy next to him.

"Is Sheriff Avery in?"

"He's busy," said the elbow-jabber.

"Maybe one of you could tell me if the autopsy's been done."

No answer, no "tells," not even a shifting of feet. There was a lot of tension in the room for a dead illegal, even though the illegal was a child. Before I said anything else, the door at the far end of the room opened and Sheriff Avery stuck out his head. "Ms. Jones, go back to Scottsdale. We may not be as flashy as you folks up north, but we can handle this."

Nothing like a warm welcome. "I just want some information about that little girl."

"She's not your problem." Although his face bore a neutral expression, it appeared even more drawn than before, which I thought odd if the girl had simply died of natural causes. But as he had noted yesterday, border crossings were hard on kids.

"All I want is to find out her cause of death, if you don't mind. You'll have to release the information to the media, anyway. If they ask." I tried to sound polite, not confrontational.

A slight narrowing of his eyes. "What makes you think we already know?"

From the tension in this room, I started to say, but stopped myself just in time. "I'm an ex-cop, remember?"

"Very ex. You left the job years ago."

Recognizing the stall, I took evasive action. "Okay. What's the medical examiner's name? If you don't tell me, I'll just call my office and find out."

"From that Pima Indian partner of yours."

At least the sheriff's background check had been thorough. "That's right. Give my partner a computer and before you can say 'somebody's keeping a secret,' he'll have your mother's maiden name and the day and time she first kissed your father."

Avery glowered, then appeared to change his mind. "The M.E.'s name is Dr. Nelson Lanphear. Now like I said, please go away."

"Is he at the hospital now?"

"You think he gives me his schedule?" Without another word, the sheriff closed his office door. At least he didn't slam it.

The deputies suddenly found business that needed attending to, so amid a great rustling of paperwork, I left.

Outside, the sun blazed down as if it wanted to bring back summer. I found Warren under the shade of a gnarled mesquite, studying the street with a worried expression. "We need to get the hell out of Dodge, Lena. These people look like something out of a Wes Craven movie."

Since I'd spent several pleasant weekends in Los Perdidos in the past, his comment surprised me. Los Perdidos residents tended to be friendly and hardly resemble characters in a slasher film. Yet when I looked around, I saw the reason for Warren's concern. On the corner, a group of men stood watching us, their body language as tense as that of the sheriff and his deputies. At the other end of the street, another group huddled together in a tense knot, glaring at Warren as if he had just insulted their sisters.

"You're right. Something's going on."

He turned away from their glares and looked longingly at the Mercedes. "An astute observation. Can we leave now?"

I wanted to, but the memory of the girl's face wouldn't let me. "Not yet."

Our stop at the hospital turned out to be a waste of time. Probably built by the same architect who had slapped together the city center's government complex, its facade was even less welcoming than most medical buildings. The only decorative touch was the bronze plaque by the front door that proclaimed: DONATED BY LEE CASEY IN LOVING MEMORY OF CAROLINE SOMERS CASEY.

Once inside, the stark interior mirrored the building's exterior, and the acrid scent of Lysol wafted along unadorned hallways painted the color of spoiled milk. In a glass booth overseeing a mostly-empty waiting room, a faded redhead informed us that today was Dr. Lanphear's day off. She added that she was swamped with work, so if neither of us was sick or injured, let her get to it. Studiously ignoring us, she began leafing through a small stack of insurance forms.

Baffled by the obvious brush-off, we returned to the car.

"This is crazy, Lena," Warren said. "That child's dead, just another victim of this mess we call a border."

By now, my sorrow had hardened into determination. "I feel like a drink, how about you?"

"Are you serious?" Warren had been in a Twelve Step program for years.

Not knowing who my parents were and fearing what kind of genetic load I might be carrying, I didn't drink, either. "Let's find a bar. The closer to the hospital, the better."

"For God's sake, why?"

"People talk in bars," I explained. "Especially when they've been there for a while. If you're too tired, I can drive."

He slid into the driver's seat. "One bar, coming up."

A few minutes later we were hunkered over Cokes at the Geronimo Lounge, which appeared even seedier on the inside than it had from the curb. Even though Arizona had passed a stringent No Smoking law, a fog of smoke and stale beer assaulted my nostrils. Someone had started to paint the cement floor a swampy green, then gave up halfway through. Moths had attacked the stuffed antelope head mounted above the cash register, and the glass had long been cracked on the large photograph of a genial-appearing Geronimo—wearing a top hat, no less—that hung on the rear wall. A damaged speaker on the juke box hissed its way through the end of a George Strait tune, then began crucifying the Rolling Stones. Still shy of ten a.m., the lounge held few customers, but the drinkers slumped over the long, scarred bar looked like they'd been exercising their elbows since sunup.

Perfect.

I found my prey, an elderly man sitting alone at a table by the men's room, his nose almost as red as the Budweiser sign on the wall behind him. By his right hand, a copy of the *Cochise County Observer* lay open to a half-finished crossword puzzle. He sipped slowly on his Molson's as if trying to make it last.

I walked up to the bar, ordered a bottle of Molson's, and took it over to his table. "Happy Birthday."

His looked up, his eyes clear. "Not my birthday, Blondie."

"It will be eventually."

"Good one. What do you want? Woman looks like you, she doesn't need to go around picking up geezers like me. Especially not with that flashy boyfriend of yours sitting over there. Or are you recruiting for some weirded-out threesome?"

I smiled. "That's a good one, too."

His grin revealed a mouth full of cheap dentures. "I wasn't always this old, Blondie."

"Don't be naughty. I just want to ask you some questions."

"That'll cost you another Molson's."

Hearing this, Warren fetched a bottle, then resumed his seat, making it clear he wanted nothing to do with either of us. I waited until the old man took another sip, then asked, "You hear about that little girl found dead in the Dragoons?"

He studied the label on his beer bottle. "Who the hell hasn't?"

"You being a local, I figure you might know where she is now."

"She ain't playing hopscotch, that's for sure." When I drew his new Molson's away, he added, "She's in that basement cooler room over at the hospital."

I shoved the beer toward him again. "They do the autopsy yet?"

"Soon's they brought her in, is what I hear." He placed a hand around each beer bottle. "Get me another Molson's."

Warren brought over two more, his face stiff with disapproval.

"I only drink in here once a week," the old man explained. "On Sundays."

"Today's Saturday."

"Yeah, well, some weeks are worse than others." With his stooped back and age-spotted skin, he probably hadn't seen a good week in years.

I leaned forward, making certain my next question didn't carry to the bar. "Do you know the cause of death?"

"What makes you think I might?"

"An educated guess. You work crossword puzzles, which means you pay attention to things."

"You some kind of Sherlock Holmes?"

"Kind of." I took my Private Investigator's I.D. out of my pocket and flashed it at him.

"Lena Jones, girl detective. Ha! You working this case?"

Case. His choice of words told me I was on the right track. "I'm not sure yet, which is why I need to know cause of death."

He picked up his beer, chugged it, then opened a new one. Halfway through that, he belched, then chugged some more.

Just as I was about to take away the other bottles, he said in a voice as low as mine, "She bled out. The assistant to the medical examiner's my nephew. He told his ex-wife, who told my sister, who told me and anyone else who would listen."

"Bled out from what?"

A subtle chorus of sounds from the bar, as if several drinkers had shifted on their bar stools at the same time. Apparently our voices weren't low enough.

My informant started to speak, stopped, then started again. "Ah, hell. The kid got cut up by some kind of sex killer. My sister said it was bad, real bad. Everybody's scared their kid's going to be next. Now, thanks for all the beer, but I need another one. I'm not drunk enough yet."

I fetched him a fresh Molson's and headed toward the door, where Warren waited, his Coke abandoned on the barroom table.

Some kind of sex killer.

Killed, mutilated, dumped like garbage in the barren waste of the Dragoon Mountains.

Sheriff Avery was wrong.

Whoever had done it didn't give a damn about her.

Chapter Three

Monday morning, after seeing Warren off to the relative safety of Beverly Hills, where only spouses sliced and diced each other, I sat in my Scottsdale office attempting to work away my grief.

For a while, the phones cooperated, conveying tales of one betrayed relationship after another. Desert Investigations is always happy to check out potential mates to make certain they aren't stalkers, serial killers, or mere garden-variety frauds, but we seldom take divorce cases. The bitterness that arises during a marriage's end stage between two people who once loved each other is not uplifting.

I stared through the big picture window as a caller confided his suspicion that his twenty-two-years-younger wife was having an affair with her personal trainer. Outside on Main Street, the sun shone down on a herd of tourists roaming from one art gallery to another. Some wore sandals and Bermuda shorts, others, East Coast wool. The shorts crowd displayed goose bumps (it was little more than seventy degrees out there), the wool crowd sweated. Only we residents ever got Scottsdale weather right.

"She says she received those marks on her neck from the Nautilus machine but I know a hickey when I see one," the caller continued in an irritating whine.

I tore my eyes away from a woman too old to be wearing the hot pants she so proudly sported, and stared at the phone. "Hickey, did you say?"

"Haven't you been listening?"

Not really, since I had heard it all before. "Mr. Gustafson, Desert Investigations doesn't handle divorce cases."

"I didn't say I wanted to divorce her. I just want to know."

"Then you need a marriage counselor, not a detective." I gave him the name of a therapist I worked with, and over his protests, hung up.

By ten, with the tide of unfaithfulness about to drown me, I begged my partner for help. "Would you take some of these calls? There's a run on cheaters today."

Jimmy Sisiwan, a Pima Indian who lived on the Salt River Pima-Maricopa Reservation at the eastern edge of Scottsdale, glanced up from his computer where he was running pre-employment checks for Southwest MicroSystems. The curved tribal tatoo on his forehead glistened against his mahogany skin. "Sorry, but I have my own problems over here. Looks like the front-runner for Marketing Director might have a history of domestic abuse."

Might have, which meant Jimmy wasn't certain yet. "Why would that matter to MicroSystems? They're in business to make money, and money doesn't have a conscience. At least, not the last time I checked."

He gave me a confident smile. "Their new vice president in charge of security is a woman. Divorced. She's taken out an order of protection against her ex."

It didn't amaze me that powerful women sometimes married creepy men, but Jimmy's naiveté did. Regardless of their own marital woes, women could be just as hard-nosed in business as the opposite sex, which meant that the applicant might get the job even if he regularly beat his wife to a pulp.

Deciding to let voice mail take my calls for a while, I picked up the morning newspaper. After sifting through front-page stories about marketplace suicide bombings in the Middle East, I thumbed to the Local section were the news wasn't much better: a drive-by shooting near Phoenix Children's Hospital, jewelry store robbery in Peoria, and the discovery of a drop house in north Scottsdale crammed with thirty-four undocumented aliens, three of them dead. Then, on the second-to-last page of the section, a headline over a young girl's photograph asked: DO YOU KNOW ME?

Those very words had once appeared over a picture of me at age four, and no one had ever responded. Today, instead of my own face, I saw the child from the Dragoons. The photographer had been kind. She no longer looked dead, just sleeping.

I must have made a noise, because Jimmy turned from his keyboard and asked, "What's wrong?"

"This girl in the paper. She's the one I found."

He rose from his seat and walked over to my desk. Picking up the newspaper, he read aloud, "*The Cochise County Sheriff's Office is asking for the public's help in identifying a young girl found dead in the Dragoon Mountains last weekend. Dubbed 'Precious Doe' by the medical examiner, the child is African-American, between five and seven years old. Wounds on her body suggest she was the victim of a crime. Anyone with information about this girl is urged to contact Sheriff Bill Avery's office at 520-555-3215.*"

Jimmy lowered the newspaper with a look in his eyes that hadn't been there before. "Sure was a pretty little thing, wasn't she?"

Was. That horrible past tense. God only knew what a few days in cold storage had done to her.

"I'm sure the sheriff will track her identity down, along with whoever did…Well, did what they did." His tone wasn't as confident as his words. We both knew that bodies dumped in the Arizona desert were seldom identified, their killers remaining free to kill again.

When I didn't respond, he said, "Lena, you shouldn't take everything so personal." An orphan himself, he knew all about my childhood, my nightmares.

Before I could remind him that I always took abused children personal, the phone rang. This time I picked it up before the voice mail did. I didn't care what kind of sad story was on the line, it would be better than the one in my head.

Desert Investigations has been in business ever since a bullet in the hip ended my career with the Scottsdale Police Department. Jimmy, introduced to me by a man whose son I had once freed from prison, joined me as full partner soon afterward. His Internet skills and my television consulting kept us flush enough to accept more pro bono cases than the average investigative agency usually took, but truth be told, we preferred those. Neither of us liked spending our time ferreting out run-of-the-mill liars and cheaters.

The office is relatively decent, as P.I. offices go, mainly because of our downtown Scottsdale location and the expectations of our clientele. None of that old Maltese Falcon grimness here, just coffee-colored walls hung with civic commendations, two tasteful blond desks with a row of matching filing cabinets, and several Western-patterned chairs scattered throughout the reception area. Comfortable and anonymous. When clients visit P.I.s, they're not shopping for decorating tips.

The day dragged on, broken up only by more paranoid spouses, and a few parents begging me to drug-test their teens. I grew so bored that by the time we closed, even the tourist parade had ceased being entertaining.

"Ready for some cappuccino at Java Joe's?" I asked, as we locked up. The art galleries were closing, too, expelling tourists onto the sidewalk, where they just stood around, wondering what to do next. Cajun fritters at Sugar Daddy's? Jose Cuervo at the Rusty Spur?

Jimmy didn't answer right away, but when he did, he sounded uncomfortable. "Ah, cappuccino sounds great, Lena, but I need to rush home and shower. I have an, um, appointment, kind of, tonight." A hint of pink began to spread across his cheeks, which was in itself strange, since Indians almost never blushed.

Such embarrassment could only mean one thing; my partner had a date. "Is she anyone I know?"

His eyes shifted away, something else that seemed strange, because he was usually the most open of men. "I doubt it."

Jimmy's love life tended to be as disastrous as mine. Among his former girlfriends were a convicted felon who'd sold him a stolen Rolex; a refugee from an upstate polygamy compound who tried to make a white man out of him; a bartender who drank more Tecate than she served. The list goes on. Always a sucker for a sob story, he had been used and abused by the supposedly weaker sex ever since we'd known each other.

As we stood on the sidewalk, tourists swarmed around us, every now and then one of them throwing Jimmy an expression of alarm. Like most Pimas, he was a big man, and his tribal tattoo made him appear fierce. Ignoring the tourists, I framed my next question cautiously. "You've known her for a while?"

A sheepish smile. "Isn't that what dates are for, to get to know someone?" This from a man whose job was dragging skeletons out of closets.

The worry-wart in me refused to let it go. Faking a conversational tone, I asked, "Where'd you meet her?"

"What, you're my mother, now? I already have two. Had, anyway."

Jimmy's biological mother, a full-blooded Pima, died of the tribal scourge of diabetes when he was a baby. Several years later, his father died of the same disease. His white Mormon adoptive parents lived in Utah, but they had kept in close touch since Jimmy had returned to the reservation to reclaim his cultural roots. The Mormons had raised him to be polite, even when dealing with snoops like me.

He sighed. "I'm sorry if I sounded rude, Lena. I know you care, but I'm a big boy and can take care of myself. Just to set your mind at rest, I met her at last week's pow-wow."

I relaxed. Most members of the tribe had their act together, so his big heart might have lucked out this time. "She's Pima?"

"Anglo, but she came with a Pima friend. We danced. We talked. We made a date. Okay?"

With that, we said good night and went our separate ways, Jimmy to seek love, and me to my lonely apartment above the office.

At one time my two-room-plus-kitchen-and-bath had been a study in beige, but earlier this year, after deciding to put down some roots of my own, I'd tricked it out in neo-Cowgirl. All that beige-ness was now buried beneath bright Navajo rugs, a saguaro-rib sofa and chair, a red Lone Ranger and Tonto bedspread, and turquoise-shaded lamps with bases shaped like horse heads.

But I'm not a purist. Although it interfered with the ambience, I still kept the "Welcome to the Philippines" toss pillow I'd stolen from one of my foster parents, either the fourth or the fifth. There were so many, I've lost track.

After nuking a Ramen noodle dinner, I settled on the sofa and stared at the wall, afraid to turn on the TV and risk hearing the news. Music, perhaps? Some blues by John Lee Hooker or Gatehouse Brown might be nice, but a glance at my CD collection revealed a tall stack of discs gathering dust without benefit of their jewel cases. I would have to clean them first, which meant that my skittery mind might fasten on subjects better left alone.

I wandered over to my book case, but nothing piqued my interest among the shelves of already-read mystery novels sandwiched between well-thumbed volumes of Southwestern history. Deciding a good movie might calm my nerves, I picked up the *Scottsdale Journal* and paged past the news section to Arts & Entertainment. Nothing interested me among the teen slasher flicks or—Scottsdale being Scottsdale—foreign films with subtitles. I hate subtitles.

Next, I tried calling Warren, but his voice mail told me that while he appreciated my call, he wasn't in right now, but if I left my name and number, he would get back to me as soon as possible. I didn't. If he was out and about with some Hollywood starlet, it was none of my business, just as what I did with my free time was none of his. Not that I ever did anything. Flying in the face of reason, I was a one-man woman.

Given my restless mood, the idea of hanging around the apartment wasn't all that attractive, so I went into the bedroom and changed into a pair of sweats. I had promised my orthopedic surgeon to go easy on the pavement pounding for a while, but right now, a re-injured hip seemed preferable to an emotional meltdown. Running settled my mind.

After transferring my .38 into its specially-designed fanny pack, I locked up and bounded down the stairs two at a time. Once on the sidewalk, I faced a decision: head east toward the Green Belt, a miles-long, path-lined arroyo that flooded every monsoon season, or south toward Papago Park, the unlandscaped piece of desert that divided Scottsdale from Phoenix. Opting for the park, I turned right on Scottsdale Road and began cutting my way through the tourists.

The park was nearby, so it didn't take me long to get there, even after stopping to assist a sunburned couple who, speaking with Brooklyn accents, asked where they might see some Indians. Amused, I gave them directions to Casino Arizona, a mile away. "Indians all over the place," I told them, "They'll be happy to show you how the new slots work." Feeling only slightly guilty, I jogged away.

The centerpiece of Papago Park is the Buttes, rough sandstone mesas erupting from the flat desert floor. Just as I entered the thousand-acre park, the Buttes caught the last rays of the sun and glowed with gaudy flashes of mauve and red. I jogged in place for a while, watching the show. Once the sun slipped behind the Phoenix skyscrapers to the west, the Buttes returned to their usual dull red, so I moved on.

For a while, other runners shared the trail, but they turned onto the wide path that ended at the south parking lot. Fleeing my sense of dis-ease, I took the more isolated path. It was one of my favorite routes, but not without danger, since this unmanicured section of the park served as home to various species of wildlife, none of them friendly. Coyote, javelina, snakes, and scorpions considered the high brush their own turf, so I wasn't too startled when I passed a sandstone outcropping and flushed an angry javelina from a creosote thicket. Mama Javelina, trailed by four squealing youngsters.

I froze.

Javelina are ferociously protective, quick to fight for their young. Whatever they fought usually lost, because a charge from even a small javelina could knock you off your feet. If you didn't regain your feet before they charged again, you might lose your intestines to their sharp tusks.

This particular javelina seemed more irritable than most. Maybe she'd had a bad day at the office, maybe Saturn was in her Pisces, or maybe her boyfriend was dating another javelina. Whatever the reason, she lowered her head and moved in front of her brood. When I took a test step back, she snorted and pawed the ground like a Brahma bull.

Then she started to circle.

Since the chances of outrunning Mama Javelina were nil, I froze again. Hardly daring to breathe, I waited while she checked me out. As I stood there the twilight faded, leaving us in growing darkness. And yet she continued to walk around me, grumbling to herself while her oblivious babies rooted for grubs in the nearby sagebrush.

If worse came to worse, I could use the .38 in my fanny pack, but the revolver was there to defend me from two-legged demons, not four-legged ones, if you could call a protective mother a demon. If more of them existed, little girls would never get shot in the face or dumped in the desert.

With that stray thought, the image of the girl in the Dragoons returned, and even the very present danger of the circling javelina couldn't chase her face away. A wave of grief, palpable as the sandy trail under my feet, swept the fear from me.

Then something changed. Perhaps the girl's ghostly presence somehow communicated itself to Mama Javelina, because she stopped circling and gazed into my eyes.

I gazed back.

She grunted, pawed the ground.

I kept my gaze steady.

After what seemed like forever, the pawing stopped. Her eyes left mine, settled on her children. With a final grunt, Mama

Javelina gathered her babies together and herded them down the trail.

I waited until they disappeared behind a butte, then turned around and jogged home.

Main Street was deserted when I reached my apartment, and so was my voice mail. Hip hurting but mind still haunted, I decided to organize my CD collection. For the next hour I cleaned discs, returned them to their proper cases, and filed them alphabetically by performer. That accomplished, I wandered into the bedroom and began straightening out my closet.

Since I don't own many clothes—one all-purpose black dress, one pants suit bought off the sales rack at Nordstrom's, and several pairs of black jeans and black tops—it didn't take long before I felt at loose ends again. Frustrated, I started vacuuming dust bunnies from under my bed but halfway through, struck pay dirt in the form of an old David Morrell novel I had never finished.

Confident that Morrell's grisly visions would keep my mind off my own, I tugged the book out and began to read. But fictional killers can only do so much to calm a troubled mind. Somewhere after one o'clock, I fell asleep…

…and woke up on the white bus. The white bus that rocketed along a dark Phoenix street, the white bus filled with singing people whose voices almost, but not quite, drowned out my mother's screams…

…the white bus where my mother held the gun against my forehead…

…the white bus where the gun went off and I fell away into the street…

There was something different about the dream this time. My sleeping self studied the small body on the pavement and discovered that the injured child was, for once, not me.

She was a different girl, a dark, tiny thing so beautiful she made my heart ache. As she lay bleeding on the street, she looked up at me, her eyes filled with the terrible knowledge that she was dying. Her lips formed two words, but the people on the bus sang so loudly that I couldn't hear.

The girl's lips moved again. This time, all the way down through the years, I heard.

"Help me," she whispered.

Then my own bullet came for me and I fell into the street beside her.

Chapter Four

When I drove into Los Perdidos late the next afternoon, five days after finding that sad little body, tension filled the air. A woman leaving a children's used clothing store clutched her toddler tightly, her eyes darting like a feral animal's. Scant inches in front, two older children held hands, the same anxiety on their faces.

In contrast to their fear, Avery's annoyed expression when I walked into the sheriff's office appeared normal. "Can't say I'm glad to see you again, Ms. Jones."

He hunched over a deputy's desk, going through some papers. The deputy looked no friendlier than his boss. They both wanted me to go away, but I couldn't, not if I ever wanted to sleep again. Nearby, I heard the dispatcher calling out codes over the squawks of squad car radios. From a bulletin board on the far wall, the child known as Precious Doe gazed down at me. I stared at the photograph in silence for a moment, then drew out the article I'd clipped from the *Scottsdale Journal*.

"You haven't been able to I.D. this girl yet, Sheriff," I said to Avery, trying to squelch my own annoyance. "Maybe I can help with the legwork."

Not even glancing at the clipping, he said, "I have plenty of men in the field so we don't need any help. At least not from any Scottsdale private detective." He was obviously one of those people who thought all we ever did in Scottsdale was lounge around resort swimming pools, courting melanoma.

"I'm sorry you feel that way, Sheriff, but now that I'm here, I plan to make myself useful. Anything I find out, I'll share. Okay?"

"I told you, we're fine."

The deputy, not quite as tall or weather-browned as the sheriff, spoke for the first time. "Otherwise we'd be thrilled to pieces by your offer of help."

"Jim. Go easy," Avery warned.

The deputy humphed and went back to shuffling paperwork.

The sheriff studied me. When he finally spoke, it was with the easy confidence of a man used to being obeyed. "We can handle the investigation, so why don't you play nice and go on home?"

"No can do." I would never forget the wind rippling through the child's white wrappings, the growls of the coyote as it scurried away.

Time to share some knowledge. "If the girl was an illegal, like most people seem to think, her family could be a thousand miles away working in some sweatshop. Or, and this is what I suspect, she might not have been an illegal after all. This morning I had my partner do some checking on past crimes in Cochise County and he found something interesting."

It has always amazed me how quickly handsome men can turn ugly, but Avery accomplished just that. His mouth hardened into a dangerous line. "We're done here."

I stood my ground. "A couple of months before 9/11, a little girl named Tujin Rafik went missing from Los Perdidos. Her family had recently immigrated here from northern Iraq to work at that insecticide plant. You were new on the job then, and maybe not as sharp as you are now. The night she didn't come home from school, you released a statement that she probably just ran away, since you'd been told that with her language difficulties and all, she was having trouble in school. I'll bet you regret that statement now."

No answer.

Taking his silence for agreement, I continued. "After Tujin had been missing for several days without a sighting, you realized you'd screwed up big time and initiated a house-to-house search. You never found her."

Jimmy had shown me a picture of the girl printed in the *Cochise County Observer* at the time of her disappearance. The expression on Tujin's face hinted at a difficult life. I'd never seen such sad eyes.

The sheriff wasn't impressed. "That partner of yours ought to try out for a job down here. If he can stand the pace."

I ignored the barb. "Tujin Rafik was seven when she disappeared. Precious Doe looked around seven, too." Seven. The same age I'd been when…Best to keep my mind off that terrible memory.

"What does the age matter?" Avery was determined to give nothing away.

"Come on, Sheriff. Everybody in law enforcement knows that most child molesters have individual preferences for certain age groups. Looks like you've got one who likes seven-year-olds."

"Maybe."

I finished summoning up the Tujin Rafik case. "Several months after Tujin disappeared, those planes flew into the World Trade Center. A couple of months after that, her family returned to Iraq."

His eyes flickered. "Can you blame them?"

"Usually with these child disappearances, the parents stay in the same house until it falls down around their ears, hoping the missing kid will eventually find his or her way home."

A bitter laugh. "Oh, come on, Ms. Jones. You know as well as I do that the mood toward anyone who appeared Muslim turned pretty ugly after 9/11. A lot of Middle Easterners got roughed up, even killed. Some of ours split for Phoenix, where they wouldn't stand out quite so much. A few, like the Rafiks, returned to their home countries. They were just part of the general exodus."

I didn't buy it. "Let's see if I have this straight. Several years ago, an Iraqi child went missing from your area, and this past weekend we found a dead girl of about the same age who just happens to be black. That makes *two* girls, *two* minorities, *both* around seven years old. I've been doing some thinking about the white cloth on Precious Doe, and I'm no longer sure it was just some anonymous wrapping or shroud. Maybe it was tribal dress. You not only have a sizeable Mideastern community here in Los Perdidos, you also have a lot of Africans, all lured by the jobs at the insecticide plant."

Avery answered quickly. "Nice theory, but after 9/11, the traditionals were the first to leave town. By and large, the Africans who stayed turned more Western than Wyatt Earp. They hang out at the library and volunteer during Los Perdidos Apache Days. As for their dress, most of them wear tee shirts and jeans, just like you."

The American stewpot, with various nationalities blending merrily away, *if* the sheriff was to be believed. But one young girl was dead, another missing and presumed dead. I didn't believe in coincidences, and told him so, finishing with another question. "Have you contacted the FBI?"

"Of course, and they have the investigation well in hand." He didn't sound like he believed it. He checked his watch. "Well, it's been real, Ms. Jones, but I have to get to work. Do us all a big favor and go home."

With that, he retreated into his private office and closed the door.

His deputy gave me an I-told-you-so smile.

Motels with empty rooms being as rare as helpful sheriffs in Los Perdidos, I'd booked myself into a guest ranch two miles out of town. As the Jeep sped along the highway paralleling the San Pedro River, tall cottonwoods threw deep shadows on the asphalt, making it difficult to find the turnoff to the Lazy M Ranch. Just as I began to worry, I saw an unmarked, narrow dirt track.

On one side of the road, a herd of Black Angus grazed contentedly behind barbed wire, while on the other side, the San

Pedro River looped its lazy way to Mexico. In the distance, the Dragoon Mountains humped up from the desert floor, their summits lit with gold from the rapidly disappearing sun.

The ranch house emerged from a stand of towering cottonwoods. A relic of Arizona's territorial days, it was built of whitewashed adobe brick, topped by a red tile roof bristling with chimneys. When I stepped from my Jeep, a stiff wind from the river raised goose bumps on my uncovered arms. Nights grew cold at this elevation, especially in winter, so old ranch houses like these generally had more than one working fireplace. To my relief, a propane tank near the side of the house hinted that modern comforts were also available.

A brown-haired woman waited for me in a glider on the porch, a cell phone at her ear, her feet tucked under as she swung back and forth. Middle-aged, she wore ragged jeans and a purple sweater that wasn't in much better shape. Spotting me, she ended her call and uncurled herself from the glider. Dirty, down-at-the-heel boots encased her narrow feet.

"Selma Mann?" I asked, stepping out of the Jeep.

"That's me." As she shook my hand, I noticed that her nails were unmanicured and her palms covered in calluses. This woman actually worked her ranch.

"Welcome to the Lazy M," she said. "That's quite some vehicle you have there, sort of a traveling petroglyph."

My sandstone-colored 1945 Jeep, which I'd rescued from its pink-painted days with a desert tour company, was covered with Pima Indian symbols. On the driver's side, Earth Doctor, the father-god who had created First World, surveyed his children: Elder Brother, Coyote, Snake, and Eagle. Splashed across the Jeep's hood was the labyrinth where Earth Doctor sought refuge after being overthrown in a power struggle. Along the passenger-side door rose the waves which destroyed First World. Sly Coyote rode the waves in his reed boat while Night Singing Bird and Sky Hawk clung to the sky with sharp talons.

I smiled. "People seem to like it."

She chuckled. "I doubt if Sheriff Avery does. Los Perdidos has grown a lot in the past few years, but not enough that we've learned to mind our own business. I know you're the one who found that child's body, and why you're back. By the way, we don't have any other guests right now, so it should be nice and quiet. Most people just come down for the weekend, bump around on the horses for awhile, then go home thinking they've experienced the Western life."

She laughed again. "Say, you hungry? The ranch hands have all been fed, we eat early out here, but I kept something in the warming oven for you."

Due to my hypermetabolism, I'm always hungry, but contented myself with a nod. When she led me inside, I found a living room crowded with furniture so authentic it might have been transported West in covered wagons. Family portraits in silver frames covered every polished table, but they didn't capture my interest as much as the antique rifles bracketed on the rough adobe walls. Among them glistened several Winchester level action rifles, a Colt Lightening Express, a Rideout Trade Musket, a Springfield 45-70, even a German Short Yeager. Near them, framed and encased behind glass over the fireplace, hung a faded black-and-white wool square that might have once been a saddle blanket.

"The family story goes that it once belonged to Geronimo," Selma explained. "He gave it to Ezra, my great-great-grandfather, who ran a trading post near Tombstone and who'd always treated him and his band with respect. The blanket's a ragged old thing, but I keep it up there just in case the story's true." Her face took on a thoughtful expression. "You know, Cochise was every bit as great a warrior, but Geronimo wound up with the lion's share of fame. You've probably noticed that half the businesses in Los Perdidos are named after him."

I had my own theory about that. "Geronimo was the last Apache to surrender, which sounds pretty romantic, at least to Easterners."

She nodded. "After his surrender, the Indian Wars were over. Theoretically, anyway. Apparently he became an ideal prisoner, and even turned up at political rallies and county fairs."

My stomach growled, cutting her off in mid-lesson.

She smiled. "Well, so much for history. Now for more immediate concerns." Ushering me into a large, eat-in kitchen, she motioned me to a long trestle table. Delicious cooking smells permeated the air, making my stomach growl even louder. Bending down, she peered into the oven. "I hope you like chicken stew. We raise most of what we eat—the beef, the chickens, the vegetables, the herbs, right down to the olives on the salad."

"We?" The ad for the Lazy M Guest Ranch had just mentioned, SELMA MANN, RANCHER. No Mr. Mann.

"Me and the ranch hands. Marriage isn't for me, too many compromises. As for children, well, that's another story." She said no more, and I didn't ask. Her personal life was none of my business as long as it wasn't connected to the investigation, and I didn't see how it could be.

The chicken stew was delicious. Not a gourmet recipe, perhaps, but due to the ingredients' freshness, more flavorful than many meals served in Scottsdale's high-end restaurants.

While I scarfed up some apple cobbler, she said, "I've done a lot of thinking about the child they're calling Precious Doe. People see places like Los Perdidos, the pretty mountains, the river, they hear the big silence and think the town's as benign as Walden Pond. But this is rough country and a lot of rough people live around here. You know about that other girl, the one who went missing a few years ago?"

I nodded again.

"Bill considers her his personal failure."

"Bill?" If she and the sheriff were close friends, I'd chosen the wrong guest ranch.

A wry smile. "We used to date. But unlike me, Bill's the marrying kind, as evidenced by two ex-wives." She shuddered. "He wants a third, the idiot, but it won't be me. Anyway, we're not on good enough terms that you have to worry about him dropping by to chat, so you'll be able to use the Lazy M without any interference from him. Or me, for that matter. I don't care who finds out who's killing little girls, or what they have to do to find the creep, just as long as he's stopped."

Her phrasing intrigued me. "You say 'killing little girls.' Plural. Then you think that other child, Tujin Rafik, is dead."

Her long fingers worried at a loose thread dangling from her purple sweater. "If she wasn't, she'd have been found long before now."

I thought of Elizabeth Smart and other missing children who turned up after being gone for months and even years. "Maybe you're wrong."

Troubled eyes met mine. "Nothing would make me happier."

We talked a while longer, until a call of nature made me ask the whereabouts of the bathroom. "Down the hall, second door to the left," Selma said.

The hallway, not visible from the more public areas of the ranch house, was decorated not with Old West paraphernalia, but with a collection of African masks, shields, and spears, along with several photographs of assorted African wildlife. One picture showed Selma in a crowded village, holding the hand of a dark child. Neither looked particularly happy.

Upon returning to the kitchen, I asked Selma about her African vacation, but she seemed disinclined to talk about it, saying only, "Even ranchers like a change of scene every now and then." Then she steered the conversation around to Geronimo and the Apaches again, regaling me with more tales of bloody raids and even bloodier reprisals. "Did you know Geronimo was considered fairly peaceful until his wife and children were murdered by Mexican troops while he was away conducting peace talks?"

I nodded. Warren had discovered that relatively unknown piece of history while researching his documentary.

"That's what turned him, I think, because after that, he couldn't get enough blood," she said. "He and his band began slaughtering every settler they ran across. Even here. If you walk south along the river, and you should because it's gorgeous this time of year, you'll see the remains of a burned-out farmstead and six graves. The Johnston family. Geronimo himself massacred every last one of them, including the baby. The other settlers vowed to avenge them. Wyatt Earp even rode up from Tombstone to join the search party but didn't have any luck. Two months later he—Earp, that is—shot up the Clantons down at the OK Corral."

Through the kitchen window I saw the Dragoons rising into a crisp sky. They looked so peaceful. "A lot of history in the area."

"Yeah, and most of it violent."

After several more stories about Apache and Anglo ferocity, Selma must have noticed my flagging interest, because she offered to walk me over to my quarters. I smiled with relief.

The guest house sat to the east of the main building, far from the ranch hands' quarters but close enough to the river that I heard water rushing against rocks. The small cottage was no more elegant than the house, but that only added to its charm. A hand-made quilt lay across the bed, a rag rug covered the scarred oak floor, and a big armoire—as scarred as if it had lain out the yard for a century or two—stood against a whitewashed wall. There were no guns or other implements of destruction here, just photographs of various Apaches, including one of Geronimo standing in a garden, proudly holding a big watermelon. Beside him stood a woman and a child.

Geronimo the family man. Geronimo the gardener.

Apaches weren't the only stars of the photo display. I also saw a picture of a uniformed Bill Avery accepting a plaque from a smug-faced man.

"You keep a picture of your ex-boyfriend?" With me, when a relationship was over, it was over. Well, usually. I talked to Dusty, one of my own exes, from time to time.

Selma laughed. "You'll notice it's not in my living room. But my guests like it, probably because that Smokey-and-Stetson outfit of Bill's makes him look like their idea of an Old West sheriff. That's Lee Casey next to him, Los Perdidos' richest man.

He owns Apache Chemical, the big insecticide plant on the edge of town. He talked Bill into being Guest of Honor at the company's annual banquet."

Tujin Rafik's father had worked at the plant, I remembered. And hadn't I seen Lee Casey's name on the bronze plaque at the hospital? When I studied the photograph more closely, I noticed that the sheriff's body language resembled a virgin trying hard not to let her horny date get too close.

Selma's next words affirmed my observation. "Lee's not one of Bill's favorite people, but the picture was taken soon after the election, while he was currying favor with county movers and shakers. Lee's turned out to be a real pain in the butt for him, always expecting special favors, like making his speeding tickets go away. Not that Bill ever complies."

"Why would a chemical plant want a sheriff as guest of honor at a company banquet?"

"Right after 9/11, Bill rode herd on the White Power types around here who were making life miserable for the immigrants, and suggested strongly that they vamoose. Most of the outright thugs did leave, the guys who'd been convicted for assault at one time or another. Because of his actions then, reasonable people—and for all his faults I include Lee among them—believe Bill kept a bad situation from getting worse."

I remained confused. "I still don't see why the sheriff's efforts would be cause for celebration at Apache Chemical."

"Because half the chemists and engineers on staff up there are from points east. *Way* east. Indians—the New Delhi kind, not the Apache kind—plus a bunch of folks from Africa and the Middle East. The company recruited them because they have all the brains and education of our own college grads, but work for half the money and under worse conditions."

Life had never been easy for immigrants, but that didn't make it right. "What about OSHA?" The Occupational Safety and Health Administration tried to keep the workplace safe, but it did have blind spots, especially where immigrants, legal or illegal, were concerned.

"OSHA does what it can, but there's a lot of ground to cover out here, lots of new plants springing up in the desert, industries that cities like Scottsdale don't want in their own backyards because of the pollution factor. Maybe I shouldn't paint such a bleak picture. Apache Chemical is pretty safe as these kinds of plants go, and hasn't been hit with many citations. Oh. Come to think of it, there was a bad accident a couple of years back, when one of the immigrants, an African, lost his hand."

That didn't sound "pretty safe" to me. "Why wasn't the plant closed down?"

"If OSHA closed plants every time there was an accident, there would be no industry in America today. They just fined the company, the guy received Workers Comp, and Casey gave him a payoff. Since then, conditions up there have changed for the better, partially because Casey's been more careful, but also because some people around town started paying more attention to what was going on up there."

That sounded promising. "Who in particular?"

"A group of community activists, mainly retired legal types, social workers, store owners, even a rancher or two. Not me. I stay out of politics. Horse manure's cleaner."

With that, Selma helped me unload my luggage from the Jeep, and we returned to the main house where we spent the rest of the evening in friendly chat over coffee so thick it could have fueled a Stealth Bomber. By the time she excused herself to attend to some paperwork, I knew enough about Los Perdidos to add some perspective to my investigation.

Best of all, she had confirmed information Jimmy had provided me with that morning.

The names of the town's two convicted child molesters.

Chapter Five

"When the Iraqi girl went missing, Floyd Polk and Duane Tucker were the first people my predecessor questioned," Sheriff Avery said, sliding the men's mug shots across his desk. He wasn't happy talking to me, but once I convinced him that I'd paid my guest cottage tab two weeks in advance and wasn't going anywhere until the case was solved, he relented.

Somewhat, anyway. The hostility in his eyes remained.

Avery's office displayed no I'm-A-Big-Shot certificates on the pine-paneled walls, just a large studio-posed photograph of him with three blond children who had his eyes, and one tiny brunette who appeared partially Hispanic but had his firm mouth. The fruits of different wives? I knew from my own years on the Scottsdale Police Force that due to the tension of the job, cops had trouble staying married. Things appeared no different here in the boonies.

I studied the mug shots. Polk, who appeared to be around seventy, squinted at the camera through his one good eye while the other, cataract white, walled out to the side. Tucker was younger and looked fairly normal, except for the puckered scar on his forehead. It resembled my own.

"Considering that Polk's been in and out of prison all his life, he's pretty healthy," the sheriff continued, tapping his finger on the old man's picture. "At least healthy enough to snatch a kid. He's a serial child molester, but thanks to our so-called justice system, his longest stretch was only eleven years, and that for the rape of a nine-year-old. Nice, huh?" Avery made a disgusted sound. "His parents died while he was in prison, left him their place, so he moved back here once he was released. The house isn't much more than a shack, really, right up against the Dragoons and secluded as hell. Anything might go on out there. He was a prime suspect when Tujin Rafik disappeared, too, but nothing came of it."

Tujin. The girl with the sad eyes. "You sure you asked him the right questions?"

He turned surly again. "How's this for a question: why don't you go home?"

I could have kicked myself for endangering our truce. "Sorry, that didn't come out right. For reasons I'd rather not explain, I feel personally involved in this case."

At this, Avery moved the papers on his desk, uncovering a folder labeled, JONES, LENA. Spilling from it were xeroxed copies of two old newspaper articles, both dated thirty years earlier. One asked the public to help identify a four-year-old girl found on a Phoenix city street, because the bullet that had almost killed her left her with amnesia. The other was a copy of the article reporting my knife attack against the foster father who'd raped me when I was nine.

"Not the world's greatest childhood, I see," he murmured, his voice turned gentle. "You ever regain your memory?"

I shook my head. "Just fleeting visions." *My father dying in a forest clearing. A white bus carrying me away. My mother aiming her pistol at my head.*

He opened the folder and stared at the article. When he looked up, his hard eyes had softened. "Let's try this again, Ms. Jones. If you stop being a smart ass, I'll stop being a prick. Bargain?"

"Bargain."

"Truce, then. Friday afternoon, as soon as the judge faxed me the search warrant, we went out and tossed Polk's place but he came up clean. The guy's either real smart, which I doubt, or he's innocent. Of this particular crime, anyway."

Now that sentencing standards against serial child molesters had become more rigorous, Polk might have killed his latest victim to make sure she couldn't testify against him. "What about Duane Tucker?"

Avery grimaced. "Ah, yes. Duane Gerald Tucker, one of Los Perdidos' most notorious imports. Born in Cheval Blanc, Louisiana, moved to our fair city with his mother when he was twelve. Began having run-ins with the law right away, mainly shoplifting and a few school fights. There was some problematical stuff early on with girls, too, but nothing serious until he was caught having what he called 'consensual sex' with a thirteen-year-old. At the time he was fifteen. The county attorney piled on a few other charges and the court shipped him off to juvie until he turned eighteen."

"How old is Duane now?" The face that peered at me from the photograph was so lacking in character that he might have been anywhere from his early twenties to his late thirties.

"Twenty-three but still a bad boy. He's suspected in a few recent break-ins, but we haven't been able to pin anything down. It's just a matter of time. Talk about your basic bad seed."

"Meaning?"

"His father, the illustrious Gerald Tucker, was executed in Louisiana a couple years ago for murder following a rape."

I sucked in my breath. Sex offenders frequently practiced on their own kids, who in turn, sometimes took up the practice themselves. "Was the victim a child?"

"Convenience store clerk. Gerald carjacked her, took her out to the bayou, did his freak thing, then carved her up. Duane was almost eight at the time. After Daddy took up residence on Death Row, his mom, Joleene, started seeing some guy who moved them out here, where he had family. Couple years later, the guy took off, stranding them. Not that it made any difference to Joleene, because she's been on Welfare all her life. What with the government's money and her turning a trick every now and then, they get by."

I stared at Duane's picture, thinking about bad childhoods and what they could do to a child. "Tell me, was he in or out of juvie when Tujin Rafik disappeared?"

A faint smile. "Now there's a good question. He'd been released a month earlier, and yes, we questioned him and came up with nada, just like we did the other day."

I touched the mark on Duane's forehead. "How did he get that scar?"

For a brief moment the sheriff gazed at my own scar, a visible record of the bullet that had condemned me to fourteen years' worth of foster homes. Then he looked away, as if embarrassed to be caught staring. "His father beat him, his mother never interfered."

Usually it took two people to turn a child's life into a living hell: a violent man and a weak woman. Or, as in my own case, terrified children screaming somewhere in the distance, my mother carrying me silently through the dark woods. The rest? It was probably just as well my memory was a blank.

"Does Duane have a long history of violent outbursts? That's a not-uncommon side effect of brain injuries." I'd had some trouble along those lines, myself.

He nodded. "We always know when our boy's out drinking. Miracles begin to happen, like chairs flying through barroom windows."

Brain injuries and booze, a bad mix. Another reason I didn't drink.

After some pleading, the sheriff gave me both men's addresses, if you called the map to Polk's desert shack an address. Its location, less than five miles from where Precious Doe had been dumped, gave me pause. Duane lived in a Los Perdidos trailer park close to the center of town.

"Don't bother going by Duane's place yet," Avery volunteered. "He's working on a yard maintenance crew and won't be home until sundown. Joleene, if she's not off drinking somewhere, won't tell you squat. Polk's 'retired,' and is home all day. A real gentleman of leisure."

Returning the mug shots to their respective folders, he asked, "Is there anything else?"

"I'd like to see Precious Doe's autopsy report."

Some of his earlier hostility returned. "Forget it."

"Why not?"

"Because you don't need my nightmares."

I could have told him I had nightmares of my own, but didn't bother. Recognizing that his cooperation was at an end, I said good-bye.

An hour later, after wrestling the Jeep over several miles of rutted dirt road and a bottom-scraping dry wash, I spotted Polk's shack hidden behind two sickly mesquite trees. The tar-papered walls listed to one side and rust spotted the tin roof. Trash blown about in the hard wind funneled down from the Dragoon Mountains littered the front "yard," which was nothing more than bare desert heaped with filled garbage bags. In the rear, near a faded pickup truck, stood a line of jerry-built cages housing rabbits. The drying skins tacked to the side of the shack told me they weren't pets.

Polk met me at the door, a huge butcher knife pointed toward me. "You get." He didn't really need the knife for protection because the odor emanating from his body could have killed the average pro wrestler.

I copied the conciliatory smile I'd used with such success on the sheriff. "Mr. Polk? I just wanted to ask you some questions."

"You and the rest of them fools in Los Perdidos. All's you need to know, bitch, is that I didn't touch no kid. Now get the hell out of here before I shove this knife up your ass." His right eye looked straight at me, his left at the ground. His face appeared closer to ninety than seventy, but muscle roped his chicken-thin arms. Some strength there, at least enough to overpower a small child.

In situations like this, being a P.I. instead of a cop comes in handy, because unlike cops, P.I.'s needn't stick to the truth. Ignoring the knife, I said, "You have it all wrong, sir. I think you're being railroaded and I'm offering my help."

The blade lowered an inch. An eye, the good one, twitched. "You one of them social workers? Or the press? 'Cause if you're a reporter, I'm carvin' you up right now." The knife lifted again.

I broadened my smile, not that it mattered. Polk liked kids, not women. "Nope, not a reporter. I'm just an advocate, of sorts, a person who wants to hear your side of things. It's a disgrace when a man who's already paid his debt to society gets hounded day after day. What is this country coming to?"

He must have liked the idea of himself as victim, because the knife swung all the way down. "I already got me a lawyer, if that's what you're after."

"And a good thing, too. But you also need a friend, someone who cares about what happens to you."

"You one of them do-gooders in that 'Nice Neighbor' bunch?" A gust of wind kicked more dust through the arid air, making him sneeze.

Nice Neighbor? I had no idea what he was talking about, but went with it anyway. "That's right, Mr. Polk. I am. And I'm confident we can come up with something to exonerate you."

After taking a moment to consider my offer, he said, "You want some tea? It's powdered, but I got some good bottled water. No lemon." A snicker.

Although I would rather drink rattlesnake venom than share tea with him, I enthused, "That sounds just wonderful!"

I waited for him to fetch me a glass, but instead he gestured for me to follow him into the darkness beyond the door. Now I faced a choice: enter a knife-wielding convicted felon's lair and get information, or stay outside in the blowing dust and get zip. Remembering Precious Doe's face as she lay in her hastily-dug grave, I stepped inside.

"Don't trip over nothing," he said, as he kicked trash out of the way. "I ain't big on cleaning."

Once my eyes grew accustomed to the dim light, I saw that almost every inch of floor space in the one-room shack was piled with old newspapers, empty beer cans, plastic Circle K bags stuffed with rags, and most worrying of all, unopened boxes of Teddy bears and Barbie Dolls.

Bait.

"Sugar or plain?"

Jarred out of my shock, I answered, "Plain, please." The fewer contaminates, the better. "By the way, I don't think I introduced myself. Lena Jones is the name."

As the desert wind moaned against the shack, he handed me a dingy glass filled with undissolved instant tea scum floating on top of muddy water. "Whatever. Have a seat, Miss Nice Neighbor, and tell me what you're gonna do for me."

After watching him plop down on a stack of newspapers, I did the same, studiously avoiding looking at the toys. "First off, Mr. Polk, I want you to tell me about yourself. You have an interesting place here, very…" I paused. He wasn't a stupid man, just a bad one. "…very rustic. I take it you raise your own meat?" I remembered the rabbit pens outside.

"Yeah, why buy what you can get for nothing? I trap them, bring them home and let them get it on. Got myself quite the breeding stock now. Ever had fried rabbit? You might say I'm what them newspapers call a 'survivalist,' and proud to be one. It's the American way."

Ah. A patriot.

For the next half hour, Polk treated me to a rambling biography, leaving out his prison record and his liking for children. In his sanitized version, he had spent an unblemished life shooting game and trying to grow a vegetable garden in a landscape that really didn't want him to. He was fishing for compliments, so I duly rendered them.

"You're a true original, Mr. Polk," I said, pleased to come up with a comment that wasn't an outright lie.

He smiled, revealing tea-colored teeth. "That's what they tell me."

Outside, the wind increased, making the shack creak alarmingly. Worried that it might fall down around our ears before I was finished, I hurriedly began asking my questions. "Most people admire your type of self-sufficiency, Mr. Polk, so what's the problem? Why is the sheriff always after you?"

He looked me straight in the eye, a trait perfected by habitual liars. "Beats me."

"Maybe because that child's body was found nearby?"

"Don't know nothing about it."

It. Not *her*. Child molesters never saw their victims as human. "Of course you don't, Mr. Polk. I know an innocent man when I see one. Now, what can I tell the good citizens of Los Perdidos that might set their minds at rest about you?"

"I don't give a shit about them folks."

My smile grew more difficult to maintain. "As much as I admire your independence, popular opinion often motivates law enforcement, which is why image is so important. And right about now, yours needs work." And wasn't that the truth? "Some good PR, if you will."

His face lit up. "Ain't never thought about that! Here." He reached to the side, grabbed a soiled Teddy bear, and thrust it at me. "Donate this to the hospital, the whatta-you-call it, peedtrics' wing."

"Pediatrics?"

"Yeah. Make sure everybody knows it came from me. How's that for good PR?"

"That should do it." I picked up the bear by the edge of its ear. God knows what was on there. Having learned as much from the old man as possible, I set my untasted tea on the floor next to a gray heap of something that resembled a dead mouse, and stood up. Was it my imagination, or had the wind grown stronger? It seemed determined to blow the shack right off the desert. Even Nature wanted Polk gone.

Polk's next words stopped me half way to the door. "Say, Miss Nice Neighbor. All this time you was here I been thinking. How'd you get that ugly scar on your forehead? You coulda been a pretty woman but that thing makes you look like crap."

I had long since stopped being self-conscious about my scar, so—curious as to how a child molester would handle it—I gave him an abbreviated version of my story. When I was through, he leered, flashing those terrible teeth again.

"Your Mommy shot you, huh? Oooh, you musta been a *bad* little girl."

Somehow I made it to my Jeep without throwing up.

Chapter Six

The sunny streets of Los Perdidos were a relief after Floyd Polk's dank shack. I pulled into the small parking lot next to the offices of the *Cochise County Observer* and before going in, tossed the Teddy bear into a litter can near the entrance. I would replace it with a new one, then drop it off at the pediatrics ward with no gift card attached. Damned if I would credit Polk.

The *Observer* was housed in an ancient adobe. In keeping with Old West style, the porch's overhang was held up by thick cedar posts, but the THIS IS A NO SMOKING ESTABLISHMENT sign on the front door, with the NO crossed out, added a rakish, contemporary touch.

The newspaper's receptionist, a bone-thin woman with sagging jowls and an unlit cigarette dangling from her lips, motioned for me to sit down on a cheap Naugahide sofa while she finished a phone call. The man on the other end must have been unhappy because she was doing her best to pacify him.

"Look, Max, your editor's over at that Chamber of Commerce meeting and he'll take it up with you as soon as he comes in, but for now, do what you have to do to write the article. No. No. Yes. No. C'mon, what difference does that make? Carolyn doesn't give a rat's patootie that you're scared of heights, so if you want to keep your job, strap yourself into that hang glider and get the story. Just don't get killed, 'cause then you'd miss your deadline. Oh, yeah? Same to *you*, too!" She slammed down the phone, then growled at me, "State your business!"

With a manner so casually rude, she had to be either the publisher's wife or his mother, so I trod carefully. "I need to see some back issues of the paper. If it's not too much trouble."

Behind her, hidden from view by a gray felt partition, a man in the newsroom swore at someone. The victim, a woman, not only returned his curses but added a few of her own. The cussing competition stopped only when a phone rang and the man answered it in a suitably honey-tongued voice.

"Reporters," the receptionist muttered, glaring at the felt partition over her bifocals. "Mouths like Marines on them, especially the women. Would you believe that one went to Catholic school? Nuns must be different than when I was a kid. What dates did you say you were interested in?"

Jolted from the image of potty-mouthed nuns, I studied my notes. "Two-thousand-one, June 25 through September." After talking to Selma, I wanted to read those articles again. I had a feeling I'd missed something.

The woman's glare didn't soften. Instead, she aimed a battery of questions at me so quickly I didn't have time to answer. "Then you're hunting information about that Iraqi girl who disappeared, right? You think she's linked to Precious Doe, right? Who the hell are you? A reporter from somebody else's newspaper, a paper whose circulation maybe overlaps ours? If so, get the hell out of this office and go do your own research!"

Properly cowed, I handed over my private investigator I.D. card.

Her abrasive manner underwent an abrupt change. "Ah. In that case, I wish you and the sheriff all the luck in the world 'cause you're gonna need it. Children going missing or turning up dead, it doesn't come any uglier than that. Who've you talked to so far? Floyd Polk, I hope?"

I nodded.

"A piece of work, huh? How about Duane Tucker?"

"He's on my list."

"Hm." She sounded noncommittal.

On the other side of the partition, the cussing started up again, but without true animosity.

Bernice smiled indulgently. "They're like children, aren't they? Now, about those old issues. The morgue at this office only goes back a year. Anything older you have to look up on microfilm at the library. Hang on a minute."

She picked up the phone again, punched in a number, and told whoever answered that a private detective would be stopping by. "Let her use that room near the administrative offices, the one with the coffee pot. She's interested in Tujin Rafik." She stopped, listened. "Yeah, poor kid. Why don't you pull the film and get her off to a running start? Why, bless your sweet heart!"

Smiling, she hung up. "Library's next to the Wal-Mart. When you go in, ask for Martha Green. She's agreed to set you up with everything you need. The coffee's not bad, but stay away from the baked goods."

I turned to go, then had a thought. "Is there some group in town called the Nice Neighbors?"

She sputtered a laugh. "I think you mean the Los Perdidos Good Neighbor Society, but yeah, they try to be nice neighbors, kind of a combination Welcome Wagon and Anti-Defamation League rolled into one. They formed right after 9/11, when we had some nasty racial incidents in town. Anything you want to know about them, just ask me, Bernice Broussard, publisher of this fine newspaper."

She stuck her hand forward to shake mine, her fingers resembling dried-out twigs banded with antique gold rings. "Our receptionist is out sick. Again. Small paper like this, everybody wears several hats. Say, you up for an interview? If my reporter survives his current assignment I can send him over to wherever you're staying. A pretty thing in your nasty line of work, hoo boy, I bet you have stories to tell. Better say yes, 'cause we'll get them anyway, but you'll like the article more if you cooperate."

Having known more than a few newspaper types in my life and what they could do to you if you played the No Comment card, I mumbled a grudging yes, but added that it would be better to talk with her reporter, if he survived his hang-gliding assignment, but only after the Precious Doe investigation was resolved.

"I'll give him an exclusive then," I promised.

"You'd better," she warned, but with a smile. "Expect a call from one Max Broussard."

"Broussard?"

"My son, the baby of the family. Still a bit of a wuss, but I'm working on that." Her hands twinkled gold as she waved me good-bye.

In the parking lot, I checked my voice mail and saw a message from Jimmy, none from Warren. Angelique "Angel" Grey, the actress who had snagged me a consulting job on her television series, had called three times. Since I was due in L.A. Friday for a *Desert Eagle* script meeting, I suspected all this phone activity forecasted stormy weather ahead. I liked Angel and respected her acting ability, but dealing with her could be difficult. The fact that she was Warren's ex-wife and the mother of his twin girls complicated our professional relationship, but in Hollywood, business was seldom strictly business. Still, the fat monthly check I received from *Desert Eagle*'s production company more than financed all my pro bono work.

Deciding to return the calls in the order of their probable ease, I rang Jimmy first and discovered that MicroSystems had turned down the wife-beater's job application.

"I found out there had been ongoing petty cash shortages in the PTA group where he served as treasurer, and that's what did him in," he said, a bad connection breaking up some of his words. "Not his propensity to beat up women."

"Like I told you, in the end it always comes down to money. By the way, how was your date the other night?" The question slipped out before I could stop it.

"With Lydianna? We had a great time, talked for hours," he enthused. "She's as smart as she is pretty. Even owns her own company!"

If Jimmy's luck ran the way it normally did, Lydianna's company was either fraudulent or teetering on the verge of bankruptcy. After our last dust-up, though, I knew better than to share my cynicism. "Just take it slow, okay?" It wasn't unheard of for Jimmy to show up for a fourth date with an engagement ring.

He laughed. "Have no fear, kemo sabe. I've learned from my mistakes."

Knowing that neither of us ever did, I rang off and placed more calls. Warren wasn't answering, neither was Angel. I left messages for both. On the way to the library, I stopped off at the Wal-Mart and picked up some Teddy bears and, not being a fan of a certain clotheshorse named Barbie, a couple of Dora the Explorer dolls. For good measure I also bought a Tickle Me Elmo, figuring hospitalized kids could use a few laughs.

The Cochise County Library, Geronimo Branch, a sleek but characterless building, not only had a bike rack out front but also a hitching post to which was tied a scruffy pinto. Side-stepping the road apples the pinto had deposited on the cement, I went inside.

The library was relatively small, so it was easy to find Martha Green, a tall, slender woman with short black hair and dark hazel eyes that didn't miss much.

After I introduced myself, she said, "You're staying in Selma Mann's guest cottage, aren't you?"

Word sure gets around. "Yep. Nice place. Quiet."

"Better watch it or you'll gain ten pounds. Selma's one fierce cook."

She abandoned the books she was shelving and showed me to a room no larger than a closet, but nevertheless decorated with a large photograph of Geronimo. This time the old warrior sat behind the wheel of a Model T, looking like he was on his way to a business meeting. On the desk below rested a microfilm reader, a printer, a stack of film canisters, a Mr. Coffee, some mugs, and a dish of irregularly-shaped cookies that nevertheless made my mouth water.

Seeing the direction of my glance, Martha said, "I don't recommend them. Our head librarian bought that cookbook Daughters of the Desert published last month, and she's working her way through the pastry section with *very* mixed results. The coffee's okay. If you need anything else, just ask." She paused, and added. "You know, we're all heartbroken."

"Over Precious Doe?"

"Of course, the poor lamb. But over Tujin, too." With that, she closed the door, leaving me alone.

Thanks to the film Martha had preselected, I immediately found what I needed. The first mention of the missing Iraqi girl was tucked in the bottom right corner of the front page of the Monday, June 25, 2001, edition of the *Cochise County Observer*. Underneath the same, sad-eyed school photograph I had seen earlier, the story read:

GIRL MISSING

Los Perdidos—The parents of Tujin Rafik, a seven-year-old Los Perdidos girl, reported her missing last night when she failed to reach a friend's house where she was supposed to attend a birthday party.

Her father, Meki Rafik, 46, who works at Apache Chemical Company, said, "This is a safe neighborhood, and Tujin told us she would be fine to walk there. When it grew dark and she was not back, I called the parents. The mother answered and told me Tujin was not expected at the party. I asked to talk to the father, but he said the same. Why would my daughter lie to me about this? I do not understand."

Tujin's mother, Ciwangul Rafik, 22, was unavailable for comment.

Sheriff Bill Avery said that if the girl wasn't found soon, he and his deputies would conduct a house-to-house search. "The father told us that because of her language difficulties Tujin was having trouble in

school, so there's every chance that this
is just a runaway. We'll probably find her
at a friend's house. But don't worry, we'll
stay on this until the child is reunited
with her family."

Yes, I'd missed a couple of things when Jimmy had shown me
the articles back in Scottsdale. For starters, the age of the missing
girl's mother—twenty-two—meant that she had given birth at
fifteen. Her husband was more than twice her age.

Another thing that made me uneasy now was Sheriff Avery's
quote about Tujin's supposed language difficulties. The girl's
father certainly spoke fluently enough in the article, and I knew
from my own experience that immigrant children learned new
languages even more quickly than their parents. Perhaps the
reporter had tidied up the father's quotes, a not-uncommon
journalistic practice.

For the rest of the week and the weeks thereafter, the *Observer*
expressed increasing concern over the missing girl. The Sunday
issue on September 9, 2001, ran a large feature about Tujin. The
headline over her picture said it all:

HOPE FADES FOR TUJIN

Los Perdidos—Although searchers have followed numerous leads and repeatedly combed
the area for clues leading to the disappearance of Tujin Rafik, 7, who went missing from
Los Perdidos three months ago, no trace of
her has been found.

"We're not giving up," said Sheriff Bill
Avery, who was interviewed at his office for
this story. "My deputies and I, along with
hundreds of volunteers, have contributed
thousands of man hours to the search, and
we'll continue to search until we bring
Tujin home."

Requests for interviews with Tujin Rafik's
parents went unanswered. Their neighbors say
they are too devastated to speak.

"Those poor people," said Janice White-

wood, 33, who lives next door to the Rafik
family. "They went through hell with that
awful Saddam, then they escaped to Turkey
where they were treated like dirt because
they belonged to some kind of minority. They
expected a better life here, but instead,
they've lost their little girl. Now they
won't even come out of their house. So much
for America being better than any place
else, huh?"

Here the day-to-day coverage about Tujin Rafik's disappearance ended, because two days later, planes flew into the World
Trade Center, the Pentagon, and a Pennsylvania pasture. Among
the dead was a Los Perdidos native, an Iranian-American busboy
working at Windows on the World.

The next time Tujin's name appeared in print was when her
family returned to Iraq. Then it was buried in a six-line blurb
on B-6, below the fold.

But the day after I found Precious Doe, the headline on the
Cochise County Observer screamed:

SECOND CHILD, SECOND TRAGEDY

Chapter Seven

"Did you know the Rafik family?" I asked Martha Green, after paying for the copies I'd made in the microfilm room. Since Los Perdidos only had two libraries, the Geronimo and the smaller Cochise, there was a chance she had at least met the missing girl.

She continued to shelve books. "I ran into them every now and then at Safeway, but we weren't exactly friendly. They were reclusive, very Old World, and I never saw the girl out on her own."

I knew what she meant. In Phoenix, where there was a size-able community of newly-arrived folks from Middle Eastern countries, a few had trouble blending in. Unlike the European immigrants who entered the U.S. over the past few centuries and were eager to dive into the melting pot, some Muslims, concerned about what they saw as Americans' lax morals, were loathe to do so.

The upside was that their children tended to be better behaved than most kids. You never heard about roving gangs of Muslim toughs painting graffiti on fences or participating in drive-by shootings. The downside was that some traditionally-oriented Muslims made no effort to enter into the chaotic raucousness of American life. After the events of 9/11, their refusal had brought about increasing government scrutiny, which in turn, made the traditionals withdraw even further.

But Tujin had disappeared *before* 9/11. Remembering her father's seeming fluency in English in the earlier article, I asked the librarian, "Did you ever hear Tujin talk?"

She gave me a baffled look. "What a strange question. She came in here with her mother and father once, asking if I would help her find a book for some class assignment. There was nothing wrong with her voice, if that's what you mean."

Had Tujin's father lied to Sheriff Avery? "Then you had no trouble understanding her."

"Of course not. She didn't even have an accent. Her mother was a different story. The poor woman couldn't speak a word of English but the father was fairly fluent. Say, what's this all about?"

"Just a discrepancy I'm trying to clear up. By the way, I'm curious as to why this is the first I've heard that a child's been missing from this area for several years? Why didn't the state media cover it more thoroughly? If she'd disappeared right after 9/11, I could understand, but it happened months earlier."

A bitter laugh. "See the color of Tujin's skin?"

I studied the girl's photograph again. She was dark. Very dark.

Martha explained, "The local media's about the only coverage Tujin received, because the same day, a blond-haired, blue-eyed ten-year-old went missing in Maine. The media, even the Arizona media, were all over *that* girl's case." Her mouth twisted. "Not that color had anything to do with it, of course."

The more things change, the more they stay the same. Missing blondes of whatever age received the most press. Something else puzzled me. "None of these articles mentioned anything about brothers or sisters."

She slid another book onto the shelf, "I hear she was an only child."

Recently, I'd worked a case in Phoenix, a hate crime against a Muslim Circle K clerk, and had noticed that Muslims enjoyed large families. "Isn't that unusual, for a Muslim girl to be an only child?"

"Oh, yes. Family is very important to those folks, but Tujin was a Kurd. I'm not certain she was Muslim."

"The newspaper said she was Iraqi."

The librarian in her emerged. "The Kurds are from northern Iraq, but a lot of them left after Saddam tried to wipe them out. Remember his mustard gas attack against one of their villages? Genocide rears its ugly head again. You would think that after Hitler, the world would have learned better, but apparently not."

She shook her head, as if trying to clear it of demons. "Anyway, as I was saying about Tujin being an only child, I think her mother had health issues and couldn't have any more children. She sure didn't look healthy. When she was here with Tujin that day, I saw her wince a couple of times, like she was in pain."

Had there been violence in the Rafik household? "Did you mention that to the sheriff?"

"In retrospect, maybe I should have." She shelved the last book and stood up with a groan. "My back isn't what it used to be. Tell you what, you want to talk to someone who actually knew Tujin, let me set you up with Peggy Binder. She was one of Tujin's teachers."

Stuffing the microfilm printouts into my carry-all, I said, "I'd appreciate that. She might be able to give me the names of Tujin's friends, or those of any adults she might have been acquainted with."

She gave me a thoughtful look. "I've read that most victims know their killers. Is that right?"

I nodded.

Her dark eyes clouded over. "That just makes it worse."

Having known and trusted a murderer or two myself, I agreed. No one wants to think that the person they invite to dinner is capable of horrific crimes. We prefer the representatives of evil to arrive as strangers.

A glance at my watch revealed why I had been tempted by the ugly cookies in the microfilm room. I'd worked through both breakfast and lunch. After thanking Martha for her help, I headed for the nearest fast food drive-through.

Since the Jeep is a stick shift I never eat while driving, so I gobbled down my Big Mac in the parking lot. The McDonald's sat at the top of a hill, and unlike most fast food restaurants, actually had a view. As I ate, I looked down along the length of Los Perdidos' main street. In the city center, saloons and adobe-housed businesses comprised the usual Western mix-up before the southern end of town degenerated into car lots and railroad tracks.

For all its ungainly growth, Los Perdidos had yet to birth a real mall. No movie houses, no game arcades or bowling alleys, just a few strip malls containing Blockbusters, mom & pop restaurants, and nondescript businesses. I wondered what the local teens did for fun. Stayed home and read *Moby Dick?*

To the east a series of ticky-tacky housing tracts and a small apartment complex sprawled across the desert. In the foothills rising toward Geronimo's rugged peaks, Apache Chemical pumped white vapor from its smokestacks into the azure sky. Located conveniently nearby, as if purposely built there to treat the victims of industrial accidents, sat Los Perdidos General Hospital, its steel-and-glass facade gleaming in the sun.

After finishing my Big Mac, I wiped dribbles of Secret Sauce off my fingers with a skimpy napkin and headed to the hospital to deliver the toys purchased at Wal-Mart.

This time I bypassed the receptionist and took the elevator straight to Pediatrics, where I handed the toys to a nurse. As she thanked me, a speaker set high on the wall announced that Dr. Nelson Lanphear was needed for a consult in Radiology. I recognized the name as that of the medical examiner who performed the autopsy on Precious Doe.

Radiology was on the second floor, where a helpful orderly identified Lanphear for me. The doctor, a beefy man with a bald head, stood quietly in the hallway while a younger doctor stabbed his forefinger at a clipboard. From what I could hear, the younger doctor disagreed with the older man's diagnosis.

Lanphear waited patiently, then when the other man wound down, said, "Oh, yes, that's what I thought, too, at first. But then I noticed..." He saw me listening and lowered his voice. After a minute, the younger doctor took his clipboard and moved off, pacified.

Lanphear approached, a frown on his face. "If you're looking for the nurses' station, it's that way." He gestured toward the elevators.

Although the chances of getting him to share the results of the dead child's autopsy were zero, I made the effort, but the minute the words "Precious Doe" emerged, he shut me down. "Anything you need to know about the autopsy, Sheriff Avery will tell you."

There seemed no point in telling him that the sheriff had already declined to share information. "If you change your mind, here's my card."

"Good day, Ms. Jones." Refusing my card, he stalked down the hall, not before I had seen a muscle twitch underneath his eye. Either he had a bad case of nerves, which seemed unlikely given his patience with the younger doctor, or something about the child's autopsy bothered him.

Before leaving the hospital, I rode the elevator up to Pediatrics, where I was gratified to see several children already cuddling their new stuffed toys. "How many kids are usually in here?" I asked a passing nurse.

"Anywhere from five to twenty," she replied, before moving on. "Right now, there's six. When summer comes and school's out, the accidents increase. As well as other things."

By "other things," I knew what she meant. Most parents control their tempers, some don't. In case there was a sudden increase in broken arms, I returned to Wal-Mart and filled my shopping cart with any toy that did not seem sexist or foolish. Then I headed to the hospital again and handed the shopping bags over to the same nurse.

What now? Duane Tucker would not arrive home from work for another couple of hours, so after reaching the parking lot, I used part of the lag time to check my voice mail. Angelique Grey had called twice, not a good sign. Her persistence probably meant trouble on the set of *Desert Eagle*.

The fact that Angel was Warren's ex-wife no longer fazed me. They had both moved on emotionally: her, to another actor; him, to a string of actresses, then me. Working with Angel had its challenges, though. She tended to be overly dramatic, which I found tiring. But business is business, so I hit the redial button.

She must have been holding the phone in her hand, because her answer interrupted its first ring. "Lena, you have to fly out here right away." Her voice, so melodic in her films, had taken on an edge.

I leaned back in the Jeep's seat, making myself comfortable for what promised to be a long, stressful conversation. "What's going on? Did *Desert Eagle* lose one of its sponsors?"

Since being hired on as a script consultant to the TV show, I had learned that sponsors were more important to the networks than sensible plots. My contribution to the series was to make certain the storylines did not become too ridiculous, always an uphill battle. For instance, during the first season, the producers saddled Angel's character, a half-Cherokee private investigator living in Arizona, with an ex-convict for a partner. The fact that no felon was allowed to have a P.I. license didn't matter to the show's producers.

At least not until "Giff" Gifford, the actor cast as the felonious P.I., got caught driving a hundred-and-five miles per hour along Pacific Coast Highway, his glove compartment filled with cocaine. After Giff checked into rehab, his character "died" saving a woman from a cougar attack. The producers had wanted to make it a shark attack, but I managed to dissuade them by explaining that Arizona had been sharkless for several million years.

Given the program's history, I was not astounded when Angel wailed, "They're messing with the storyline again, Lena!"

Same old, same old. "Calm down, Angel. Nothing could be worse than Giff and we survived him, didn't we? How's he doing, by the way?"

A theatrical groan. "Same as always. Talking Twelve Step, gulping Stoli. But that's his problem. Our's is that the producers want to replace him with a kid as a continuing character. One of our new sponsors has a microwave snack line, Cheezy-O's or something like that, and they want to appeal to the under-twelve demographic."

"*Under twelve?*" The show was one of television's darkest crime dramas. Past plots had featured bondage, necrophilia, and once, a graphically-filmed murder by an old Chinese torture called The Death of a Thousand Cuts. "You can't be serious."

"Oh, but I am. That's why I need you here. Speerstra won't listen to a thing I say." Hamilton "Ham" Speerstra was *Desert Eagle*'s executive producer, a ferret-faced man with a false smile and avaricious eyes.

"Since the Giff thing," she continued, "which you warned him about from the beginning, he pays more attention to you than anyone, so can you take the next flight? Spend the night at my place and we'll corner him first thing tomorrow morning. Once everything's straightened out, you can fly back. Or stay for a few days and we'll go shopping."

I shook my head, then remembering that she couldn't see it, said, "Sorry. I'm working a murder case in Southern Arizona." I didn't add that the way things were going, I might not even make our regular Friday script meeting.

"But they'll have him in war paint by then!"

An ambulance screamed by on the way to the hospital's emergency entrance, drowning out her next sentence. When it pulled up to the doors and cut the siren, I said, "Repeat that. It sounded like you said something about war paint, but I probably heard wrong."

Another theatrical groan. "You heard me right. The new story-line calls for a ten-year-old Indian boy who solves crime by communicating with his long-dead ancestors. If Speerstra gets his way, *Desert Eagle* will take a sharp left turn toward Woo-Woo City."

I enjoyed my first laugh in days. "A baby shaman is going to be your new partner?"

"It's not funny, Lena. I'm supposed to be fighting crime, not spirits."

At her distress, I sobered. "There's nothing I can do. The case I'm working, it's a murdered child, possibly two."

"Oh." Her tone changed. She might have been an actress, but she was also a mother. "Okay, I'll try to stall Speerstra, but whatever happens, be here Friday, promise?"

With reluctance, I promised. It was the third mistake I would make that day.

We chatted for a few more minutes about Warren, the twins, the L.A. smog, the decaying freeways, the rising crime rate. She ended the conversation by saying that she was thinking about moving to Scottsdale after the *Desert Eagle* franchise died its natural death. At that pie-in-the-sky pronouncement, I reminded her that Scottsdale now enjoyed all the standard urban problems: smog, terrible traffic, and yes, a skyrocketing crime rate. Scottsdale husbands were killing their wives on a regular basis. The only difference was that Arizonans used guns, not knives.

"Thanks for those bright words of cheer," she said bitterly, then rang off.

After talking to Angel, I needed a bit of cheer myself, so I pushed the rapid-dial button and within seconds connected with Warren.

"I called earlier, but your voice mail picked up," I told him, attempting to hide my tension. I knew he wouldn't be comfortable with my involvement in the Precious Doe case. Or any murder case, as far as that went. Understanding how my childhood had wounded me, he believed the rougher side of P.I. work only added to my nightmares. Once, after a particularly bad night, he told me I needed forgetfulness, not reminders.

Like Angel, Warren was only a couple of hundred miles away in L.A., but from the distance in his voice, he might have been on the moon. "Sorry, but I've been in and out. You know how it is."

"Sure do."

When only silence was forthcoming, I asked, "So what's happening?"

"Not much." I could almost hear his shrug. Something was wrong.

He always liked talking about work, so I gave that a try. "How's the Apache Wars documentary coming along?"

His answer stunned me. "It's scrapped."

"When you've almost finished the preproduction work?" I could hardly believe it. Warren had been enthusiastic about resuming his series on American history told from the Native American point of view. He saw Geronimo as a freedom fighter and was determined to correct the one-sided history we'd all learned in school.

"Yeah, I know," he said, "but I'm kind of off Arizona right now."

"What do you mean, 'off'?" How could a person be "off" an entire state?

A deep breath, then, "I just don't want to be reminded about, well, about what we saw out there in the desert. It's not as if I'm in your line of work and stumble across dead bodies every day." Then he caught himself. "I'm sorry. I didn't mean to say that."

There was no arguing the fact that detectives saw more dead bodies than the average person, so I accepted his apology, and for the sake of peace, changed the subject. "How are the twins?"

Warmth returned to his voice. "Precocious as always." Ever the proud father, he bragged about his girls for a few minutes, then asked, "Angel said she was going to ask you to fly out here tonight."

Since they shared the twins, living memories of their five-year marriage, Warren and Angel were always on the phone with each other. "Yes, she did," I told him, "but I had to turn her down."

Now he sounded exasperated. "Angel *needs* you, Lena. That series of hers is in trouble. The only taste Speerstra has is in his mouth, and even there, nada. Blindfolded, he couldn't tell a taco from a turd."

A pithy observation, but irrelevant. Even though it would upset him, I decided to be frank. "I can't fly out there right now because I'm in Los Perdidos trying to find out what happened to that little girl."

"You're involved in *another* murder case?" His exasperation mutated into fear. "Don't you remember what happened last spring?"

It's hard to forget almost being killed, but that's the risk P.I.'s take, I reminded him.

He groaned. "Then move to L.A. and work in the film industry full-time."

I would rather be dipped in honey and staked to an anthill, but this was hardly the time to admit it, because my refusal to abandon Desert Investigations was becoming an increasingly sore spot in our long-distance relationship. "I'll think about it."

Warren was no fool. "Lena, you might not mind living like a nun, but I'm no monk. There's a limit to how…" He didn't need to finish the sentence. "Do you understand what I'm saying?"

I certainly did, although I would describe the exclusivity of our relationship less religiously and more militarily, sort of like the Army's don't-ask-don't-tell policy. In other words, don't ask me if I'm screwing around, Lena, and I won't have to tell you the truth.

"Understood, Warren, and remember, the agreement works both ways." Not that I had any candidates in mind.

He didn't like my answer, and his voice turned frosty. "Well, it's been nice chatting with you, but I've got places to go, people to see."

I hated to leave the conversation on that note, but another ambulance came screaming up the hill, so I shouted a good-bye and rang off. The ambulance pulled up to the emergency entrance and paramedics jumped out, ran around to the rear doors, and jerked them open. I was parked at least twenty yards away, but could still hear moans emanating from the ambulance's interior. Carefully, but with great speed, the paramedics eased out a stretcher. On it lay a woman with hair as blond as mine. The sheet covering her was soaked with blood.

Something terrible had happened to her, but at least she was alive.

It being the middle of the week, I figured the chances of catching my elderly informant at the Geronimo Lounge were slim, but I stopped by the bar anyway. Since Dr. Lanphear had refused to tell me anything about Precious Doe's autopsy, another run at the old guy was in order.

I fought my way through the smoke and beer fumes to the long bar, ordered a Coke, and as soon as my eyes accustomed themselves to the dim light, looked around. He wasn't there. Swallowing my disappointment, I called the bartender over and described the man I was searching for.

"You must mean Clive Berklee," the bartender said, a thin man whose bushy salt-and-pepper hair harkened back to the Afros of the Seventies. "Old guy, drinks Molson's, always working a crossword puzzle? Usually comes in Sundays?"

Thank God for bartenders. "That's him. Do you know his nephew, by any chance, the one who's the medical examiner's assistant?"

He shook his head. "All I know, his name's Herschel and he's some kinda lab tech or male nurse. Not a lot of the hospital crowd comes in here. Any drinking they do, they do at home."

At least now I had a name. Herschel. I already knew that the medical examiner's assistant had a loose lip. Maybe, with the proper incentive, he would tell me more.

Before hunting Herschel down, I drove by Geronimo's Rest Mobile Home Community, where Duane Tucker and his mother lived. I've seen better trailer parks and I've seen worse. Near the entrance perched several rows of double-wides, most of them in fairly good shape. Some even boasted tiny, picket-fenced yards filled with flowers and whirligigs.

As the lane wound its way through the park, however, the real estate degenerated into single-wides so battered they might have been plundered from salvage yards. At the end of a line of particularly damaged trailers was a deserted play area with a slide and creaky swing set. I saw no children anywhere.

Even more worrisome were the suspicious faces that watched from trailer windows as the Jeep crept down the lane, so it came as a relief when I finally found Duane's rusting single-wide. His trailer was anchored next door to a sleek Airstream, against which leaned a wrecked Harley-Davidson partially covered by a tarp.

Two little girls, both freckled redheads, sat on the steps of this gleaming paragon, engrossed in what appeared to be homework. When I pulled my Jeep to a stop, the older girl passed her notebook to the other, and stood up.

"If you're huntin' Duane, he ain't home." She was about ten, wearing clean but frayed slacks and a sweater several sizes too large.

The curtains in the trailer twitched. Someone was inside, listening.

"How about his mother, then?"

The girl snickered. "Joleene's 'asleep.'" Her hands made the common quote gesture. "You their friend?"

"Just somebody who wants to talk to them."

Another snicker. "You must be a cop, then, 'cause Duane ain't got no social worker no more. Hey, that sure is a pretty Jeep, all painted up with them Indian signs and everything. Would you take me and Labelle here for a ride?"

Given the circumstances of my visit, her over-friendly attitude worried me. "Didn't your mother tell you it was dangerous to get in a stranger's car?"

"Got no mother. So what's your name, pretty lady?"

I guessed where this was going and I was right. As soon as I told her my name, she said, "I'm Ladonna Lundstrom, I'm ten, and that there's my sister Labelle, she's eight. Now we's friends, so can we go for a ride?"

"Sorry. The answer's still no."

Her Cupid's bow mouth turned down. "You're a bitch."

"And you have a dirty mouth."

"Screw you."

At that, the curtains gave a final twitch. The door opened and a man wearing a torn Foo Fighters tee shirt hobbled out, his leg encased in a thigh-high cast. In his right hand he carried a baseball bat. "Ladonna, what did I hear from your mouth?"

Ladonna didn't flinch at the sight of the bat. "Labelle said two dirty words."

"Did not." Labelle, sounding bored.

The man, who had the same red hair as the girls, had obviously been around this block before. Scowling at Ladonna, he said, "You think I can't tell your voices apart? Get your lying butt in here."

Ladonna threw me a look that blistered paint and slunk into the trailer.

Foo Fighter Man turned his attention to me and raised the bat. "You'd a started to put them in that Jeep, I'd a bashed your ass."

I so admire protective parents. "Sir, do you have any idea when Duane will be home?"

"Never, I hope. You a friend of his, you better not let me catch you talking to my babies again." He grabbed the other girl by the arm and pulled her into the trailer.

So much for a minor's arrest record being expunged when he turned eighteen. The whole nosy trailer park probably knew about Duane's background, but being poor and powerless, they could do nothing to rid themselves of his presence. I wondered how Duane was faring now that Precious Doe's body had been found. For that matter, I also wondered about Floyd Polk's safety.

How long would it be before a Los Perdidos vigilante took matters into his own hands?

Chapter Eight

While waiting for Duane to get home, I killed time with a cup of coffee at a nearby Burger King. The coffee was fine, but the view from the parking lot lacked the scenic scope of that from McDonald's, and all I could see was the back end of a feed store. I sipped until six, then zipped my jacket against the cooling October air and returned to Geronimo's Rest Trailer Park. This time I struck lucky, if you can call talking to the town tough and his drunken mother lucky.

"I never touched that kid," Duane Tucker said, leaning against his trailer door as if to block me from entering. His mug shot had not revealed his lack of height or eroded teeth, the kind that came from smoking crystal meth.

His mother, Joleene, reached around him and snatched my I.D. out of my hand. Her lips moved as she read. Handing it back, she told him, "She ain't a cop, just some kinda private detective like the ones on TV. We don't have to talk to her." A bleached blonde, an inch of gray-brown roots showed at the base of her stringy, shoulder-length hair. She swayed, one hand on her son's arm, the other wrapped around a Budweiser.

"That's true," I told her. "You don't have to talk to me, but the sheriff sees Duane as a possible suspect in the girl's death. Maybe I can help straighten things out."

Duane sized me up with a practiced sneer. I must have passed inspection because despite his mother's protests, he invited me in. The trailer smelled almost as foul as Floyd Polk's place.

Flies buzzed merrily near the tiny kitchen's sink, where a pile of food-encrusted plates moldered away. Budweiser cans littered the avocado shag carpet, and the pink floral sofa boasted almost as much rotting food as the plates in the sink.

Someone had at least made an attempt at decor, if not cleanliness, by taping a large, brightly-colored cartoon strip over the sofa. The artwork appeared to be original, and while gory in subject matter—a werewolf chomping his way through a teen slumber party—it had been rendered with obvious skill.

"Can't nobody prove I done anything," Duane said, stepping over a crushed beer can.

I forced a smile. "I'm sure you didn't, but do you have an alibi? The girl died sometime late Friday night or early Saturday morning. Where were you then?"

"With me," his mother said, flopping down on the filthy sofa. Due to health concerns, I remained standing.

Duane threw her a sour look. "I was with Shirley."

"That slut." Joleene took another swig from her Budweiser and belched.

"Ain't no worse than you, Ma."

I interrupted this jolly family interchange. "May I have Shirley's address?"

Duane, who at least wasn't illiterate, picked up a pencil and paper, and in delicate script, wrote MRS. GENEVA ROUSSE, 4210 SO. WICKIUP. "We was at Happy's Cantina til they closed down Friday night, then we followed some friends over to their apartment and partied til noon. They'll back me up. And yeah, you can talk to Shirley's mom, too We had a big fight over me keeping her out all night, so she's sure gonna remember. If that kid died when you said she did, I couldn't a done it. I told the sheriff as much when he came nosing around."

Joleene spoke up again. "That bastard's always been after good people like us."

I kept my smile in place. "Cops are like that, aren't they?" I produced the newspaper clipping with Precious Doe's picture. "Have either of you seen this girl?"

The mother gave it a brief glance and snorted a negative, but Duane surprised me. "A few months ago I saw somebody like her standing in front of that mosque-thing they rigged up by the Unitarian Church." He darted a quick look at his mother. "I used to go to Al-Anon meetings in one of the buildings." He stopped, flushed, then tried again. "Anyway, she was talking to an Egyptian girl around the same age. The Egyptian kid was wearing one of those head scarves."

"Do you mean a *hijab*?"

"Yeah, that's the word. A black one."

Interesting. "Did you tell the sheriff this?"

Joleene answered for him, a self-satisfied smirk on her face. "I told Duane not to ever tell the cops nothing."

Not even when the information might help clear him? I didn't know which infuriated me the most, the woman's hostility or her prideful ignorance. She had accomplished a minor miracle by actually making me feel sorry for Duane. When I glanced at the cartoon strip above the sofa again, I saw that one of the teens being chomped by the werewolf bore a strong resemblance to her.

"Your work?" I asked Duane, pointing. "It's very good."

His false sneer slipped into a genuine smile, but before he answered, Joleene snatched the artwork off the wall, crumpled it into a ball, and tossed it to the floor. "Shit stuff. Any five-year-old can do better."

A millisecond of hurt flashed across Duane's face as he bent to pick up the cartoon.

The corners of my mouth began to cramp, so I let my smile go. "Well, thanks for the help. I'll check with Shirley and her mother, and if Duane's story holds up, I'll pass that along to the sheriff."

Joleene belched again. "Suit yourself, Miss Fancy Pants."

Fighting the urge to smack her, I asked Duane, "Anything else you know that might help?"

He held his crumpled artwork in his hands and smoothed it the best he could. When he looked at me again, the sneer had returned to his face. "I told you everything I know, so why don't you just leave?"

With great relief, I did.

From the trailer park, I drove to Happy's Cantina, where the bartender said that, yes, the night Precious Doe died, Duane and his girlfriend stayed at the bar until closing time, when they left with a crowd of other drunks. He directed me to a booth toward the rear, where a group of Duane's friends were sharing a pitcher of beer.

Three were sober enough to agree that, yeah, the dude and the hot bitch had spent the rest of the night at their apartment, and by the way, why didn't I join them 'cause I wasn't half bad myself. After declining their gracious offer, I drove to the Rousse house. While Shirley, clad in a skimpy middy top and crotch-hugging jeans, sulked in the background, Mrs. Rousse confirmed Duane's alibi.

"He brought Shirley home drunk past noon, for Christ's sake. You tell him if I ever see his meth-smoking face again, I'll take a shotgun to it."

Unless they were all lying, Duane was in the clear.

By now it was almost seven, but on the off chance Sheriff Avery was still in his office, I stopped by. He was there, all right, standing in the reception area, staring at the picture of the dead child tacked up on the bulletin board. His blue eyes were blood-shot, and his already craggy face seemed to have lost flesh.

"What do you want now?" Even his voice sounded tired.

"Duane has an air-tight alibi."

He eased into a chair across from a just-as-tired deputy. The deputy's desk was piled high with Precious Doe's DO YOU KNOW ME? fliers. Since my newspaper cutting was getting ragged around the edges, I helped myself to several.

Avery frowned but didn't take them away. "An air-tight alibi? Lot of those going around, these days. Floyd Polk's pickup truck hasn't been running for a couple of weeks. I know because we checked it out ourselves. The guy had no way of transporting anyone's body, not even his own. He's been hitching into town for his provisions."

Comparing notes wasn't the only reason I had decided to brave Avery's hostility. "Sheriff, given the mood of the town, perhaps you should arrange for some sort of protection for those two. Polk, especially." I remembered that isolated shack and the old man's vulnerability. A knife would be inadequate defense against an angry mob.

The deputy started laughing but Avery silenced him. "Believe me, we would if we had the manpower, but unfortunately, we don't. With this cooler weather, crime is up. Car thefts, break-ins, and old ladies spooked by illegals cutting through their yards on the way to Tucson. It's all we can do these days to keep the Mexes from getting shot."

"What about the FBI? Didn't you tell me earlier that they've taken an interest in the case?"

He snorted. "That turned out to be just so much hot air. Thanks to the Patriot Act, the Feds are too busy opening everybody's mail than to help us catch child killers. A couple of agents did show up yesterday, asked a few questions, then drove back to Tucson, probably to sneak-read their neighbors' credit card bills. Like I said, we're swamped. Polk and Duane have to fend for themselves."

A common excuse, but true. If the police had enough manpower, there would be no crime. Of course, there would be no freedom, either, but that was another issue entirely.

"Duane said he saw someone resembling Precious Doe talking to another girl of her age at some mosque near the Unitarian Church. An 'Egyptian kid' is how he described her." Too late I wondered how Duane could tell the difference between an Egyptian, an Iraqi, or any other Middle Eastern person. Then I remembered his beautifully-detailed cartoon. He had an artist's eye.

Avery shook his head. "There's no real mosque in town, not enough Muslims, although Lee Casey up at Apache Chemical is doing what he can to change that. They're cheaper labor and less trouble than the locals. The Unitarians let them use their hall for Friday services and various social get-togethers. Maybe that's what Duane meant."

"Do you have any idea who the Egyptian girl might be? She wears a *hijab*." Most Middle Eastern immigrants I'd met in Phoenix eschewed traditional dress, so there was a good chance this detail might help identify her.

He thought for a moment. "I wonder if he means the younger Wahab girl. Aziza, I think her name is. Her father, Dr. Kalil Wahab, is one of those Egyptian chemists Casey sponsored. Talk about strict! From what I hear, Wahab really makes his kids tow the line."

I fought down my excitement because the tip might turn out to be nothing. "Would you give me their address?"

Avery's face closed down. "They're in the book."

Détente was canceled. Hostilities had resumed.

As revealed by the tattered telephone directory I found hanging from a payphone outside a nearby Circle K, Dr. Kalil Wahab and family lived on Broken Arrow Avenue in an upscale area of town. The house probably wasn't more than five years old, but was designed to look like a Territorial relic, with faux logs protruding from faux adobe and a faux ladder leading up to the roof. A satellite dish perched incongruously atop the tile roof.

After my third knock, a dark-skinned man dressed in navy wool slacks and a pale blue cashmere sweater answered the door. The scent of something wonderful drifted out from the kitchen.

"May I help you?" the man asked, in lightly-accented English.

Dr. Wahab, I presumed. Not tall, but handsome, with a slim build, chocolate-colored eyes and short black hair.

I introduced myself and explained my mission.

He confirmed that he was, indeed, Dr. Wahab, then shook his head. "Our Aziza knows no such person, Miss Jones."

"She was seen talking to the girl." Why reveal that my informant was one of the most disreputable men in town?

Wahab started to shake his head again, then thought better of it. "Surely there has been a mistake, but perhaps you should come in while I ascertain the truth of this? I do not wish you to wait alone on our doorstep in the cold air."

The temperature hovered in the low sixties, but we do get spoiled up in Scottsdale. Grateful for his Middle Eastern courtesy, I stepped into a living room furnished with exquisite Persian rugs and high-end electronics. A large plasma television screen tuned to an Arab satellite TV station hung on the wall, while a scattering of Bose speakers, a Metronome Technologie CD player, a Game Boy, a Wii and other toys occupied the ebony entertainment center below. Despite what I had been led to believe, Apache Chemical paid well enough.

In a nearby alcove, three boys of stair-stepped ages played Scrabble at an intricately-carved game table. The smallest, a boy of about eight, had put down ZOOSPORE, much to the annoyance of the others. At my entrance, they rose, nodded a polite hello, then resumed their game, but not before the oldest kicked Zoospore Boy's ankle.

"Kalil?" A beautiful woman wearing an ankle-length *abayah* muted the TV and placed the remote on a rosewood coffee table. This hospitable gesture revealed a greater racket. Thundering down the hallway came an avalanche of traditional Middle Eastern music backed by a dance beat, with the female singer's voice raised in ululation. Aziza, rocking out to an Egyptian version of Beyoncé?

Dr. Wahab said to the woman, "Quibilah, this woman has a question about Aziza."

Quibilah Wahab's hushed beauty came as a welcome relief after the hapless Joleene, but concern filled her dark eyes as she stepped toward us. "Has she done something wrong?"

Halfway through telling her the same thing I'd told her husband, Dr. Wahab interrupted, saying something in Arabic to his wife.

She blinked. "Oh, Kalil, I do not think…"

He interrupted again in more Arabic, and with a chagrined expression, Quibilah hurried out of the room.

Extending a hand toward the crushed velvet sofa, Dr. Wahab said, "Please be comfortable, Miss Jones. I will now view this picture of which you speak."

When I sat down, I sank several inches into down-filled cushions. After recovering my balance, I rummaged through my carry-all, pulled out a flier, and handed it over. "This is the girl I'm talking about."

He studied the picture carefully. "I do not know this child."

"Your daughter might."

He shook his head. "Aziza knows only those people I wish her to know, and this dead girl, of whom I have heard much, does not belong to that select group. We Egyptians do not allow our children make their own friends or run loose in the streets to find trouble. We keep them close at home, near our hearts, *and* our eyes and ears!"

Considering the high delinquency rate in the U.S., his was a sensible philosophy, but a disappointing one. "Are you sure she, or even perhaps one of your sons, hasn't seen the girl around?"

With a grunt, Dr. Wahab took the flier over to the boys, who after a brief look, all shook their heads.

"You see?" he said, returning.

Just then, a girl of around fifteen bearing a strong resemblance to Mrs. Wahab, and also wearing an elegant *abayah*, limped into the living room carrying a silver tray loaded with a full coffee service. Carefully, she placed the tray on the coffee table, then hobbled away without once meeting my eyes. Birth defect? Accident? Mrs. Wahab, who stood in the doorway watching her, nodded approval. With a tremulous smile, the teenager vanished into the kitchen. Her job of culinary supervision finished, Mrs. Wahab eased herself down on the sofa.

Dr. Wahab gestured toward the tray. "Please try the coffee. Shalimar, our older daughter, whom you have just seen, brews it Egyptian style, not Starbuck's. You will find a great deal of difference."

After only one sip of the diesel-strength brew, I felt adrenaline dancing through my veins. I took a larger sip. "Addictive!"

Dr. Wahab inclined his head. "You see? Sometimes the ways you Americans consider foreign have much to be admired."

True, but I refused to be sidetracked. "Perhaps I might ask Aziza if she recognizes the girl?"

He frowned. "Impossible. Aziza has a test tomorrow, so she may not receive visitors. In the old days, education was not considered necessary for girls, but as a modern man, I do allow her that privilege."

"My husband speaks wisely," Quibilah put in. "My own degree is in mathematics. And Shalimar is already taking college-level courses. Not that it will make a difference." She glanced toward the kitchen. Problems with Aziza's older sister? From my own experience, I knew teenagers could be tough, especially the girls.

Dr. Wahab gave his wife a doting smile but continued addressing his comments to me. "Like my sons, Aziza studies well with music, so I allow her that small pleasure, also. While it goes against my better judgement to interrupt her, you are anxious to discover this dead child's true identity, so I will show her the flier. The girl appears to be only sleeping, so I do not believe viewing the picture will cause my daughter undue sorrow. If you would wait here, please?"

With that, he disappeared down the hall.

The Middle Eastern music boomed out twice as loud as before when Dr. Wahab opened the door to his daughter's room. "*Aziza!*" he shouted. Then I heard an irritated spate of Arabic.

"Oh, *Daddy!*" A young girl.

After another gruff command from Dr. Wahab, the music lowered enough for me to hear murmurs of conversation, but as soon as he returned to the living room, the music rose to its previous level. Aziza would be lucky to reach the age of ten with her hearing intact.

He handed the flier to me. "Aziza says she has never met this person."

Not liking other people to ask my questions for me, I remained dissatisfied. "Are you certain I can't talk to her, just for a minute?"

His tone was polite but firm. "I am sorry, but the answer remains no."

In the kitchen, the teenager had begun rattling pots and pans. "How about Shalimar? She might have seen the girl."

He said to his wife, "Quibilah, take the picture to Shalimar."

As Mrs. Wahab stood and held out her hand, I said hurriedly, "I would prefer to ask her myself, if you don't mind."

Dr. Wahab shook his head. "Unlike Aziza, who becomes more American every day, our oldest daughter is uncomfortable in the presence of strangers."

Defeated, I handed the picture to Quibilah Wahab and watched her take it into the kitchen. She returned a moment later shaking her head. "Shalimar says no, Miss Jones."

"You see?" Dr. Wahab said, nodding at the flier. "Our daughters move within a strictly supervised circle of friends, and this poor girl was not among them. It is unfortunate that you have wasted your time with us since we have been of no help, but perhaps you would like more coffee to warm you against the cold night?"

Although courtesy itself, he preferred to be in control. Fine. Tomorrow I would waylay Aziza and Shalimar on the way to school, show them the flier, and find out the truth.

By the time I made it back to the Lazy M, the sun had lowered behind the cottonwoods. Eager to stretch my legs after spending so much time in the Jeep, I transferred my handgun into its fanny pack, slipped on a light jacket, and set off for a quiet stroll, hoping to find the ruins of the old Johnston farmstead Selma told me about.

The banks of the San Pedro River were famed for their varieties of songbirds. Within a quarter mile I had identified—besides the usual modest cactus wrens and grackles—a gray-blue kingfisher, a bright yellow warbler, and several species of hummingbirds. The hummingbirds, some iridescent turquoise, some sporting rosy throats, siphoned nectar from late-blooming flowers, then flew into the dusk.

Ahead of me, a startled jackrabbit hopped away and small lizards scurried deeper into the brush. Less nervous, a small, yellow-and-black gila monster sat unconcernedly on a rock, soaking up the last heat of the day.

The evening produced a symphony of sound. Crickets chirped, dragonflies hummed, the river danced. Overhead, cottonwood leaves brushed softly together, stirred by a breeze scented with sage. As I continued my walk, twilight closed in, bringing with it the yips of a nearby coyote and the deep-throated squawks of a great blue heron.

Reality trashed this bucolic dream when I rounded a stand of low-hanging willows and entered a clearing. Circling out from the ashy remains of a bonfire were a series of shelters constructed of plastic sheeting draped over low-hanging branches. Within the shelters, moth-eaten blankets and an assortment of mismatched toss pillows made up rough beds.

At first the place appeared to be just another homeless encampment—the area near the Mexican border was littered with them—but as I poked through the makeshift tents, the magazines I discovered made me reconsider. *Hot Rod. American Chopper. Cosmopolitan. Teen Graffiti.* Investigating further, I found a shopping bag filled with empty beer cans and Hostess Twinkie wrappers, and a tin box hidden underneath a nearby pillow revealed a baggie half-filled with marijuana. Another tent held a small sack of fruit-flavored condoms.

Now I knew what the town's teens did for amusement. They snuck off to the river and behaved like teens the world over; they drank beer, smoked weed, and practiced their night moves. Not wanting to be present when the Youth of America showed up for their evening revelries, I hurried away.

A quarter mile further on, I found the remains of the old Johnston farmstead. Nature had finished what Geronimo started, and a thick carpet of vines now covered the cabin's charred foundation. I poked around for a few minutes, finding only a rusted tool too far gone to identify. In case it had belonged to the Johnstons, I left it where it had fallen.

Several yards behind the cabin stood a grouping of grave markers, little more than rocks with inscriptions smoothed by time. But Los Perdidos had not forgotten the lost Johnstons. A contemporary granite obelisk rose behind the markers, the six victims' names carved on its glossy surface.

ELIAS JOHNSTON, 28
MARTHA HOLMES JOHNSTON, 25
ABEL JOHNSTON, 6
SUZANNAH JOHNSTON, 5
PETER JOHNSTON, 2
LOUIZA JOHNSTON, 3 MONTHS

Below the names, their epitaph read: MURDERED BY GERONIMO, 1881.

Upon returning to the guesthouse and checking my messages, I found one from the sheriff. In a voice made strident by fury, he told me to get my ass over to the Wahab's place before he sent his deputies out to drag me there.

Dr. Kalil Wahab had just accused me of kidnapping his daughter.

Chapter Nine

The first thing Sheriff Avery did when I pulled up in front of the Wahab's house was stare at my feet. "Sevens? Eights?"

At five-eight, I'm not a short woman, but I am fine boned and my feet are accordingly small. "Seven-and-a-half, but what does the size of my feet have to do with Dr. Wahab's accusation?"

Between the time the sheriff left the message on my cell phone and my arrival here, he had brought his anger under control. Police radios squawked around him and deputies and crime techs muttered worriedly to each other as they carried bags of evidence from the house, but he stayed steady.

"The footprints in the flower bed underneath the Wahab daughter's window were at least nines, maybe even tens. Medium. Could be a man's, could be a woman's. My techs are taking casts."

"Aziza's really gone, then?" I had not actually met the child, but remembered her girlish voice and spirited music. I tried not to remember the Iraqi girl who had vanished and was never found, or the coyote tugging at Precious Doe's body. This was a time to hope, not grieve.

"Looks like someone gained access through her bedroom window, then carried her away. Dr. Wahab claims it was you." Avery watched for my reaction.

"That's bullshit and you know it."

He nodded. "As a matter of fact, I do. Not that I think you're above breaking the law if it suits your purposes, but sneaking a little girl out of her window isn't your style."

"So why did he make such an outrageous claim?"

He sighed. "When people are upset, they don't think very clearly. Or don't you remember that from your own days on the force? Anyway, when his daughter disappeared, he thought back to your visit and must have decided that your insistence on seeing her was suspicious."

"Insistence" was hardly an accurate representation of our conversation, but I let it go. "Those footprints. Nines or tens, did you say? Mediums?"

I reminded him that neither Floyd Polk or Duane Tucker were large men. As far as I was concerned, Duane did not fit the profile of a molester, but Polk was another child rape waiting to happen. The old man might somehow have managed to get his hands on a vehicle, too. Then again, even if he had wheels, why would he drive all the way into Los Perdidos and pick an upper-middle-class enclave for the scene of his crime? Molesters usually liked to nab their victims on the way to or from school.

"I'm with you on that," the sheriff said. "But I've sent deputies to both men's places. Either of those bastards has that kid, we'll find her."

Any good lawman would have done the same, but Polk's shack was isolated, surrounded by miles of empty desert. If the old man had Aziza, she could be anywhere. As for Duane, there were a couple of reasons he was probably innocent of this particular crime.

"Duane was home with his mother when I talked to him earlier," I told Avery.

"And she wouldn't let her darling boy do anything nasty, right?"

Actually, I didn't think Joleene would, but not from altruism. For whatever reason, the woman hated cops, and anything that might draw their attention would send her into a frenzy. There was one more thing. If I was wrong about Duane and he *had* taken Aziza, he wouldn't be stupid enough to hide the girl in his tiny trailer with all the nosy inhabitants of Geronimo's Rest watching his every move, not to mention the bat-wielding Foo Fighter Man.

Flashers from the cruisers flickered across the Wahab house. Along the street, neighbors assembled on their porches in tight knots, clutching their children to them in an outpouring of love and fear. I could only imagine how the Egyptians felt. Every window in their house blazed with light, as if they hoped all that wattage would reach out to their daughter like a beacon, guiding her home.

As the sheriff turned away, I begged, "Please don't go yet. Tell me how this went down, everything, step by step."

He halted, appeared to think about it for a moment, then said, "All right, Lena. After giving you such a rough time, it's the least I can do. The family discovered Aziza missing right after supper. Dr. Wahab told us she was studying for a test, so as soon as she ate and helped her mother with the dishes, which was around seven o'clock, she went back to her room."

He took a breath, then continued. "About an hour later, when Mrs. Wahab opened the door to tell the kid to switch off the CD player and turn in for the night, she was gone. They tore the house apart searching for her, then did the same with the garage, but she was nowhere to be found. We're now in the process of canvassing the neighborhood, but so far, no one's admitting anything. And before you ask, yes, we've already issued an Amber Alert. Her name and description is already doing crawls on the bottom of TV sets across Arizona."

"Maybe Aziza snuck over to a friend's house to play." Children were prone to stunts like that. I told him about the time when I was a Scottsdale police officer and my unit had scoured the streets in search of a "kidnapped" boy found several hours later enjoying a forbidden game of Dungeons and Dragons at a friend's house.

"Let's hope that's all this turns out to be. I'd like to believe she climbed out that window on her own, but there was only one set of footprints, an adult's."

"So someone definitely went in after her."

He started to answer, but suddenly a horrible sound from the Wahab residence tore at the night, the kind of sound you hear when a coyote captures its prey. Avery jerked his head around. "What the hell was that?"

The sound came again. A woman. Keening.

I'd heard women mourn like this over the bodies of children and lovers, but experience didn't make the sound easier to bear.

The sheriff and I both knew that if a missing child wasn't recovered within the first twenty-four hours, the odds of her safe return dropped drastically, so after a hasty good-bye, I hurried to my Jeep and headed toward Polk's. With the Jeep's four-wheel drive, I could at least go into the desert and listen for a child's cries.

As it turned out, others had made the same decision. A caravan of trucks and four-wheelers sped along the dirt road leading to the shack, the beds of several pickups loaded with rifle-toting men. If they caught Polk with Aziza, I doubted they would attempt to take him alive. No fan of vigilante action, my real concern was that the mens' rage might hinder their aim, causing them to accidentally shoot the child, too.

If Polk had her, which was far from certain.

By the time I reached his place, a pair of tense deputies were stuffing a shaking Polk into the rear seat of their cruiser, which was already surrounded by a group of men baying for his blood. Fortunately, they turned out to be relatively law-abiding, so when the deputies ordered them to stand down, they did.

"We've searched the cabin and she's not there," one deputy shouted to the crowd. "Now, please, folks, if you want to help, split up and comb the surrounding area. Keep the noise down so you can hear her if she calls out." They weren't worried about the men trampling over clues. Right now they were more interested in finding the girl than prosecuting her abductor.

Grumbling, the crowd edged away enough to allow the patrol cruiser to ease onto the road. Then the men, and a few determined-looking women among them, duly piled into their vehicles and headed into the desert.

After fetching a canteen and flashlight I kept in the Jeep's tool box next to a battery-powered police scanner and other tools of the P.I. trade, I started my own search on foot. Not that the more deliberate pace made any difference in the end.

The night stretched long and fruitless. The desert, so open during the day, is secretive when the glaring sun goes down. Even with the beam of my flashlight and the faint glimmers of lights from other searchers, the deep arroyos yielded nothing. Yet I refused to give up. Propelled by the memory of Quibilah Wahab's screams, I stumbled along in the darkness, every now and then calling, "Aziza! If you can hear me, shout! I'm here to take you home!"

Nothing. Always nothing.

When the sun finally rose, I had covered an area slightly more than a half-mile square, shining my flashlight into creosote thickets, between boulders, and crawling down into ravines. The only thing I found was the body of a dead javelina being eaten by a coyote. At least it wasn't a little girl.

As the first rays of the sun glimmered across the tin roof of Polk's distant shack and another fleet of searchers arrived, I gave up. Some of the people who had been out there all night did, too, and as we hobbled back to our cars, we shared exhausted glances. When we reached the road, the one deputy remaining pointed to his radio and gave a slow shake of his head. Apparently Sheriff Avery's men had not been successful, either.

Wherever Aziza Wahab was now, she was beyond our help.

By eight o'clock I was in Los Perdidos, footsore and heart-sore. On the way to grab a couple of hour's sleep at the guest ranch, I stopped by Avery's office. The dark circles under his eyes proved that he hadn't slept all night, either.

"Polk swears he didn't take the girl," he said, "and you know what? I believe him. He's not acting self-righteous like molesters usually do, just scared. Somehow I can't see him hitchhiking into town, kidnapping the kid, then hitchhiking back without somebody noticing. Just in case, we're putting his picture on TV at noon. And our boy Duane? Yet another alibi tighter than a crab's ass. Your visit upset him so much that as soon as you left, the creep drove down to Happy's Cantina and started downing tequila. You have quite the effect on men, don't you, Lena? The guy was butt-bouncing drunk when we showed up."

Not only was Avery still using my first name, but he was sharing information again. Next thing you know, he'd deputize me. But this was no time to celebrate the lessening of hostilities. "He might have snatched Aziza on the way to Happy's."

"Timeline doesn't fit. Lester Lundstrom, his next door neighbor? He has two little girls, so he keeps a close eye on Duane's movements. He told us that our boy took off at seven twenty-five, and he's sure of the time because he was watching the local wrap-up on Headline News. Five minutes later, Duane was down at Happy's. The bartender knows *that* because ESPN had just begun a bottom-of-the-hour segment on that Vegas fight where the heavyweight was killed."

That's modern life for you. Everyone tells time by what's on TV.

Avery wasn't finished. "I sent some deputies out to organize the searchers. Here in town, I've got more going door-to-door. I promise you, if that kid's within ten miles of Los Perdidos, we'll find her."

His face didn't match the optimism of his words. Like me, he was probably thinking of the desert, the river, the mountains, a silent van speeding along I-10—all the hidden places a child might disappear into and never be found.

"How are the Wahabs doing?" I asked.

"The father's bearing up, the mother's under sedation."

There was nothing more I could do, so I headed toward to the Lazy M. Staggering through the day with a numbed mind wouldn't help the missing child. When I reached the guest cottage, I didn't even bother with a shower, just fell across the bed fully clothed in the dusty jeans and tee shirt I'd worn throughout the night's futile search. Before sleep claimed me, my cell phone rang. I thought briefly about switching it off, but just as quickly changed my mind. The caller might be the sheriff with news of Aziza. Not bothering to glance at the display, I answered.

It was Angelique Grey, in Beverly Hills. "Sorry to call so early, Lena, but we've got an emergency here."

I groaned. Hollywood's idea of an emergency wasn't the same as mine, especially now. "Angel, I can't…"

Over my protest, she continued, "Yes, I know I told you that arriving on Friday would be all right, but the situation's beyond insane. Last night I had dinner with Brad Speerstra and the other producers and the kid's crazy mother and she…"

"Angel, not…"

"It was like something out of an old Peter Sellers comedy, only so not funny. Everyone was smiling as if there wasn't anything wrong and that bringing her on board was the greatest idea since cheek implants, but she's the world's biggest pain, and she's going to be on set all the time. You wouldn't believe, I mean, really not believe! She actually said…"

"Angel, shut up!" I yelled.

That got her attention. "What?"

Before she started in again, I told her about Aziza's disappearance, and concluded with, "As soon as I get some sleep, I'm rejoining the search party."

Never an insensitive woman, she realized that the rest of the world didn't turn upon Hollywood's axis. "That poor child. How old did you say she was? Seven? That's about the same age as the girl you and Warren found, isn't it?"

"Correct."

She fell silent, obviously pondering this, then spoke in a more reasonable tone. "It's a tragedy, but surely the officials out there are doing everything they can. And you said yourself that there's a big search party combing the area. What difference will one person make?"

Although her logic made sense, sense wasn't the only thing that counted in this world. "At least I'm doing something. Look, Angel, I promised I'd fly out tomorrow and I will. Hold on until then." All this fuss about a dumb television show was so insignificant it would be funny if I were in a laughing mood. "If you see Warren before I talk to him, give him my..." Give him my best? Too lukewarm. My love? Too strong, especially in light of our last conversation. "Tell him I said hello."

I ended the call and turned off the cell. Angel was nothing if not persistent, but *Desert Eagle's* script problems no longer mattered to me.

Before lying back down, I rummaged through my carry-all and pulled out one of the fliers with Precious Doe's death photograph. I propped it up on the bedside lamp next to the picture of Tujin Rafik. Now the two children would be the first thing I saw in the morning, the last thing I saw at night.

Sad-eyed Tujin, who had been missing for years, was silent. But Precious Doe asked, *DO YOU KNOW ME?*

After a short nap that made me feel more groggy than refreshed, I showered, changed into clean clothes, and drove to the sheriff's office. Except for the dispatcher and a deputy handling the phones, the place appeared deserted. Empty coffee cups sat on the desks and cigarettes butts littered the carpeting, many of them right under the NO SMOKING sign. On the bulletin board, another picture had joined that of Precious Doe: Aziza. Her *hijab* accented dark-lashed brown eyes, a sculpted nose, and a wide smile. At seven, she hovered on the edge of her mother's beauty.

Seven. The age when so many terrible things might happen to a little girl.

I shook the memory of my own childhood away and headed toward the rear, where I found Avery in his office, slumped over his desk. The place was half-buried in paper, with printouts slopping across the floor and every other available surface.

"What do you want now, Ms. Jones?" he asked, raising his weary head.

The return to formalities worried me. "I'm here to help, Sheriff. If you'll let me."

He shook his head slowly. "I've done some thinking about that, and the answer's no. What with Dr. Wahab's accusation, you've become part of the problem. Besides, another girl's gone missing."

"*What*?!" Surely I hadn't heard right.

His eyes were so sunken they looked like a one-hundred-year-old man's. "The call came in right after you left the Wahab's house. Her name is Nicole Hall and she's sixteen. Her family lives just the other side of the Lazy M Ranch. This morning her parents found her bedroom window open—sound familiar?—and she was gone. So was one of the family cars."

My fear for the girl lessened. "Does she have a boyfriend?"

"Not currently. Her father's the Reverend Daniel Hall, who runs Freedom Temple. He's stricter than Dr. Wahab, which is saying a lot."

A teenager. A strict father. A missing car. You didn't have to be a genius to figure that one out. But I'm not much on coincidence, and two young girls disappearing at the same time bothered me. "What's being done?"

"I've pulled men in from Benson, Tombstone, Bisbee, even Sierra Vista. Before you say anything else, let's go outside. I want some fresh air." He pushed his chair away from his desk

Curious, I followed him out into the "fresh" air, where the exhaust of automobiles headed for the day shift at Apache Chemical overwhelmed the more subtle perfume of the desert. After glancing up and down the street, he said, "Things are getting worse here, and your situation with the Wahabs just adds to the general deterioration. That's why I'm telling you again, go home."

Whatever I'd been expecting, it wasn't this. Angered, I snapped, "Worried about reelection, are you?"

"That was uncalled for, Ms. Jones. I've been busy trying to hold things together while you've been running around the county getting people even more riled up. Now, don't start a fight you're bound to lose. Get in my way and I'll lock you up."

"For *what*?"

"Interfering with a police investigation." With that, he spun on his heel and went back inside.

I stood there a moment, trying to figure out my next move. Going home was out of the question, but in a way, Avery was right. So far, I'd accomplished nothing other than putting certain people on their guard. Yet with one girl dead and two more missing, I couldn't bring myself to walk away.

Not and live with myself, I couldn't.

Chapter Ten

When I returned to the guest ranch, I found Selma Mann in a paddock, working with a recalcitrant Appaloosa colt. She wanted to saddle it, it didn't want to be saddled. A few ranch hands sat on the fence's top rail, grinning at the spectacle. She finally got the saddle on, although the colt wasn't pleased. Leaving him alone to contemplate this new addition to his life, she walked over to the rail.

"Horses. Can't live with them, can't live without them." She brushed dust off her face, then her shirt. "Say, there's a FedEx package waiting for you inside the cottage. Sent from a Beverly Hills address. I signed for it and put it on your bed."

The latest *Desert Eagle* script, no doubt. Oh, joy. I would have to read the thing before leaving for L.A. the next morning. But not now. There was a reason I'd returned to the ranch before heading to Freedom Temple. A fifth-generation Arizonan, Selma knew about everyone local, living or dead.

"What can you tell me about Reverend Hall?" I asked. "Sheriff Avery says he lives nearby."

She grimaced. "Yeah, a quarter mile down the road. The parsonage's in the rear. Why? Is he implicated in Aziza Wahab's disappearance? It's been all over the news this morning. Hall's a major asshole, but I never heard he had issues with kids, if you know what I mean."

I did. After the Catholic Church's sex abuse scandal, ministers of all denominations had come under increasing scrutiny, some with good reason. Power corrupts, and spiritual power was no exception. I remained shocked, however, at hearing Selma refer to a man of the cloth as "a major asshole." Harsh words, even in these disrespectful times. Maybe she just had a thing about religion. Lots of people did.

"Nothing like that," I assured her. "His daughter's disappeared, too. The sheriff's hoping she just ran away."

Shock replaced the grimace. "Nicole? Disappeared? It's happened before, but I'm concerned about the timing. There was that Iraqi girl a few years ago, then Precious Doe, then Aziza Wahab, and now Nicole. It's terrible!"

There's terrible, and then there's terrible. At sixteen, Nicole Hall was almost ten years older than Tujin, Aziza, and Precious Doe. Yes, most pedophiles did specialize in one particular age group, but not always. The timing of the teenager's disappearance worried me, too. Less than a four-hour drive away, in the border town of Juarez, Mexico, hundreds of young women had disappeared over the past decade. A few mutilated bodies had been found in the desert, but most victims remained lost, the perps unknown. Had Juarez's serial killer, growing bored with grown women, moved to Los Perdidos? Had he begun preying upon children, killing an older girl every now and then as a refresher course?

Then I remembered that one of the Hall's cars was missing, which made it almost certain Nicole was a runaway, but it wouldn't hurt to make sure.

"Maybe I should pay the Reverend a visit," I told Selma, curious to see her reaction.

She snorted, sounding just like the Appaloosa. "Good luck."

"What do you mean?"

"You'll see." Shaking her head, she went back into the paddock and tried to horse-whisper a colt that wanted nothing to do with it.

Freedom Temple was an unprepossessing cinder block building, its whitewashed walls unrelieved by decorations of any kind, not even a cross. The signboard in front announced services at nine a.m. and six p.m. every Sunday; seven p.m. every Wednesday. The Women For Freedom study group met at eleven Monday and Thursday. Today. A political group? I'd always believed religion and politics made a dangerous mix. Checking my watch, I found it was already ten-thirty, which meant that I'd have to conduct this interview in record time.

The driveway wound around the church and ended at a gravel parking lot separating it from the parsonage. The small house was no more attractive than the church, just a plain wooden structure with a deep eave jutting over a slightly raised cement pad that passed for a porch. There were no shutters, no flower boxes, none of those friendly, human touches normally seen at rectories. Except for the lacy tracings of cottonwoods against the sky at the rear of the house, the entire property was composed of sharp, stern angles.

The Jeep crunched across the gravel until I braked next to a ten-year-old Taurus that was a candidate for the wrecking yard. After climbing out, I approached the house, but before I reached the porch, the door opened and a tall man peered out. White teeth flashed.

"May I help you?" His voice was as melodious as a good Shakespearean actor's, and as mannered as a bad one's. He started to add something, then halted, an expression of shock crossing his face. But it disappeared quickly and the phony smile returned.

"Excuse me for staring, dear. That scar on your forehead. A car accident?"

I phonied a smile back. "An old bullet wound, and no accident." While he digested this, I studied his too-perfectly chiseled features. He would have been handsome except for the coldness of his blue eyes.

"Did you receive counseling, dear? If not, perhaps I can help. Freedom Temple is happy to offer those services, for a sliding fee, of course." He didn't invite me in, just stepped onto the porch, closing the door behind him.

"No counseling necessary, Reverend. I'm here to ask a few questions about your daughter."

His smile faded when he noticed my Jeep. In the bright morning light, the Pima Indian signs that decorated it from bumper to bumper fairly glowed. "That's not one of Sheriff Avery's vehicles."

I was getting tired of standing at the bottom of the steps, and wanted to hurry this along, but I dutifully handed up my card.

He gave it a quick glance. "You drove all the way down here from Scottsdale to investigate Nicole's disappearance? Oh, I don't think so."

Stretching the truth until it howled, I said, "I'm helping the sheriff with another missing girl case. Aziza Wahab."

Raised eyebrows. "What does she have to do with Nicole?"

"Probably nothing. Look, my questions will only take a minute and after that, you can get on with your day. Otherwise, Sheriff Avery might have to question you himself."

He didn't like that. "Get it over with, then." Still no invitation to enter the parsonage. Maybe his wife was lying on the floor, drunk.

"Is it true Nicole's run away before?"

"Many times." His frosty calmness stood in direct contrast to the grief experienced by the Wahabs the night before.

"How is Mrs. Hall holding up?"

He seemed taken aback by my question. "Olivia? She accepts all her trials, of course."

All her trials. What an odd phrasing. I decided that I needed to see Olivia Hall, too, but for that I had to get inside the parsonage. "May I come in, Reverend? I hate standing around in parking lots."

"The Women For Freedom will be here soon."

"Yes, I know. They're meeting in a half hour." To force the issue, I placed my foot on the bottom step. Now he would either have to allow me access or the two of us would share a three-foot-wide section of concrete.

Gracelessly, he gave in. "Really, Ms. Jones, the parlor is rather untidy."

I gave him what I hoped was a non-threatening smile. "If it's good enough for the Women For Freedom, it's good enough for me."

To my admittedly non-discerning eye, the parlor didn't appear untidy, just naked. It boasted no rugs, no flowers, no lovingly crocheted doilies, and still no crosses in sight. Cheap linoleum covered the floor, and a long table testified to the room's sometimes use as a banquet hall. A half-dozen worn upholstered chairs and two equally worn sofas hugged the walls, which were decorated with photographs of various churches. Curious, I approached for a closer look.

In a photograph so old it had faded to sepia, a teenage version of Reverend Hall stood in front of an ornate church door, next to a grim older man wearing a cassock. His father? Probably, since the resemblance between the two was strong. In another faded picture, this one color, a slightly older Hall stood among a group of ethnically-diverse people near a white bus, with chaparral-sprinkled mountains rising in the background. Other photographs showed him posed in front of a series of churches, chief among them an elegant seaside edifice with a hint of ocean twinkling through Monterey pines.

Most were humbler postings. A wood-planked church nearly eclipsed by oaks draped in Spanish moss; a bare bones church in the middle of a rocky field, and a mud-and-wattle hut in a village surrounded by goats and dark children in African dress. Unlike the bleak cinder block the reverend now served, each managed to present a stoic dignity.

"You have five minutes," Hall said, closing the parlor door behind me. Once we both settled into sagging chairs, he made a great show of checking his watch.

No time for guard-lowering pleasantries, then. "Okay, Reverend. I'll be brief. Did anything unusual happen last night?"

"No."

"Did your daughter act unhappy lately?"

"Nicole was always unhappy." For all his emotion, he might have been talking about the scuffed linoleum.

I had run across cold men like him before but their frigidity hadn't annoyed me nearly as much. Some other element seemed to be at work here. "What was bothering her?"

"She was sixteen. That's enough, isn't it?"

Having a father like you probably doesn't help, either, I wanted to say, but with only four minutes remaining, I didn't want to spend them trading insults. "Was she active in your church?"

His eyes weren't just cold, they were mean. "Of course."

On the other side of a door at the far end of the room, someone began to make coffee. Mrs. Hall? The aroma seeped into the room and due to my near-sleepless night, I could barely restrain myself from falling on my knees and begging for a cup.

The reverend stood up. "If that's all, I'll see you to the door."

I stayed put. "When did you notice Nicole was missing, Reverend?"

He sat back down with ill-concealed impatience. "Not until this morning. When my wife went to wake her, she found her gone, along with her clothes and our new car. I called the sheriff and gave him the license plate number. Do you want that?"

"It would help."

He checked his watch again. "Buick LeSabre, dark green, Arizona plate MFK 762. Freedom Temple bumper sticker."

I wrote it down. "Description, please."

"I already gave it to you. Dark green Buick LeSabre."

"No, I meant a description of Nicole. Tall? Short? Thin? Plump? Hair color? Any identifying birthmarks, scars, tattoos or piercings?" I added the last to shake him out of his cold calm.

His eyes became slits. "Certainly not!"

I softened my approach to throw him even further off-balance. "Probably due to your good influence. By the way, Reverend, may I see some photographs of her?" He had so many of himself plastered all over the walls, surely dozens of his daughter were stashed somewhere in the parsonage's private quarters.

Wrong.

"My faith isn't into self-glorification," he said, apparently forgetting his own pictures. "I gave Sheriff Avery the only photograph we have, taken at Los Perdidos Elementary when Nicole was twelve. She's taller now but looks pretty much the same. Long brown hair, brown eyes, pale complexion, about your height. Bigger-boned, though."

I wrote that down on my notepad. "Braces?"

"As I said before, our faith concentrates on the inner self, not the exterior."

This from a man whom I suspected had undergone considerable cosmetic surgery. Those pearly whites were capped, too. "What faith is that?" I asked, while writing, NO BRACES.

"Non-denominational."

"Protestant," I muttered, writing it down.

He shook his head. "Non-denominational."

Raising my eyebrows, I gestured with my pen toward the photographs. Crosses were clearly visible on all the church buildings, including the African hut. He had once been a missionary, and not for the First Church of Satan.

"I've moved on."

To what? Some religion he'd invented all by himself? Arizona was filled with nutso cults, but with only two more minutes left on the clock, I didn't have time to explore his beliefs, and I doubted I'd be thrilled with them, anyway. "Do you have any idea where Nicole might have gone? The names of friends who might be hiding her?"

"None of our friends would be so foolish."

Remembering that gathering place near the river, I said, "Most teens have friends their parents don't know."

"Not Nicole. We've been home-schooling her for the past two years."

I was about to point out that home-schooling needn't isolate a child, but just then a side door opened and a tall wraith of a woman stepped hesitantly toward us. She might have been pretty once, but her hair had faded to an unattractive gray almost the same color as her eyes, and her height was diminished by rounded shoulders. The dress she wore, a dowdy print that had seen too many washings, sagged on her as if she had recently lost weight. Dots of flour sprinkled her frayed apron.

"Daniel? I heard voices," she said, almost inaudibly. Her eyes were as pale as her husband's, but unlike his, they were rimmed in red. At least someone in this household mourned Nicole's disappearance.

Irritation flickered across Hall's face. "Didn't I tell you to stay in the kitchen?"

"But I wanted to…"

"Don't argue with me, Olivia." He didn't raise his voice. He didn't need to.

"I'm sorry, Daniel." She exited, closing the door softly behind her.

Her departure made up my mind. I saw no kidnapping here, only a rebellious teen desperate to escape her bully of a father.

The bully rose to his feet. "Your five minutes are up."

Realizing there was nothing to be gained by arguing, I rose too. Hall marched me to the door. Before he opened it, he took my hand.

"You need counseling, Miss Jones. That scar harkens back to a troubled past. While we were talking, I noticed that you are somewhere in your thirties—am I right?—yet you wear no wedding ring. Perhaps I can help with whatever is keeping you from maturing into a true woman. Counseling women is my specialty."

I wouldn't let him counsel me for a stubbed toe. Not caring if he noticed, I pulled my hand away and wiped it on my jeans.

He was so intent on delivering his message that he didn't catch it. "Women like you try to get through life alone, which is always a mistake. Women simply aren't capable of living a normal life without a man's wise oversight. Independence in a woman is the root of all evil. Why, look at what happened in the Garden of Eden when Eve decided to act on her own. Mankind has been paying for it ever since!"

I knew a little bit about the Bible, myself. "Adam wasn't at all culpable, Reverend?"

"Adam was blinded by love, Miss Jones. Women and their unholy desires will do that to a man. That's why they need to be controlled."

Unholy desires? Eager to leave, I opened the door. Seeing that I was about to escape, he said one final thing, but in my rush to get away, I wasn't certain I'd heard him right.

"Control women and you control the world."

In the parking lot, a group of women were walking toward the parsonage, several of them wearing the kind of cowled white robes I'd seen on Trappist monks. The Women For Freedom? Most were fairly young, in their twenties or thirties. With one exception, a fragile redhead with a lost expression, none were even remotely attractive. Like all hucksters, the Reverend knew how to target an audience.

As I crossed the parking lot to the Jeep, I glanced behind me and saw him with his arms spread, a movie-star smile on his face, all traces of his former coldness vanished. The overt bully replaced by a slick manipulator.

A mile down the highway, I pulled into a rest area and checked my messages: one from my partner at Desert Investigations, and one from Martha Green, the librarian who had been so helpful the day before. No calls from Warren. Deciding to worry about him later, I returned Martha Green's call first. She whispered into the phone so she wouldn't disturb the library patrons, but I had no trouble hearing her, even with the traffic rushing by.

"Can you meet me for lunch at the Nile Restaurant, on the south end of town?" She asked. "The elementary school's only holding a half-session today, and Peggy Binder's anxious to talk to you."

It took me a moment to remember that Binder had taught Tujin Rafik, the first child to disappear from Los Perdidos. Believing Tujin had been taken by the same person who killed Precious Doe and kidnapped Aziza, I agreed, and we made a date for noon.

Then I called my partner and discovered that Jimmy wanted to join me in Los Perdidos. "Lena, I've been watching the local feed on CNN. One dead child and two more missing? Why don't I pack my laptop and continue these background checks down there? It sounds like you need all the help you can get." His voice softened. "Besides, I'm worried about you."

I missed his company, but he needed to stay in Scottsdale. "Jimmy, you're more useful up there. Those background checks you're doing for Southwest MicroSystems will pay the rent for the next six months."

"The money from your TV show's already paid it for the next two years. Besides, I'm portable."

Unsettled as I was after my visit with Reverend Hall, I had to smile. "MicroSystems feels more secure knowing you're within badgering distance. But there is something you can do for me. Run a check on a Reverend Daniel Hall, leader of a Los Perdidos church called Freedom Temple."

"Non-denominational?"

"And how."

"Don't like him, eh?" We had been partners so long he could read me through the phone.

"You might say that. His daughter vanished last night."

"*Another* missing girl?" he all but yelled. "Lena, you're in danger. You need to come home. Or at least let me join you down there and give you some protection."

"Calm down, Jimmy. The girl's sixteen and probably just a runaway—the family car's gone—but Hall was so creepy I want him and his church checked out. Get what you can on Mrs. Hall, too. Something there doesn't add up." Like two pale-eyed parents having a brown-eyed child.

"I'll call as soon as I find out anything, but are you sure you don't want me there?"

"I'm sure." Knowing that I shouldn't ask my next question didn't keep me from asking, "By the way, how's things with what's-her-name?"

"Lydianna?"

I didn't even like her name. It sounded too contrived. "Yeah. The gal you met at the pow-wow."

"You asked the same question yesterday."

I forced a laugh. "Maybe, but you move pretty fast."

"Compared to you, a snail moves fast."

"Do you mean Warren? C'mon, that's not my fault. He lives in L.A., so we can only see each other every now and then." We'd spent what, six weekends together since we'd met last spring? Half the time when I flew into L.A. for the *Desert Eagle* script meetings, he was so busy with his own projects that he didn't have time to see me. Or at least, that's what he said.

"How about Dusty?" Jimmy reminded me.

"That's different." Dusty, who cowboyed on a dude ranch north of Scottsdale, had been my first real love, but his bad habits—booze, gambling, and women—kept me from making a commitment until that relationship blew up in my face. What sane person moved fast with a man like that?

Jimmy spoke into my silence. "Let's make a deal. You won't ask about my love life and I won't ask about yours."

Now I felt hurt. "You make it sound like I'm always poking my nose into your business."

He laughed.

"Okay," I said, chastened. "No more questions. About women, anyway." But I reserved the right to ask if he'd seen any good date movies recently. Or ate dinner at some candle-lit restaurant.

He must have known the way my mind was working, because he spoke quickly. "I'll talk to you tomorrow. In the meantime, you take care. Los Perdidos sounds about as safe as a nest of rattlesnakes."

Swearing I would watch out for myself, I hung up.

By the end of the day, I had broken my promise.

Chapter Eleven

When I strode into the Geronimo Lounge, I saw Clive Berklee, my elderly informant, sipping slowly at a Molson's while he worked a crossword puzzle.

"It's not Sunday," I said, sliding into the chair across from him.

"I'm pretending it is." He drained the rest of his glass, then called to the bartender, "Another beer. And put it on the blonde's tab."

"You'll need to work for that."

He called to the bartender again. "Make that *three* Molson's, but keep two on ice." Then, to me, "Whatcha want?"

"Your nephew, the one who assists the medical examiner. Where can I find him?"

"Herschel? At the hospital. He works all the time except for Sundays, and sometimes even then. Why? You wantin' a date?"

"Funny man. All I want is his home address. I want to talk, not go to the prom."

He grinned. "You're pretty funny yourself." Before I responded, he tore off a strip of newsprint and wrote down the information. "It's in that new tract on the east end of town, where all the houses look alike. He works nights, so don't go waking him up until around three or he'll tear your head off, then mine."

We bantered until it was time for me to meet Martha Green for lunch at the Nile Restaurant, a tiny but crowded Middle

Eastern place that came as a relief from the town's ubiquitous fast food joints. When I entered, I smelled the tang of mysterious spices. The gleaming copper hookahs and pots that shone down from shelves high on the burgundy-colored walls were considerably more attractive than prints of Ronald McDonald.

"Nice choice," I said to Martha, after finding her at a table with the woman I took to be Tujin Rafik's teacher. Peggy Binder was a dark, attractive brunette well into her forties, and as soon as we ordered from an elderly waitress—shish kabob for me with a couscous side, pita sandwiches for the others—I asked her how well she knew the first missing girl.

"As well as most teachers know their students," Peggy answered. "She was sweet but shy. The family was in the first wave of immigrants to work at the chemical plant, and some of them had trouble fitting in. Tujin especially."

"Any particular reason why?" As other diners came in, the noise level in the restaurant rose.

"She felt self-conscious about her clothing. Her family was very traditional and refused to let her wear Western dress. You know how girls are, they want the latest fads, no matter how ridiculous."

Following up on the inconsistencies in the *Observer* newspaper article, I asked, "Was she having trouble in school? Her father was quoted as saying she did because her language skills were poor."

When Peggy shook her head, a wisp of glossy black hair fell across her cheek. As her fingers pushed it back, I saw a large, silver-and-turquoise ring that matched her earrings and bracelets. Studying her more carefully, I noted the bronze skin, high cheekbones, and narrow nose. Her vowels weren't quite as soft and broad as a Navajo's.

Apache. Perhaps a descendant of Geronimo's band. Today they sold insurance, ran casinos, and taught Iraqi immigrants.

"Poor language skills?" Peggy remained oblivious to my musings on the strange pathways of societal evolution. "Ridiculous. Tujin's English was as good as the other children's, better than most, actually. Like a lot of my English-as-second-language students, she took more care with her grammar than the aver-age American does. As for having trouble in school, she was a solid B student."

So Tujin's father *had* lied to the sheriff. I would have pon-dered this development further, but the next thing Peggy came as a shock.

"Speaking of missing girls, are you aware that Aziza Wahab is one of my students? And that her sister, Shalimar, used to be, too?"

Martha and I both stared at her. "I didn't know that," the librarian said.

Peggy nodded. "They were both in my Advanced Learners Class. I called Sheriff Avery this morning and told him how alarming it was that two of my students were missing. Each one a minority, too, like Precious Doe."

She went on to say that while Los Perdidos was an open-minded town, as Arizona towns went, it didn't mean there were no pockets of racism among its populace. "The more traditional the immigrants appear, the bigger targets they make for assaults."

"Aziza's parents seemed pretty assimilated to me," I said, remembering the electronic gear in their living room, the boys playing Scrabble.

Peggy shrugged. "They've been here six years and they're pretty well assimilated, although Mrs. Wahab and the girls still wear the *hijab*. Look, something else has been bothering me. Aziza's very attuned to her environment, so I can't believe she just sat there passively while someone came through her window and snatched her. she would have fought back, or at the very least, screamed her lungs out."

I had a ready answer. "Maybe she did, but no one heard her." I described my visit to the Wahab's house the evening before, and the music blasting out of Aziza's bedroom. The Nile wasn't that much quieter, I noted. Over the loud conversations of a room full of customers, Middle Eastern music played on the restaurant's sound system. In other circumstances, I might have enjoyed the friendly din.

Remembering how shy the older Wahab girl had seemed, I said, "Aziza sounds a lot more outgoing than Shalimar." I raised my voice as a quartet of diners near us began to laugh uproariously.

The noise didn't bother Peggy. "God, yes. Shalimar, is shy and very restrained. I'm not sure she has many friends to speak of, at least few at school. Aziza's just the opposite. She makes friends everywhere she goes, and she's so smart a lot of them are years older than she is."

The laughter died down and I was able to speak in a more normal voice. "Did Aziza have any black friends?"

"Plenty. We have a small Somali and Ethiopian population and most of them have kids. They attend prayer services on Fridays with the other Muslims. You'll see them standing around outside the Unitarian Church where they meet, some of them in tribal dress. It's very colorful."

When I told her that Duane Tucker said he'd seen someone who looked like Aziza talking to a dark girl who might have been Precious Doe, she grimaced. "Oh, geez. Duane. There's a hat full of trouble. He used to hang around my kid sister until Dad ran him off. Half the time the guy's *non compos mentis*, if you get my meaning, so don't put too much stock in anything he says. But I'll say this about Duane. If he's a child molester, I'm a Swede. He likes them young, but not *that* young."

A conclusion I'd reached myself. "The victims were around seven years old, unless you count the last one."

Both women shot me startled looks. "What are you talking about?" Martha Green asked.

"You haven't heard?"

The librarian shook her head. "I've stopped watching the news. Too depressing. I get up, eat breakfast, go straight to the library."

For her part, Peggy offered, "I was out late last night with one of the search parties, and I overslept this morning. By the time I hauled myself out of bed, I didn't even have time for breakfast, let alone the news."

I started to explain. "A girl named Nicole Hall…"

"Not Nicole!" Peggy looked distraught.

Several Nile patrons turned to stare, including our elderly waitress, who had just arrived with our meals. No, not just waitress. Her name tag announced: ASENATH NOUR, MANAGER. Eyeing Peggy carefully, she asked. "Are you all right, Miss Binder?"

Peggy gave her a wan smile. "Thanks, Mrs. Nour. I just learned something disturbing about one of my former students."

"Ah, yes," Mrs. Nour said, sympathetically. "Children can break your heart, but Allah be praised, I have been fortunate in mine." With a glance at Peggy's slightly trembling hands, she added, "Today I suggest Seven-Up for your drink, not tea. It appears you need no more caffeine."

When Mrs. Nour went to fetch Peggy some Seven-Up, I eyed the teacher with curiosity. "I thought Nicole was home-schooled."

Peggy picked up her napkin, fumbled with it for a second, then placed it in her lap, making no move toward her sandwich. "I taught her from first grade until she entered middle school. She's a sweet girl, one of my favorite-ever students. I used to have high hopes for her. Please don't tell me something's happened to her, too."

I did my best to reassure her by saying that so far, the girl was suspected of simply being a runaway. Then I remembered something. "Didn't you say you teach advanced students?"

She finally took a nibble from her pita sandwich, but with an expression of regret, put it down. "Guess I'm not hungry, after all. Yes, I teach the advanced class, which is how I wound up with Tujin and Aziza. Nicole, too, because believe me, that girl's as smart as they come. But as she grew older, she became a real handful. That's why I wasn't surprised when…" She hesitated.

"When what?" I urged.

Mrs. Nour arrived with a Seven-Up. After thanking her, Peggy drank half the glass, then with a nervous gesture, tucked her hair

behind her silver-studded ears. "It happened when Nicole was
fourteen. She ran away from home and was gone for a couple
of days. Nobody knows where she was during that time, but she
eventually turned up at her boyfriend's house."

"A boyfriend?" Why hadn't Reverend Hall given me that bit
of information?

"She and Raymundo Mendoza had known each other since
first grade, and you know the way these things go. She was
pretty, he was gorgeous, and their hormones were raging. But as
it turned out, she ran away because she'd skipped her period and
knew that if she was pregnant, her parents would have a fit."

Another item Reverend Hall had neglected to mention. "And
was she pregnant?"

"Yes."

"At fourteen?" My already dark feelings about Hall grew
darker. "Whose baby was it?"

Peggy must have guessed where my thoughts were heading
because she didn't let me complete the question. "The baby, a
girl, was Raymundo's. He admitted it. As for Reverend Hall, while
I'm no fan of his or that weird Freedom Temple, in all the time
I taught Nicole, I never saw any indication of abuse, sexual or
otherwise. She was well fed, and wore clean, if somewhat dowdy,
clothes. There were no 'she-fell-down' bruises, either, and that's
something I'm always on the alert for. You can never tell with
parents, can you?"

Taking our silence for agreement, she continued, "Nicole's
middle school teachers said the same thing, that they never
saw any reason to suspect abuse. But back to the pregnancy.
Raymundo and his family wanted to raise the baby, but Hal
shipped Nicole off to an aunt in Idaho or Montana or someplace
like that, and the baby was put up for adoption. The Mendozas
were beside themselves and even made noises about contesting
the adoption—after all, the baby was their granddaughter—but
by the time Nicole returned to Los Perdidos, they'd decided not
to break the adoptive parents' hearts."

"Raymundo himself could have contested it."

"He was only fourteen, remember. Anyway, Reverend Hall pulled Nicole out of public school, and that was the end of that. Since then, on occasion I've seen the poor kid around town with her parents, but she's different now. It was like she'd always blazed with light, then someone turned off the switch."

A pregnant teenager, a powerless boyfriend, and an out-of-state adoption agency—the same old sad story. "Losing your first love and then your baby would be traumatic," I told Peggy.

She nodded. "If you ask me, I'd say her very soul was damaged."

I had no rejoinder for that. "Does Raymundo's family live near by?"

"Sure. The Mendozas are descended from one of Los Perdidos' founding families." She gave me a half-humorous, half-bitter smile. "In fact, they like to brag that one of their ancestors shot one of my ancestors. Anyway, they own a pottery business at the edge of town and live right behind it. If Nicole did run away, and I hope that's all this is, she'd head straight there. Especially now that Raymundo's graduated."

"I thought he was only sixteen."

"Yes, but he's as bright as Nicole and was able to skip a couple of grades. He's working at the shop with his mother until he starts U of A this fall on a full-ride scholarship."

I thought for a moment. When Nicole ran away the first time and turned up at Raymundo's house, his father turned her over to the authorities. If she was as smart as Peggy said she was, she wouldn't repeat the same mistake. Still, I needed to find out what was what. By now, Raymundo might have resources of his own.

Before I attacked my shish kabob, I asked Peggy one final question. "Is there any possibility that Nicole knows Aziza Wahab?"

She shrugged. "Nicole was friendly with Shalimar, her older sister, but as for knowing Aziza, I can't say. I guess it's possible their paths crossed, but I doubt if Nicole and Shalimar had any sleep-overs or anything like that. The Wahabs aren't the type, and neither are the Halls. Since that pregnancy business a couple of years ago, Nicole's father keeps her pretty much under wraps."

I was sliding meat off the skewer when she added, "Come to think of it, Nicole did know Tujin Rafik, that Iraqi girl who disappeared."

I put my fork down. "How?"

"When Nicole was around ten, we used her as a tutor in our Peer Program, where kids help kids. She drilled some of the immigrant girls on their reading, and Tujin was one of them. They were pretty close, and when Tujin disappeared, she took it so hard her father kept her home from school for a few days. When she returned, the school provided what counseling our budget would allow, which admittedly wasn't much, and she seemed to get over it. At least she stopped crying all the time."

There it was. A connection between the runaway Nicole and one of the missing girls.

Chapter Twelve

As soon as we finished our lunch, I paid the tab over Martha's and Peggy's protests and drove to Mendoza's Mexican Pottery.

The store, only a few minute's drive from the Nile Restaurant, was a large one, stocking not only pots of all shapes, sizes, and colors, but also Navajo rugs and groupings of hand-carved Mexican furniture. Among them I recognized the night stands in the Lazy M's guest cottage and the large coffee table in Selma's living room.

As I approached the counter, where several smartly-dressed customers stood filling out forms, I saw a sign announcing "SÍ! WE SHIP!" Another sign said that they were delighted to accept American Express, Visa, MasterCard, and out-of-state checks. Situated as it was on the tourist trail to Tombstone, Mendoza's was doing a brisk business.

I waited until the customers were taken care of, then asked the middle-aged Hispanic woman running the register where I might find Raymundo. In unaccented English, she told me he was in the storage area out back, and how about a nice Navajo rug today? They'd just received a special shipment from their supplier in Window Rock. "We have a wonderful selection, including Teec Nos Pos, Two Gray Hills, and Raised Edge. And, of course, the usual Yeibichai. Commercial but lovely, and priced just right."

Shopping sometimes lifted my spirits and I'd seen a beautiful red-and-black Klagetoh that would partner nicely with the Two

Gray Hills rug I already owned, so after hauling it from the large pile it crowned, I handed over my Visa.

As she rang me up, I filled out a shipping label. Shipping arrangements completed, I stepped out to the storage yard, where a handsome young man who strongly resembled the woman at the counter was rolling a large terra cotta pot across the cement floor. He was Nicole's age, sixteen, but his height and muscular physique made him appear much older.

"Raymundo?"

He turned around and threw me a dazzling smile that didn't quite overcome the worried expression in his eyes. "How may I help you, ma'am? Are you looking for natural terra cotta like this or something more colorful?"

"Neither. I want to talk to you about Nicole Hall."

The smile disappeared. "Don't know where she's at."

"But you know she's run away."

He glanced around to make certain no customers were near by. "You a social worker or something?"

I showed him my I.D. card.

Disbelief showed on his face. "Oh, c'mon. I can't believe that toxic father of hers went and hired a private detective! Don't take this wrong, but even if he did, he'd hire a guy. Reverend Hall doesn't believe girls have enough brains to come in out of the rain. Sorry. I mean *women*." Someone in his family, probably his sales-conscious mother, had tutored him on political correctness.

"I don't work for Nicole's father, Raymundo. I don't even like him."

After giving me a piercing look, he nodded. "Okay. I believe you. But if you're not working for Hall, why're you here? Somebody else hire you? The sheriff, maybe?" He vented a snort of laughter.

"I'm the person who found Precious Doe."

"Oh. The dead girl." He swallowed hard. "That must have been rough."

"It was. And now two more girls have disappeared. Aziza Wahab and Nicole."

His eyes shifted. "I don't know anything about that other kid, but you don't have to worry about Nicole."

Teenagers can be so transparent. "And I don't have to worry about her because...?"

"Because she's all right. I've just got a feeling."

Like hell he had a feeling; he *knew*. I pulled the cell phone out of my carry-all, flipped it open, and pretended to punch in a number.

"Who are you calling?" Raymundo cried.

"The sheriff, of course. Since you won't tell me, you can tell him."

He reached out his hand and grabbed my wrist. A lot of strength there. "Nicole's safe. She called right after she took off, but wouldn't tell me where she was. All I know is that she said she'd contact me later. She had to do something first."

I closed the cell but didn't put it away. "When was this?"

"Yesterday, some time after eight. We'd just closed."

Reverend Hall had told me his wife didn't discover the girl was missing until this morning. Upon reflection, I remembered how much noise the gravel parking lot outside the parsonage made when cars crunched along it, so Nicole's departure hadn't been silent. Why had her parents waited until the morning to call the sheriff? Under ordinary conditions, I would have questioned Hall about this discrepancy, and at the same time, tell him his daughter had contacted a friend and was safe. But this situation appeared far from ordinary. Hall seemed more concerned for his missing car than his missing daughter.

"Did she say how long it would take, to do whatever it was?"

Raymundo shook his head. "Naw. When I tried to talk her into coming over here, she hung up on me."

"You and Nicole had a baby together, right?"

His face turned defiant. "Everybody knows about that."

"And the baby was adopted out."

"Ancient history." Sullen, now.

Time to unsettle him further. "How did you feel about losing your baby, Raymundo?"

"How do you think I felt?" He was as disdainful as only a sixteen-year-old can be.

I pushed again. "That first time Nicole ran away, she vanished for a couple of days before turning up at your house. Don't tell me you didn't know where she was during that time."

His eyes shifted to the terra cotta pot. He leaned over and with a fingernail, flicked off specks of dirt. "Nope. I didn't."

He was smart, but a bad liar. "Maybe I won't phone the sheriff." I watched him relax. "Instead, I'll just go talk to your mother, tell her you know where Nicole is, and that you're hampering a police investigation."

He straightened up, his face pale. "All right, but you've got to promise not to tell anyone else. I don't want to get them in trouble."

"If whoever she's staying with has a record of endangering kids, I can't do that."

"Endangering kids? They *save* them!" He glanced toward the shop where his mother was working with another customer. "Follow me. I want to make sure my mother doesn't hear what I'm about to tell you."

With that, he opened a wooden gate and stepped onto a brick path which led toward a tidy adobe. La Casa Mendoza. To the side of the house, under a lush ironwood tree, stood a picnic table. No one seemed to be around. Presumably the younger Mendozas were in school, the older ones at work.

He waited until we'd settled ourselves at the picnic table before saying anything else. "That other time she ran off, she borrowed a friend's cell and called me right away. She hadn't told her parents yet about the baby because she was afraid what her father might do if he found out she'd been sneaking out her window at night to meet me down by the riv…well, at our regular meeting place. I swiped my father's truck and picked her up. I drove her, well, I drove her some place."

Driving around at fourteen, he'd been lucky not to get picked up by the cops, but where Nicole was concerned, he didn't seem to worry about what was legal and what was not. I thought his admission might be all the information he was willing to give, but he added, "There's this ranch, a big secret, but some of the guys at school know about it, kind of a safe haven for kids in really bad trouble. I mean, *really* bad, not just shoplifting or stuff. I figured this thing with the baby was really bad, so that's where we went."

When he ducked his head in embarrassment, he didn't seem so mature any more. "She stayed with them two days then started feeling guilty, so she called me and had me pick her up. I didn't know what else to do, so I took her to my house and asked my father if she could live with us and we'd all raise the baby."

I told him I knew the rest, that her father had immediately called Reverend Hall. Any responsible parent would.

"Pop screwed up." His voice was bitter. "The next day Reverend Hall shipped her off to Idaho and when she got back, it was all over between us. I'd go to where we used to meet and wait there for hours, but she pretty much stopped showing up. When she did, she wouldn't let me anywhere near her. She never even called me again until yesterday."

"Raymundo, where's that 'safe house?' "

Hope lit his face. "Do you think she's there?"

There was a strong possibility, and I told him so. I dug into my carry-all and brought out a notebook and pen. "Write down the address and phone number."

"I never knew the phone number, and the address won't do you any good, 'cause it's way out in the boonies the other side of Sierra Vista." But he drew a map and jotted down the directions. "When you get there, don't tell them who told you, okay? And don't tell anyone else. Swear you won't! They help people, not hurt them."

I gave him a conditional promise. "If what you say is true, I'll keep quiet. But if there's the slightest hint that kids are being exploited, I'll tell every law officer in the state."

He nodded. "You'll see."

Before I left, I asked, "Do you have a photograph of Nicole? I don't even know what she looks like."

He tugged a fat wallet out of his pocket and opened it. Several packets of plastic sleeves were filled with pictures of Nicole, both casual and posed. Here was Nicole as a freckled child of around ten, her glossy brown hair in braids. There was Nicole a few years older, in braids again but somehow much more mature, a secretive smile playing around her heart-shaped lips. Then Nicole as a middle-schooler, the freckles gone, her hair shorter, spirit evident in lively brown eyes.

The last few pictures were taken outside a supermarket as Nicole helped her mother load groceries into a car. Seemingly unaware of her photographer, Nicole, now around sixteen, wore a dress as shapeless as the older woman's, and her beautiful hair was twisted into a severe bun. Her eyes were dull.

Peggy Binder had been right: Nicole's light had dimmed.

"May I have one of these if I promise to bring it back?" I asked Raymundo, but he snatched the wallet away, as if fearing I'd run off with it. I told him I understood, then gathered my things.

The expression on Raymundo's face just about broke my heart. "Ma'am, if you find her before she calls me again, tell her…" He stopped, as if he was having trouble expressing himself, then finished with a simple, "Tell her I still love her."

When three o'clock rolled around, I headed over to Herschel Berklee's house. As his Molson-drinking uncle had informed me, the medical examiner's assistant lived in a tract of homes so alike only their inhabitants could tell them apart. Fortunately, Herschel's house was situated on a corner, its address painted both on the curb and emblazoned in three-inch-high numerals on a front porch post. Like many savvy health care workers, he'd made certain the EMTs would find his house in case of emergency.

It took a while for Herschel to answer the door, and when he did, he looked like he'd just crawled out of bed. An even scrawnier version of his uncle, his hair stood on end, and rumpled pajamas peeked out from under a moth-eaten bathrobe.

His bleary eyes gave me a slow up-and-down. "Honey, if you're sellin', I'm sure buyin'."

When I flashed my I.D. and told him his uncle sent me over, his leer faded. "You don't exactly look like Mickey Spillane, but come on in. Just don't expect any smarts on my part. I worked fourteen hours straight last night. I'm so damned tired I can barely think."

Like his uncle, Herschel's wolfishness was all talk, no action. With an almost formal politeness, he led me to a comfortable chair in a newspaper-littered living room, then offered me coffee. "Bought one of them new machines puts it on a timer, so when I crawl outta bed, it's fresh ground and hotter'n a whore on payday." He flushed. "Oops."

To settle him down, I said coffee sounded fine, and when he hustled into the kitchen, I took a look around. Like most bachelor pads, the room was devoid of decorations except for the two photographs of a dark-complexioned little girl that rested on an end table. In one, she smiled in his arms. In the other, she wore a soccer uniform and a determinedly fierce expression. His daughter?

Shortly, Herschel returned with two steaming mugs. As I sipped, I tasted mocha hazelnut with a sprinkling of cinnamon. Quite the gourmet.

"What can I do for ya? Uncle Clive didn't send you over just to say hi."

After I explained my connection to the Precious Doe case, he said, "Musta been rough. Guy who did that to her, I hope he slow-boils in Hell." Then his face changed. "Hey, wait a minute! You came over here to pump me about the autopsy, didn't you? Dr. Lanphear warned me some nosy woman's been asking questions around the hospital. Was that you?"

I admitted it. "Every killer, especially a child killer, has an individual M.O. that helps investigating officers link one crime to another." Knowing there had been scant publicity about the Juarez killings, I filled him in on the hundreds of young Mexican women who had been mutilated and murdered in Juarez. There might be a link, I pointed out.

"You saying there's hardly been any investigation over there?" He looked furious.

"Correct."

"Let me guess. Nobody cares because the girls are just Mexicans, right?"

"That might have something to do with it." To everyone's shame, including even the Mexican government's.

He muttered something about "damn racists," then gestured toward the photographs. "Jewell, that's my kid, she's half-Black. Her mother and me, my hours and some other shit split us up. I get Jewell every single weekend. I painted up her room with that special pink she's so crazy about and put a buncha Barbies in there. My ex-wife complains I'm spoiling her rotten, but that's my job, right? If a daddy can't spoil his little girl, he ain't worth being called a daddy."

He fell silent for a moment, then asked, "You're trying to connect Precious Doe to that Juarez mess? Seems to me Doe's the wrong race. Those women were all Mexican."

"I'm also interested in ruling out the connection."

He sipped absent-mindedly at his coffee. With one last glance toward his daughter's photographs, he said, "The sheriff sure as hell hasn't been getting anyplace with this, so I'll tell you what you want to know. Just swear you won't let on where you heard it, okay? You do and my ass is fired. If that happens, I'll come hunting you, don't think I won't."

I swore eternal silence.

"Precious Doe bled to death, you know that much?"

I nodded.

"No sperm present."

Thanks to television programs like *CSI*, killers had learned how not only how to clean up a crime scene, but how to keep from dirtying it in the first place. That's why condoms were now commonplace during rape.

"Interesting. Anything else?" I waited, convinced more was on its way.

Herschel took a deeper drink of his coffee, then said, "Her killer hacked off all her external sexual organs."

"*What?!*"

"All of them. Everything. He *amputated* her! Then, if that wasn't enough, the sonofabitch stitched her up like he was trying to stop the bleeding or something. Stitched the vagina closed, too, *after* he stuck some kinda narrow tubing up in there. Stitched her up with thick black thread, the kind you'd used to fix torn upholstery. Nice touch, huh? Probably, he was just getting himself more kicks. And you wanna know the worst part? The poor thing was still alive when he did it."

Somehow I managed to ask the next question. "Were the amputations made with something like a scalpel? Perhaps by someone with medical knowledge?"

"Didn't you hear me? I said *hacked,* lady! *Hacked!* A real butcher job. You know what I hope?"

He took a deep breath. "I hope the perv who did that to her gets caught by some little girl's daddy."

Chapter Thirteen

After leaving Herschel Berklee's house, I sat in my Jeep for a few minutes staring at nothing in particular. Cars purred along the street as the first commuters arrived home from work. Somewhere a dog barked, more in excitement than threat.

When I had calmed down as much as possible, I reached into my carry-all and pulled out the photograph of Precious Doe. Her delicate face gave no hint of the torment she had endured. Instead, she looked as serene as the angel she'd become.

Only slightly comforted by the thought that the child was long past her sufferings, I headed back to the *Cochise County Observer*. There I found Bernice Broussard once again manning the receptionist's desk as she marked up the morning newspaper with a red pen.

"Tell me the truth," I said. "You don't really have a receptionist."

"Not anymore, I don't," she grumped. "That 'sick' business? Turns out she went on a shopping trip in Nogales with her boyfriend, so I told her to find another job. Not because she wanted to shop—hell, all she had to do was ask—but I can't stand being lied to. Enough about my employee problems. What do you want this time?"

Without going into the specifics, I asked if there had been any reports of animal mutilations in the area during the past few years. She was no dummy and immediately guessed what I was getting at.

"Mutilations? Like what happened to Precious Doe?" Gold rings twinkled as she clenched her fists. "Christ, no. This isn't Texas. Or New York."

"How about missing pets?"

She shook her head. "Nope." Then her face changed. "Wait, let me rephrase that. We lose a few cats and small dogs to coyotes every year, but that's normal when the desert's your backyard."

In the West, people tend to attribute the loss of pets to raids by neighboring wildlife and discounted the possibility that something more sinister could be on the loose. I knew that serial killers often began with animals. "Has the number of lost pets increased lately?"

"We're not dumb down here, Ms. Jones. If somebody in town was having that kind of serious trouble, we'd know it."

I pointed at the marked-up newspaper. The headline read: NO LEADS IN PRECIOUS DOE CASE. The subhead was, AZIZA STILL MISSING. A separate article discussed Nicole Hall's disappearance. "You don't call that 'serious trouble'?"

"You know what I meant. I've already told you we don't keep our back issues here, so if you want to run the numbers on missing pets, go back to the library. Now let me do some work, all right? Apparently, I've hired a copy editor who doesn't know the difference between *they're* and *their*."

I took her advice and drove over to the library, but even with Martha Green's help, didn't find what I needed. Yes, over the past few years there had been missing pets aplenty in Los Perdidos, but just as many pets were recovered as lost forever. The big dogs, German shepherds, mastiffs, and Irish wolf hounds, almost always returned home in one piece. Only the toy breeds and cats stayed gone, probably serving as some four-legged predator's dinner.

That avenue of investigation effectively closed, I turned on my police scanner to keep me company and aimed the Jeep west toward Sierra Vista and the safe house Raymundo Mendoza told me about. It took longer to get out of town than I would have expected. With the shift at the insecticide plant ending, the main drag was clogged by battered cars filled with dark faces, the blue-black of Somalis, and the lighter hues of Middle Easterners and Hispanics. First the Irish did America's dirty work, then the Italians, then the Puerto Ricans. Now it was everyone else's turn.

The newer cars were driven by Anglos: management. Some things never change.

After twenty minutes of driving across the desert into a pink-streaked sky, I arrived in Sierra Vista. The city of forty thousand-plus was the home of Fort Huachuca, Arizona's largest military instillation. Founded in 1877 as a product of the Apache Wars, the original fort had been erected to block the Apaches' traditional escape route to Mexico. Now the U. S. Army Intelligence Center and School had taken up residence, and God only knew what those folks were up to.

The safe house existed in a much lower-tech world, ten miles beyond Sierra Vista, nestled among the low foothills of the Whetstone Mountains. The sign on the gate announced FLYING HORSE RANCH. In the rosy glow of sunset, a herd of white-faced cattle grazed behind the barbed wire fence. More alarming was the posting, PRIVATE PROPERTY—NO TRESPASS-ING—THIS MEANS YOU!

After turning off the police scanner to save power, I jumped out, unlatched the gate, and turned into a dirt lane.

I didn't get far.

Before I had driven a hundred yards, a pickup truck topped a low rise and rushed down the road toward me. As it neared, I saw a thin man in the truck bed, holding a rifle. When the truck rumbled to a stop, he drew down on me. "Can't you read?"

A woman. The setting sun at her back cast her face in shadow, but from her voice, she was no kid. Guns have a wonderful way of reminding you of your manners, so I raised my hands. "Yes, ma'am, I can read. But I'm looking for someone, and…"

"Get off our land," she ordered.

Forcing my hands not to tremble, I tried again. "Is Nicole Hall here, ma'am?"

The rifle didn't waiver, neither did her voice. "Like hell you can read, and you obviously don't understand English, either. I *said* get off our land." The sunlight glanced along the rifle barrel aimed straight at my chest.

If the woman shot me, no one other than a few cows would hear, so the smart thing to do would be to follow orders, but that wouldn't help me find out about Nicole. Ignoring the dryness in my mouth, I said, "Ma'am, if you would just help me find her? I'm a private detective from Scottsdale—*not* hired by the Halls, by the way—and I won't tell her parents if she's here."

The truck's driver stuck his head out of the cab window. "What's your name?" Like the woman, he didn't sound young.

"Lena Jones. Want to see my I.D.?"

Instead of answering, the man called to the gun-toting woman, "Get down here for a minute."

She did, and the two of them held a low conversation. After a couple of nods, the woman, the rifle balanced along one arm and braced against her shoulder, walked toward me. She stretched out her hand. "Hand it over, but move slow."

Now that she stood along side my Jeep and the sun was no longer at her back, I saw a woman of about sixty, with dark brown hair, brown eyes, and the lined face of a long-time desert-dweller. When I reached toward my carry-all on the passenger's seat, she brought the rifle up again. "*Don't.*" I recognized the stance; she was ready to fire. Who the hell was this woman? A retired Marine?

"Ma'am, that's where I carry my I.D."

"Throw the bag on the ground."

I'd seen more expression on rocks, so I did as she said, although I wasn't happy about it. The noise my carry-all made when it landed alerted her that it held more than makeup.

"Now back up."

I did.

Keeping her stern gaze on me, she picked up the carry-all and walked backwards to the man in the truck. He took it without a word, then rooted around until he found my .38.

"I'm a Glock man, myself," he muttered, placing the gun on the seat next to him. Then he took out my billfold and flipped through the plastic photo folders until he found my State of Arizona P.I. card. After comparing my face to the picture, he said to the woman, "As they say at Disneyland, it's a small world after all."

The two held a brief consultation I couldn't hear. The man stuck his head out of the window again. "You're the detective who helped that little girl escape the polygamy compound, aren't you?"

That case, which involved the forced marriage of a thirteen-year-old girl to an elderly polygamist who already had several "wives," had earned me all kinds of publicity, some of it even positive. After ushering the girl to a save haven, I had turned over all the information I'd uncovered on the polygamy compound—forced child marriages, rampant molestation, and tens of millions of dollars in welfare fraud—to the Arizona attorney general. Prosecutions were ongoing. So were the death threats against me.

Since these people ran a safe house for runaway teens, I figured the chances of their being polygamists were zilch to zero. "Yep, that's me," I called to the man.

The woman shifted her stance slightly, and the rifle barrel lowered almost a whole inch. "Who told you about us?" she asked.

"Raymundo Mendoza."

A grunt from the truck. The woman shifted the rifle all the way down, then climbed into the pickup's bed, motioning for me to follow them. Since they had my carry-all and .38, there was little other choice. After a brief drive through increasingly bumpy ground, with the Jeep eating the pickup's dust, we arrived at a ranch complex tucked behind a grove of ancient mesquite. Off to the right, a windmill creaked, a generator hummed, and a satellite dish tilted up to a sky now turned scarlet. Chickens pecked in the yard, and from the barn, a cow lowed. I figured the outbuildings contained enough provisions to keep the ranch's humans fed for a year.

Several girls flitted between the trees in the fading light, their laughter carefree. As we grew closer, I noticed they were all young teens. Even in the dimming light, their resemblance to each other was striking: polygamy runaways, the look-alike products of generations of incest. And that was why so many girls bolted: they were fleeing upcoming "marriages" to uncles and grandfathers who already had a dozen wives.

The pickup pulled to a stop in front of a sprawling ranch house, and the man exited the cab and approached. As old as the woman, his dark hair was thick and wavy, his eyes a deep hazel. The woman jumped down from the truck bed.

"I'm Victor Friedman, Ms. Jones," the man said, handing my carry-all and handgun back to me. "Annie Oakley over there is my wife Evelyn. Let's go inside."

When we entered the house, I found more look-alike girls scattered around a large living room furnished with attractive, if mismatched, sofas and chairs. I didn't see Nicole among them, but the others were watching CNN on a large-screen television set, where a female senator was making mincemeat of a male senator over proposed legislation to curb presidential powers. Amazement showed on the girls' faces. Television—news of any kind, actually—was forbidden to women on polygamy compounds. Even more forbidden was the idea of a woman contradicting a man.

"We'll talk in the den," Friedman said. "Don't want to interfere with the girls' education, what little there's been of it."

The couple led me into a book-filled room furnished with a sturdy gun cabinet, a handsome leather sofa, and his-and-her desks, each with its own computer. One was a Mac, the other a PC. Friedman eased himself into a chair in front of the Mac, which was blinking out a green-bannered website called ValueLine. Stocks? Way out here in the boonies? Then I reminded myself that thanks to the Internet, you no longer had to be on Wall Street to run with the bulls.

As Evelyn locked the rifle away in the gun cabinet, Friedman closed down the computer and gestured for me to take a seat. "Let's hear it, Ms. Jones. If the Halls didn't hire you, why are you so interested in Nicole?"

I explained the situation, finishing with, "After Precious Doe's murder and then Aziza Wahab's disappearance, I'm worried about her. I just want to make sure she's all right."

He shook his head. "I hope she is."

My heart fell. "What do you mean? Isn't she here?"

"She called us last night from a payphone, very upset, not making much sense," he said. "You heard that she stayed with us a couple of years ago?"

I nodded and waited for him to continue.

"Nicole was pregnant then. Like so many girls, she panicked, not sure what her parents' reaction would be, but after a few days with us, she decided to go home and face the music. Judging from what she'd told us about her father, Evelyn and I weren't all that happy about her decision, but we certainly weren't going to keep her against her will. After all, she was a minor, and no crime—not one that we saw evidence of, anyway—had been committed against her, so we drove her to her boyfriend's family's house and let them take it from there. That was the last we heard from her until last night. This time she wasn't worried about herself, but about someone else."

"Did she say who?" I asked, frowning.

"She never gave us a name, just that 'this person' was about to be hurt, and she refused to let it happen. She wanted to bring 'this person' to us. Then I heard a child talking in the background, so of course I asked her how old 'this person' was."

"And?"

"She said 'this person' was a seven-year-old girl."

Aziza Wahab's age. I remembered Peggy Binder telling me that Nicole had once been friendly with Shalimar, Aziza's older sister. Had the two met through her? But what could have happened to make Nicole kidnap the girl—if it really was a kidnapping, something I was no longer certain of.

Before I shared my suspicions, Evelyn jumped in. "Victor told Nicole that if she was really worried about a seven-year-old's safety, to take her concerns to the authorities. They were the ones who should deal with it, not her."

He raised his hands in a helpless gesture. "Nicole said there was no point in telling, that nobody would believe her anyway. But she had to make sure no one else died."

My concern for the two girls catapulted into alarm. "Wait a minute. No one *else* died?" Could she have been referring to Precious Doe? Or Tujin Rafik? Or both?

"I got the impression she was talking about someone else, but maybe I'm wrong," Friedman said. "Anyway, she started crying, so against my better judgement, I told her to bring the girl on over."

Evelyn spoke again. "We waited up all night, but Nicole never showed. She didn't call again, either. Believe me, we're as worried as you are."

As I drove away from the ranch, my concern over Nicole's welfare increased. She was only sixteen, yet had somehow allowed herself to become involved in kidnapping, and possibly even murder. The more I tried to figure it out, the more frustrated I became. For some reason, the teenager seemed to believe she was *saving* Aziza, so she obviously had no intent to harm her. Since Nicole had taken the family car, maybe she and Aziza drove to a friend's house before heading to the Friedmans'. If so, I would find out soon enough, because Victor Friedman had promised to call me the minute the two showed up.

In Sierra Vista, I placed a long distance call to Angel Grey while I filled the Jeep up with gas. Yes, I reassured her, unless something broke in the case of Precious Doe, I would be in L.A. tomorrow for *Desert Eagle's* production meeting. I couldn't stay long, because as soon as the meeting ended, I needed to fly straight back. Too much was happening.

Angel sounded disappointed. We'd become friendly during the past few months and usually followed the meetings with lunch or boutique hopping, but she understood the way P.I.'s worked. After ringing off, I called Warren, but with no better luck than earlier. Before I could leave a message, the gas pump dinged, announcing the Jeep had guzzled its fill. Intending to try Warren again as soon as I reached Los Perdidos, I stuffed the cell phone into my carry-all, replaced the Jeep's gas cap, and continued on my way.

Now that the area's version of rush hour was over, I made the trip quickly, turning my police scanner down so I might puzzle through Nicole's actions, but the relative silence didn't work. Teenagers were like aliens from distant planets: completely unknowable.

When I drove into Los Perdidos, I spied a small crowd milling around in front of the sheriff's office. Had the girls been found? Or had another child disappeared? Alarmed, I pulled to the curb. The shadows of night cloaked most of the men, but the glow of a passing car's headlights illuminated old Clive Berklee.

"What's going on?" I asked, leaning out of the Jeep and interrupting him in mid-chuckle.

"You haven't heard?" He sounded quite jolly.

My concern diminished. "I was out of town for a few hours. Did the sheriff find the missing girls?"

His smile faded. "Afraid not. But at least Los Perdidos is minus one big problem now."

"Which problem is that?"

The smile returned. "Floyd Polk. Some Good Samaritan burned the sumbitch's shack to the ground. With him in it."

Chapter Fourteen

Vigilante justice, seldom more than a necktie party away from modern Arizona courtrooms, had reared its ugly head. I jumped into the Jeep and sped toward Duane Tucker's place, fearing he might be next on the revenge roster.

The minute I drove into Geronimo's Rest Trailer Park, I noticed a difference in the air. A party mood sparked the night. Couples chatted on their front steps. A group of men stood near the playground, sipping their beers and laughing. Children, no longer hidden behind closed curtains, played on the swings while their parents watched with relaxed smiles. As I rolled up to Duane's trailer, the reason for all this celebration became apparent. Most of the trailer's windows had been smashed, and the open door revealed a gutted interior.

Next door, Ladonna Lundstrom skipped rope with her sister Labelle. She gave me a wave. "Hey, lady! The perv and the bitch are gone."

Her father shouted out the window, "Mouth!"

"What happened?" I asked Ladonna.

Her smile almost reached her ears. "Some guys came by and messed up Duane's place. Messed him up, too. Then him and his mother booked. Didn't take hardly nothing, just took off in that ratty old station wagon of theirs. Now me and Sis can play outside again."

"No one tried to intervene?" I used the word before I remembered I was talking to a ten-year-old.

The precocious child understood, though. "You nuts or something? Ain't nobody gonna stand up for Duane. Or that slut Joleene."

Her father stepped out the door and glared. "You back again?" At least he wasn't lugging his baseball bat.

"Just trying to find out what happened to Duane."

"He got run off." Foo Fighter Man fell silent for a moment, then added, "I tried to make them boys leave him alone and let the law do its job, but they wanted him gone in a big way."

I noticed he hadn't mentioned Polk. "You heard what happened to Floyd Polk?"

He nodded. "Wish I could say I was sorry, but I'm not. Still, Polk shoulda been the law's problem, not some lynch mob's. This ain't the Wild West anymore. Or at least it ain't supposed to be." Then he glanced at his daughters. "You two. Party's over. Time to come in."

Grumbling, they looped up their jump rope and complied. Before their father closed the door behind them, Ladonna shot me another big smile.

Life was good once more in Geronimo's Rest.

A full moon had just cleared the peaks of the Dragoon Mountains, illuminating the desert in its pale light, so when I arrived at Floyd Polk's place I could see that his shack was all but gone. Behind fluttering remnants of police tape, the ruins smoldered as wildlife began to reclaim the land. From behind the outhouse, which improbably remained standing, several pairs of yellow eyes peered at me from the darkness. The wild rabbit pens, a safe distance from the shack, had been spared, their prisoners released into the wild by some unknown benefactor. On a nearby hilltop, a coyote painted silver by moonlight studied the scene with interest. Drawn by the odor of burned meat?

Surprised by my own pity, I hoped that Polk had died from smoke inhalation before the flames reached him.

Chapter Fifteen

My night was made turbulent by a recurring nightmare about a terrified, seven-year-old girl running across the desert. More exhausted than rested, I awoke to a pale dawn. The first thing I saw was Precious Doe gazing at me from the flier I'd propped up on the night stand the night before.

But she hadn't been the girl in my dream.

I stared at the flier, reminded that Precious Doe lay in cold storage in the hospital basement. The possibility that Floyd Polk lay near her troubled me even more than my nightmare.

Decades ago, a murder victim was often kept in storage until an arrest was made, but as people grew meaner and the body count climbed, that practice declined. Quick burial being the perfect solution to overcrowded morgues, bodies were now released to their families as soon as possible. If no one showed up to identify the victims, they were relegated to a county grave site, the final resting place of the unclaimed and unloved.

I refused to let that happen to Precious Doe.

The night stand clock told me it was too early to start calling funeral homes to find out how much it cost to bury a child, so I headed for the shower to wash the horrors away.

A half hour later I emerged from the cottage and saw Selma Mann leaving the barn. "Morning, Lena," she called. "It looks like you didn't sleep last night. Something wrong with the bed?"

I told her the bed was fine, but that I'd be flying out to L.A. for the afternoon.

She grimaced. "You'd be better off catching up on your sleep. L.A.'s got too much pollution, too many people." Then she abruptly changed the subject. "Hell of a thing about Polk, isn't it?"

"Sure is." Around us, early birds sang. The river breeze rustled cottonwood leaves. The world seemed so innocent.

"Polk's no great loss, but the whole thing stinks," she added. "By the way, I sent a couple of my men over to join the search party for Aziza Wahab. I'd go out there myself, but one of my mares is about to foal and she's prone to breech. The vet's down near Tombstone trying to keep some useless show horse alive, so I'm on my own with a long rubber glove." Her face twisted with distaste, then just as quickly brightened. "Say, want some coffee?"

Her slightly plaintive note made it sound like she wanted to talk. Or maybe she was just lonely. Ranch living could do that to a woman. "Sure, coffee sounds great."

She led me into the ranch house kitchen and poured a steaming mug of coffee so black and thick it could have walked to the barn on its own. Neither of us said anything for a while, just sat there companionably. When I decided it was time, I broke the silence. "Polk didn't kill Precious Doe, Selma. That old truck of his couldn't make it across the road, let alone out to the place where the killer hid her body. And he couldn't have carried her all that way on foot."

She nodded. "Vigilantes are good at hating, not thinking."

I agreed. Hate short-circuits the brain. "Have you thought of anything else since we last talked, something you saw or heard that might have seemed unimportant at the time?"

"Such as?"

"Anything."

She set her coffee mug down. "All right. Something has been bothering me. It probably isn't related to what's been happening, it's just that, well, there's a situation I haven't told you about before. But like I said, there might not be any connection to those girls." Her tone gave the lie to her words. She *did* think there was a connection.

"Tell me."

Her answer, seemingly out of left field, was startling. "Labor troubles."

It sounded so out of sync with what was going on that I almost laughed, but her grim expression kept me silent.

"All three girls were minorities, Lena. Have you thought about that? Aziza. Precious Doe. Tujin Rafik. Not one Anglo among them."

I told her that everyone was worried about the minority connection and that the sheriff, DPS, and the Feds were diligently scrutinizing local White Power groups.

Impatience clouded her attractive features. "No, no. I'm not talking about a *racial* crime, which would be relatively easy to solve. Just find out what local asshole has a Nazi flag hanging in his bedroom and there you are. Those jerks are too stupid to cover their tracks. I meant something else entirely. For the past few years, minorities have made up most of Los Perdidos' unskilled labor force. Hispanics, mainly, but lately more and more Middle Easterners and Africans, even a few Asians."

"So I've noticed."

"You've been around long enough to know what that means," she said. "Cheap labor for management, bad working conditions for the minorities. There have been a string of small accidents, mostly cuts and burns up at Apache Chemical, where that man lost his hand a couple of years ago. After OSHA investigated, the company did make some big changes, I'll give them that. The worker's name was Jwahir Hassan. Did I tell you he was Somali? Besides Worker's Comp, he received a small settlement, but to him, it must have seemed like a fortune."

Selma had told me some of this when we'd first met, but I knew better than to interrupt. She was building up to something.

"Anyway, Hassan and his family moved up to Phoenix. I hear through the grapevine he's attending ASU now."

We were almost there, but she needed a little encouragement. "Go on. I'm listening."

She studied the plastic tablecloth. Beige, with a raised pattern of leaves. Nothing special enough to create such apparent interest. "I've seen the girl's picture. It was in the newspaper."

Tacked on every utility pole in town, too. "And?"

"I think she might be Somali."

Frowning, I pulled the ever-present flier out of my carry-all and studied it again. Selma might be right. Precious Doe's face appeared as dark as most Somalis', although death had grayed her skin tone to the extent it was impossible to tell for certain. Color aside, the child's features exhibited that exquisite delicacy common to the North African tribe, a delicacy that led so many of its non-tribal descendants into careers as fashion models. But the dead girl's beauty proved nothing.

I voiced my concerns. "Why does it matter if she's Somali? As opposed to Kenyan? Or even African-American?"

"Because of that Somali man who lost his hand at Apache Chemical. His settlement was nowhere as high as it should have been. An attorney from Tucson wanted to represent him and raise the settlement a few decimal points, but the man and his family blew out of town in a hurry, almost as if they were afraid of something. And, Lena, I heard they had three daughters. If I remember correctly, one of them was around five, which would make her seven now."

I finally understood. "You think that girl might be Precious Doe."

"It's possible. When they left, the youngest girl was too young for school, and therefore had no teachers to recognize her. The Somalis around here pretty much keep to themselves, so she might not have had any play friends, either. Anyway, I've never been convinced of Bill Avery's pet theory, that Precious Doe was part of some family sneaking across the desert from Mexico."

I wrote down the Somali's name so that Jimmy could run a check and make certain the family wasn't missing a daughter. But I saw another problem. The time line didn't make sense.

If Selma was right, the family had left Los Perdidos two years before I found Precious Doe's body.

Selma had a theory to explain that, too. "Maybe she was kidnapped and held ransom for her father's settlement money, as meager as it was."

And buried in the desert near where she used to live? It sounded like a bad TV movie plot, but kidnapping for ransom had become common. Especially in Arizona, where coyotes, the two-legged kind, often held hostage the very people they helped cross over from Mexico, to wring more money from the families left behind.

I wasn't convinced. "If Precious Doe was kidnapped from the Phoenix area, there would have been a report of a missing child in the Phoenix newspapers, and there wasn't. The only kid gone missing up there in the last six months was the girl abducted by the mother's live-in boyfriend, and she was found unharmed a couple of days later. Whereas Precious Doe..." Belatedly, I realized that Selma didn't know the details of the autopsy, the mutilations which revealed a particularly disturbed pedophile, so I filled her in.

It took a while for her to recover. "Oh, good Lord, that poor little girl. Lee might be greedy, but he would never hurt a child. Especially not like *that*."

"Lee?" The name sounded familiar.

"Forget everything I just told you. I have an overactive imagination. Must be the stress of waiting for that damned mare to foal. I've been up all night."

Lee. Lee. The name clicked when I remembered the plaque at the entrance to the hospital: DONATED BY LEE CASEY IN MEMORY OF CAROLINE SOMERS CASEY, 1953-1998. He owned Apache Chemical, the plant where the Somali man's accident had taken place. "Does Casey have a reputation for violence? Or problems with little girls?"

Still shaken by the revelation about Precious Doe's injuries, she said, "Just for fostering unsafe working conditions." Then she added, "Well, let me backpedal somewhat. Lee's not originally from Los Perdidos so I can't be one hundred percent certain what he was like before he moved to town. He grew up on a ranch near Flagstaff and went to Northern Arizona University, where he met his wife, Caroline. When she died in a car accident, he inherited enough money to start Apache Chemical. His degree is in chemical engineering, by the way."

She seemed to know a lot about him. Then again, like most Arizona cities, Los Perdidos was small, and on the social ladder, the two probably occupied the same rung.

"If Lee Casey isn't a pedophile, why would he kidnap Precious Doe?" I asked. "Surely he doesn't need the money."

She sighed. "I was thinking he might have done it as a warning to her father, but after what you've told me about those injuries, it doesn't sound likely. I can't imagine Lee doing anything like that to a child. He's a father, himself."

My experience in law enforcement has taught me that fathers could be pedophiles, too, but I saw another possibility. Casey might have hired someone to do his dirty work, and inadvertently hired a pedophile.

Now a more likely motive had emerged. Perhaps the Somali man's Tucson attorney had finally convinced him to bring a civil suit against Apache Chemical. I pitched that possibility to Selma.

She appeared horrified. "To kill a child over *money?*"

"It's been done." Maybe Casey thought the hired hit of one little girl was cheap at twice the price.

But what about Aziza Wahab and Tujin Rafik? Dr. Wahab was one of the scientists at Apache Chemical. Tujin's father, before he took his family back to Iraq right after 9/11, had been a janitor at the same plant. Then I remembered something I should have remembered sooner. The U. S. Army Intelligence Center was located only a few miles down the road in Sierra Vista. So was Fort Huachuca.

In these days of terrorist attacks, some of the usual civil liberties protections had been suspended in the name of self-defense, and rumors abounded that biological experimentation, heretofore forbidden in populated areas, had begun again. Could

Fort Huachuca be involved? If so, had some of the work been handed off to a nearby chemical plant whose owner could pass the necessary security check? Anything was possible.

"Selma, do you know if Apache Chemical has any government contracts?"

My question startled her. "I don't think so. Why?"

"Just trying to cover all the bases."

We talked for a few more minutes until she grew fidgety about her mare and left for the barn. I returned to the guest cottage, where I placed a call to the Friedmans, only to learn that Nicole hadn't shown up yet. Next I called Sheriff Avery, who with a weary voice, told me that, no, neither Aziza nor Nicole had been found, but he and his deputies were doing their best, so would I please stop bothering him? Controlling my irritation, I rang off as politely as possible.

Taking a few deep breaths, I called a local funeral home, where the answering service connected me with a man who sounded like he'd just got out of bed. I asked if a fund had been set up to cover Precious Doe's burial expenses, and at his negative answer, gave him my credit card number, telling him to give her the best.

With nothing more to do, I threw the *Desert Eagle* script into my carry-all and left for Tucson International Airport.

Chapter Sixteen

The joke in Arizona is that it takes longer to get through the Tucson International Airport security line than it does to fly to LAX, and this morning's wait proved no exception. Due to some fool who blew through the line, we all needed rescreening, and by the time we boarded, I could have flown to Los Angeles twice and had time left over for a side trip to San Diego.

When the Southwest Airlines flight rolled down the tarmac, I hauled out the *Desert Eagle* script and yawned my way through the pages. The script, bristling with Angel's yellow Post-it notes and green highlighter, was beyond ridiculous. Crammed with technical absurdities, the thing also had plot holes large enough to swallow the entire state of California.

My estimation of Hollywood intelligence, never high, dropped even further.

Less than an hour later, the plane bumped to a landing at LAX. I shoved my way down the aisle and headed straight for the Alamo counter, where I rented something tank-like to navigate the Los Angeles freeway system. Then I girded my loins and steered through the smog to Century City.

I hate L.A. because it's a forecast of what Phoenix is becoming. Bad air, bad freeways, too many look-alike subdivisions, and thanks to current trends in cosmetic surgery, too many look-alike people.

Because of a series of fender-benders on the 405, it took more than an hour to go ten miles. When I arrived at the Century City complex, my nerves were so frayed that I snapped at the parking attendant who stared too blatantly at the scar on my forehead. His own features, of course, were movie-star perfect.

Once I entered the mirrored elevator, the better for all those perfect people to admire themselves in, I checked my watch and saw I was late. After a stomach-lurching ride, the door dinged open on the twenty-third floor, revealing the charcoal-on-charcoal offices of Speerstra Productions, Inc. Black minimalist paintings hung on the wall, and spiky constructions of various metals squatted in the corners. Furniture? Sculpture? I'd never been able to figure out which. All in all, the place was so aggressively PoMo that it made a bus station seem homey.

Stepping around a twisted metal pile that vaguely resembled a chair, I announced myself to the silicon-enhanced receptionist. Forty-five double D's, or my name wasn't Lena Jones.

Then again, it probably wasn't; I'd been named by a social worker.

"You're eight minutes late," the top-heavy receptionist pointed out while buzzing someone on the intercom. Within seconds, a woman so thin she almost wasn't there ushered me into the conference room, where the charcoal color scheme was relieved by the floor-to-ceiling windows looking out on the yellow California sky.

Angel, the Emmy-winning star of *Desert Eagle,* sat with her arms crossed near the head of the brushed-steel table. At the low end sat the writers of the series, wearing sheepish expressions.

Eight feet across from Angel—the conference table was that wide—slumped a boy of around ten who wore a severe black Armani suit more appropriate for a studio head's funeral than a script meeting. The presumptive shaman? An overly cosmeticized woman wearing a feminine version of the same suit sat so close next to him that their shoulders touched, her bejeweled hands folded neatly in her lap. Stage Mom, otherwise known as Kelli Keane, a failed actress who'd once screamed a scream or two in a Bruce Campbell movie.

"You look pretty rough, Lena," Angel said. Her beauty was flawless, with creamy skin and blond hair so glossy it reflected the room. "Those circles under your eyes are as dark as these awful walls. After the meeting, why don't you let me take you to this terrific day spa on Rodeo Drive where they can fix those without injections."

I managed a smile. "I don't need a day spa, just a good night's sleep. Where's Ham?" But I knew the answer. Hamilton "Ham" Speerstra, in keeping with that fine old Hollywood tradition of one-upmanship, would arrive exactly fifteen minutes late. We had six minutes to go.

"Maybe somebody murdered him," Angel said, hopefully. Then her expression changed. "Oh. I'm sorry. I forgot you're working on that case with the chi…" She glanced at the boy and caught herself. Like most mothers, she knew what was and was not appropriate to discuss in front of children. "…on the case with the, um, young woman."

"Yes, the case with the young woman. It's keeping me up nights."

She wasn't ready to give up on her offer. "Then you definitely need some 'me' time. The spa would do you a world of good, and afterward we can get in some shopping. It's been months since we've spent time together. Outside of work, that is."

"Maybe next visit."

The boy, who had been silent until now, suddenly spoke up. "Are you two lezzies?"

Angel ignored him. So did I.

The writers pretended they weren't there.

The boy raised his voice. "I *said*, are you two lezzies?"

I stared at him. Over-styled hair, a body too chubby beneath that too-formal suit, and a tiny Cupid's-bow mouth twisted with ill temper. Speerstra expected this brat to battle the forces of evil? At a loss, I glanced at Stage Mom, expecting her to step in and tell him to behave himself.

Then I remembered where we were: in La-La Land, where good manners took a back seat to bad scripts. Stage Mom smiled as if her son had said something brilliant. "Cory's very precocious."

Angel rolled her eyes. The writers kept pretending they weren't there.

Someone had to break the silence, so I took the plunge. "How about this weather, huh?" I said to Stage Mom. In my desperation, I was prepared to ask what her sign was, too, since they still talked about that kind of thing in California, but Hamilton "Ham" Speerstra saved me from myself by entering the room in a rush of woven silk and Moroccan leather. Even shorter than Tom Cruise, whom I had once seen toddling out of a Rodeo Drive bistro, he made up for his lack of height with a supercilious manner.

"Glad you're all here," he off-handed.

"As we have been for the past fifteen minutes," Angel groused.

Speerstra didn't reply, just opened his briefcase and removed his copy of the script, on which I recognized more of Angel's Post-it notes. "Let's start on page six, where the child shaman summons help from the local wildlife."

"No," Angel said, sidetracking him. "I want to start with the entire shaman concept itself. There are *no* child shamans, at least none who can fly and shoot death rays out of their forefingers."

The boy piped up again. "There are if the script says so, lezzie!"

Speerstra shifted his cold eyes toward him. "Let me take care of this, Cory."

"But I want to say something!"

Ignoring him, Speerstra said to Angel, "We're keeping the character because our new sponsor wants it. Moving on to page eleven, the scene where the little shaman tells the bear that Global Warming will ruin the climate for migrating buffalo."

I was just about to say that there were no bears in the Arizona desert competent to discuss Global Warming and its effect on migrating buffalo, when Cory, his face red with outrage, yelled,

"*Little* shaman? What the hell you talking about? I'm taller than you are, *Shitstra!*"

At first I thought Stage Mom would continue to ignore her son's bad behavior, but I was wrong.

"Shut up, Cory." When she shifted position slightly, he flinched. A pinch under the table? Although the woman hadn't minded him insulting the program's lead actress and its technical consultant, she apparently drew the line at insulting the money man.

After a moment, Cory said, "I apologize for what I said, Mr. Speerstra. It won't happen again. " His words were as formal as the expression on his face.

The writers looked at each other.

Angel looked at me.

I looked at Cory.

Cory looked down at the table.

Speerstra turned another page of the script. "Objection duly noted, Angel. We're having trouble finding the right bear, anyway. Let's see, page thirteen, where the *little* shaman..." He repeated the phrase. "Where the *little* shaman asks the owl to bring him the shotgun. No problem finding owls these days, fortunately, so that scene stays in and I don't want to hear any more about it."

Time to earn my consultancy fee. "Ah, Ham, an owl isn't strong enough to fly around carrying a double-barreled shotgun. And continuing this thread about the child shaman, if he can shoot death rays from his forefingers, why would he need the owl to bring him a shotgun in the first place?"

Speerstra scribbled a note in the margin. "Nice catch, Lena. Page twenty-four. The scene where Angel's character finds the dead man, that'll be a close-up, so we can see her reaction. Maybe we'll have her faint. That way we'll be able to lift her blouse a little and let the viewers see the sights."

It continued like that for the next half hour, with me suppressing yawns from the night's sleeplessness, and the writers speaking only when spoken to. As, thankfully, did Cory. Not so Angel, who argued vehemently against every child shaman scene.

The only objections Speerstra took notice of were those where the script too obviously flaunted the laws of physics, such as the levitating tortoise. Listening to all this nonsense I marveled at how far afield we'd strayed from what had once been a decent TV series about a half-Cherokee private eye. Well, kind of decent, anyway. Every now and then, the script called for Angel to flash a tit.

When the meeting ended, we all, with the exception of Speerstra, fled toward the elevators. The writers were miserable, but Stage Mom appeared gratified. None of her son's scenes had been cut.

"Holy crap," Angel muttered beside me.

"Is that a prayer or an editorial comment?" I asked, squelching another yawn, and hoping that my return flight would be smooth enough for me to catch a nap.

Stage Mom either didn't notice Angel's funk or didn't care. In a fit of après-meeting brown-nosing, she said, "Miss Grey, the meeting went by so fast that I didn't get a chance to say how honored Cory feels working with you. Isn't that right, Cory?"

"I guess." Cory didn't try to hide his malice. The bout of trouble we'd experienced with him at the start of the meeting was probably just the beginning of our woes.

Angel's face went professionally blank. Before she had time to answer, the elevator dinged open and we rode down together. Stage Mom bragged the whole way about the commercials Cody had been in, the movie walk-ons, his brief stint on a reality TV show.

Desert Eagle was to be his first "also starring" role. "He's a full-time actor now," Stage Mom said, her face smug.

Curious, I asked, "And what are you doing now? Broadway? Summer stock?"

She gave me a hard-edged smile. "I manage Cory's career."

In other words, Cory was her meal ticket.

Upon exiting the parking garage, instead of turning south toward LAX, I turned north toward nearby Beverly Hills, believing that some face time with Warren might help heal our relationship, or at least stem the hemorrhaging. The flight to Tucson didn't leave until four, so there was time to swing by his house.

Warren lived in one of Beverly Hills' oldest neighborhoods, in the same Mediterranean villa where he had been raised by his porn king father and porn actress mother. Unlike most of his neighbors' homes, his boasted no guarded gate. I had just begun to turn into the U-shaped drive when the front door opened and Warren stepped out, carrying an overnight bag toward his idling Mercedes. I was congratulating myself on arriving in the nick of time when another person, also carrying an overnight bag, followed him out the door.

A blonde.

Unlike Warren's naturally sandy mane, the woman's tresses were strictly artificial. So were her breasts, the size and shape of party balloons. Her skimpy pink dress barely reached her crotch, and when she loped toward the car, I saw a flash of lavender panties.

Not the maid.

Instead of turning into the drive, I parked across the street and watched. Warren had no sisters. Besides, the kiss the blonde planted on him as he paused to open the car door was far from sisterly. After they came up for a few gulps of smoggy air, she drew him close again. When her hips ground against his, he took a long time to move away.

It hadn't taken him long to replace me, had it?

More angry than hurt, I pulled away from the curb and headed for LAX, where at least one of my wishes came true. The return flight was turbulence free, and my seat mate, a Middle Eastern man with kind eyes, was not inclined to talk. Within seconds of the plane reaching cruising altitude, I fell asleep…

…only to awake running across the desert. Overhead, something big, black, and scary flapped down from the sky and landed on a nearby rock. To my seven-year-old eyes,

the raw-necked bird appeared the size of a dragon. I almost expected to see flames shoot from its mouth.

I veered away, and as soon as the distance between us seemed safe, turned again toward the curved line of earth where the sun rose every morning.

East.

East was home. East was where my mother and father lived. Lived! My father hadn't died in the forest, and my mother hadn't died on the white bus.

I hadn't actually seen them die, had I? Just heard the shots. Yes, the social workers believed my parents were dead, but I knew that social workers didn't know anything. My parents would never go away forever like dead people do, would never leave me to be raised by strangers. Mom and Dad were in trouble, that's all. Not dead! When they finally made it to Scottsdale to pick me up, we'd all be together again.

They were probably looking for me right now, but the social workers, those stupid, smiley-faced people who didn't know what a seven-year-old knew in her heart, had moved me around so much my parents couldn't find me. It was up to me to find them.

East.

I had to run east, east across the desert with the setting sun at my back, east until I reached the place where the trees grew thick and tall, east to the house at the edge of the creek, east where…

The bird landed in front of me again, but as I shrank back, it turned away and began tearing the flesh of something that lay half-hidden behind a stand of prickly pear cactus. I craned my neck to see.

Oh, horrible!

The vulture's dinner was a girl my own age, and not quite dead. She was beautiful, with glistening skin almost as black as the bird's feathers and delicate features that in some ways resembled my own. Like me, she must have been running across the desert, headed for home, but unlike me, she hadn't been careful enough.

Now the big black bird had her.

The girl opened her brown eyes, held out a bloodied hand, and whispered, "Help me." Then she closed her eyes again.

As the bird tore into her flesh, I screamed. The bird ignored me. Its curved beak opened, red flesh dangled, and I screamed again and…

"Lady, wake up, please!" A man's voice.

I opened my eyes to find my kind-eyed seat mate shaking me. "Wha…?" Groggy, I gazed around at the interior of the plane, saw two flight attendants hovering in the aisle, and a grim-faced man with the demeanor of an air marshal closing fast, his hand reaching under his suit coat.

"She had a bad dream, that's all," my seat mate explained. The others were staring at him, not me. Why? I was the one who had screamed.

Oh. Right. A Middle Eastern man on a plane, sitting next to a screaming woman.

Before the air marshal could take action against my seat mate, I raised my hands and said, "Please, he's telling the truth. It was just a bad dream. I have them a lot."

For a moment the air marshal's expression did not change as he looked back and forth between my seat mate and me, but then he shrugged and returned to his own seat. The flight attendants did too, but not before throwing me a matched set of frowns.

Releasing a relieved sigh, my seat mate sat back. "I am sorry for your bad dream, Miss. Do you wish to speak of it? They say that telling another our nightmares can help."

I stared out the window, where filmy white clouds trailed along the plane's wings. "Thanks, but no."

Nothing would ever help.

Chapter Seventeen

A few minutes past five Southwest Air's landing gear touched down in Tucson, with me remaining resolutely awake. On the way to my Jeep, I checked my messages. The first was from Warren, telling me how much he loved me and how much he missed me and how certain he was we could work out our relationship problems and so on and so on. By the way, he added, after ending this stream of bullshit, he'd changed his mind about the Apache Wars documentary—*somebody* had to tell the real story about Geronimo—and planned to start filming in Arizona within the month.

In fact, his message continued, he'd probably be spending so much time in Arizona, buying a home there would be a smart business move, and since I knew the area so well, could I help him house hunt?

Furious, I pressed the delete button and punched up the next message. It was Jimmy, saying he had information on Reverend Hall. I started to return his call, then realized that if I hustled, I could make it to Apache Chemical before management went home for the day. I threw the cell into my carry-all, hurried to my Jeep, and peeled out of the lot.

Forty minutes later I sat in the small Apache Chemical reception room, waiting for Lee Casey to emerge from his office. The longer I sat there, the less likely my new theory seemed. The plant didn't appear large enough to be involved in secret government research. Not only that, I had seen day care centers with tighter security.

Only one guard had questioned me when I arrived at the main gate, and after a cursory glance at my driver's license, he'd waved me straight through. To reach the executive offices, I had wandered unchallenged past a deserted loading dock. Only when I entered the plant itself was I provided with an escort, an annoyed man in a gray jumpsuit with JEFFREY embroidered over the pocket. Jeffrey ushered me into Casey's outer office, where he summarily left me.

The secretary, whose name plate announced she was JO ELLEN WOOTEN, was a pretty but vacuous young woman who didn't bother to ask for my I.D. She seemed more interested in her *People* magazine than worried about me running off with secret biological weapons.

"Shoulda made an appointment," she said, staring dreamily at a picture of Brad Pitt.

"Probably."

"Mr. Casey's a busy man."

"I'm sure he is."

She cracked her gum. "Just so you know."

While she was mooning over Pitt, the door opened and a frowning man in his late fifties stepped out. He was tall and broad-shouldered, but a considerable paunch marred his otherwise athletic physique. "Jo Ellen, you messaged that someone wants to see me?"

"Her." She pointed.

His frown disappeared when he saw me. "Well, how nice! I always have time for pretty ladies."

Casey's office was no more elegant than the reception area. The walls needed painting and the furniture looked like he'd picked it up at a garage sale. A framed diploma from NAU, several tennis trophies, and plaques from various civic groups tried to lend importance to the room but failed. On the desk sat a photograph of Casey with his arm around a heavy-set blond woman. Surrounding the couple were—I counted—eight children, evenly split between boys and girls. In age, they ranged from the tow-headed toddler on the woman's lap, all the way up to two gawky teens. Their dated clothing revealed that the picture was at least a decade old. The last family portrait taken before the wife died in that car accident?

Casey's smile grew broader. "So, Miss, um, to what do I owe the pleasure?"

When I handed over my I.D., he raised his eyebrows. "Lena Jones. Private investigator. Yeah, I heard one was in town. You're investigating the murder of that poor little girl, aren't you? Well, I wish you every success."

"Sometimes the private sector can succeed where government officials fail," I fished.

He bit. "No lie there, Ms. Jones. The sheriff is hamstrung by so much red tape he couldn't find his own ass at high noon, let alone a child-killer." He shot a worried look at the photograph on his desk. Whatever the man was really like underneath all that phony bonhomie, he did care for the welfare of his own children.

"Sheriff Avery does seem to be overwhelmed," I agreed.

"Issuing parking tickets overwhelms that guy."

Remembering that Selma had told me Casey liked to drive fast, I wondered how many speeding tickets he had accumulated. An abundance of them might explain his hostility toward the sheriff. Or was there something deeper?

While I was considering this, he asked, "Anyway, why the visit?"

I decided to be as forthright as he was, minus the smarm. "There's a theory floating around town that Precious Doe might be Somali. Don't you have Somalis working for you?"

His smile vanished. "None of them are missing any kids, and believe me, I would know. My workers are my family."

"Really? I heard one of your 'family' threatened you with a lawsuit recently."

"Oh, I see. You've been talking to Selma Mann. Running that big ranch, you'd think she'd have better things to do than obsess about what goes on in my life. Some women just can't handle rejection, I guess."

The statement seemed so strange I repeated it. "Can't handle rejection?"

He smoothed his salt-and-pepper hair, an oddly vain gesture for a man of his bulk. "We dated for a while but the relationship didn't pan out so I stopped seeing her. She wasn't happy about that."

Selma had dated the sheriff *and* Casey? For a rancher, she sure got around. "When was this?"

"Five, six, seven years ago. I can't remember exactly." He folded his hands over his ample stomach and relaxed in his chair.

"Before or after 9/11?"

"Like I said, I can't remember."

Nine-eleven had cut a dividing line through everyone's life. There was what had happened before 9/11, and what happened after. Despite Casey's obvious lie, I found his description of Selma as a spurned woman interesting, so I played along. "You might be right about her. She did exhibit a certain amount of emotion when she talked about you."

He seemed pleased.

"Another thing, Mr. Casey. Didn't the father of that missing girl, Tujin Rafik, work at Apache Chemical?"

He seemed less pleased. "What are you getting at?"

Now that I'd unsettled him, I eased up again, an old interviewer's trick. "Nothing, really. The coincidence just struck me. By the way, I was surprised to find a chemical plant all the way out here. How did that come about?"

Offered safer ground, he opened up, and with growing enthusiasm, told me about his days at NAU, his degree in chemical engineering, his marriage, the birth of his children, the death of his wife, the startup of his company. "Because of the San Pedro River, there's a lot of nearby farming, but we're surrounded by desert, and our unique soil conditions create special challenges, as do our desert insects. I'm proud to say I've devised a formula that meets those challenges, an all-purpose insecticide and our own brand of fertilizer, Apache Grow-Pro. Maybe you've seen our commercial?"

I shook my head. I always muted commercials.

Undeterred, he continued, "Picture this. A Bedouin stands in the middle of the Sahara Desert with his camel. The camel says—the commercial is animated, obviously—the camel says, 'If Apache Grow-Pro can grow stuff here, it can grow stuff anywhere.' Then the Bedouin sprinkles some Apache Grow-Pro on the sand, and giant roses spring up, singing *'Apache Grow-Pro makes us tall, Apache Grow-Pro makes us strong, Apache Grow-Pro makes us bloom and bloom, all the summer long!'* After a test run on a Phoenix station, Arizona sales jumped twenty-two point one percent. Isn't that something? We're taking it national next month."

I tried to appear impressed. "That's something, all right. How about the government? You do any contract work for them?"

He blinked. "Why would the government care about roses?"

The muscles around my mouth were growing tired of maintaining my artificial smile. "Not in growing roses, certainly, but I thought they might be interested in various applications for your insecticide."

Casey's earlier caution reappeared. "Such as spraying it on terrorists? As much as I like the concept, no. Sad to say, the Feds haven't approached me. If they were into that kind of thing, and I wouldn't put it past them, they'd develop it at their own facilities, not here in Los Perdidos where nosy people might ask too many questions." The room chilled further as he added, "Nosy people like pretty private investigators."

With that, he stood up and offered his hand. "While I've enjoyed your visit, Ms. Jones, I really need to get back to work. But feel free to stop by any time. We have no secrets at Apache Chemical."

When I shook his hand, he gripped mine so hard it hurt. Before I could respond in kind, he escorted me out the door and called to his secretary, who was packing up to leave, "Have Jeffrey accompany Ms. Jones out of the building. It would be a shame if she got her pretty face splashed with something. She already has one scar too many."

Then he closed the door.

Outside in the parking lot, where Jeffrey watched me climb into my Jeep, I thought about Lee Casey's final words.

A warning?

By now it was well after seven, so once Apache Chemical lay safely behind me, I pulled off on the shoulder of the highway and called my partner on his cell. As twilight deepened, traffic slowed to a trickle. A pickup truck, its bed loaded with day laborers, swerved around several crows picking at their supper of road kill. Racoon? Coatimundi?

Jimmy answered on the first ring. After a few pleasantries, he said, "That Reverend Hall guy? I pulled up some interesting stuff on him, but before you get all excited, he's never been convicted of anything."

As Jimmy ran down his finds for me, I listened with increasing suspicion. Hall, the son of a Presbyterian minister, had attended a fundamentalist theological seminary in Kentucky, but left after one semester.

"Woman problems?" I asked. "Man problems?" Recent events had shown the world that sinning reverends might swing either way. Or both ways at the same time.

"Neither," Jimmy chuckled. "The so-called 'secure site' I accessed just stated that he had, 'a turn of mind not desirable in a pastoral candidate.' Anyway, after Hall left Kentucky, he received a theology degree by mail from one of those diploma mills and found work at a series of small churches in Mississippi, Alabama, Idaho, and Utah, but never stayed any place long. I talked to a Deacon Wheeler at God's Light Tabernacle in Idaho, who remembers Hall quite well. He gave me an earful. Still mad, I figure."

Besides the various sexual sins, I could only think of one other sin that would piss off a deacon. "Embezzlement?"

"Naw. He just said that Hall's personal beliefs were too fundamentalist for their particular denomination. *This* from a guy who came right out and asked me if I was married, and when

I said I wasn't, wanted to know if I was gay, because if I was, I would burn in Hell for eternity."

In the past, Jimmy's soft voice and polite demeanor, common Pima Indian traits, had led other Anglos to jump to the same conclusion.

"Nasty," I observed.

Jimmy chuckled again. "But interesting, don't you think? When a guy that far to the religious right accuses Hall of being too fundamentalist, it kinda grabs your attention."

That it did. While I didn't follow any particular religion myself, I allowed that there was room enough in the world for every belief, no matter how oddball or mean-spirited. As Hall's Women For Freedom group proved, some people liked to be led. It absolved them of the responsibility of thinking for themselves.

On the highway next to me, another truck, this one loaded with cattle, swept by, briefly scattering the crows. As soon as it was gone, they returned to peck at the road kill, now flattened beyond recognition. "One last question, Jimmy. Any arrests with charges dropped, that sort of thing? Kid trouble?"

"No on both counts, just gossip. Wheeler told me Hall's wife was somewhat less than 'chaste,' as he so charmingly put it, and said the daughter didn't look anything like him."

"Maybe she was adopted."

"Nope. The daughter was born during Hall's stay in Idaho. Wheeler and his wife even visited Mrs. Hall at the hospital. The Halls wound up staying at that church for five years, long enough for Wheeler to notice that the girl couldn't possibly be Hall's. And before you ask, that particular denomination doesn't believe in artificial insemination or embryonic implantation, either. Eventually, the girl did grow to look a lot like her mother, although Wheeler said something about her eyes being wrong. Do you know what that's about?"

Whatever religious blinders Wheeler wore, he was an obser-vant man. As I had noted earlier myself, Hall and his wife both had light-colored eyes, but Nicole's were dark brown. Hall couldn't possibly be the biological father. In the face of such obvious adultery, how had he dealt with his wife? Prayed? Beat the crap out of her? As for Nicole herself, how had he treated the girl, especially when she became pregnant by her boyfriend?

Then again, maybe I judged the good reverend too severely, and his over-controlling behavior was merely an attempt to keep his wandering females in line.

"Were you able to talk to anyone else, Jimmy?"

"Sorry. Other than Wheeler, religious types tend to be tighter-lipped than the National Security Agency. But I think something weird's going on with Hall, because with the exception of the Idaho church, he's never stayed in one place for more than a year or two. He's bounced from place to place, and frankly, most of the places he's been affiliated with sound more like cults than churches. Not all, though. Before Idaho, he did manage to snag a placement with one of the more traditional denominations, the Church of the Nazarene. They sent him to the Somalia-Kenya border with a group of missionaries. Very brave missionaries. Do you know what's been going on there with all the warlords and stuff?"

"Yeah, murdered nuns and burned bodies dragged through the streets. That's why so many Somalis are trying to get the hell out of Dodge. Sad as that is, right now I'm more curious about Reverend Hall."

"Gotcha. Okay. Hall didn't stay long, Lena. After only a few months the Nazarenes yanked him back to the U.S. and left the other missionaries in place, so it sounds like he wore out his welcome again. I couldn't find out the reason, but I'm still checking. Anyway, after his African adventure, Hall dropped out of sight until he re-emerged in Los Perdidos and built Freedom Temple. Nobody's run him out of town yet, so maybe he's mellowed."

I doubted it. Leopards and jackals didn't change their spots. However, Jimmy's mention of Somalia did remind me of something. "I have a couple of new names for you. Jwahir Hassan and his family. They're Somali. They immigrated to the U.S. a few years ago and before moving to Phoenix, lived in Los Perdidos. The father lost his hand in an industrial accident at Apache Chemical and received a financial settlement. I want to know how much. Also, the Hassans supposedly have three daughters. Make certain they're okay and have actually been seen since Precious Doe turned up dead. There's an outside chance one of the girls might be her."

Our connection was good enough that I heard his intake of breath. "If that's true, why didn't the family report her missing?"

"Good question. Here's another name. Lee Casey. He owns Apache Chemical Company. He graduated from NAU, where he married a rich girl maiden name of Somers who died in a car accident a few years back. See if you can find the accident report."

"He inherit?"

"Yep." The crows in the road began fighting over a piece of intestine. Wincing—the scenario reminded me too much of my dream on the plane—I turned my head.

"Wait a minute," Jimmy said. "Isn't Fort Huachuca near Los Perdidos? And that Army Intelligence installation?"

Great minds think alike. "Yep again."

"The plot thickens. Okay, I'll get right on it."

We chatted for a few more minutes until he said he had a date and needed to get cleaned up.

"*Another* date? With the same woman?"

"That's right, Mommy. Another date with Lydianna."

Thankfully, he couldn't see my blush. "I'm not nagging." No, not at all. Just trying to keep my partner out of trouble because he had no judgement whatsoever when it came to the opposite sex.

Sarcasm is not common to Pimas, but every now and then they indulge. "Coulda fooled me, Lena. By the way, how's things with Warren?"

I recognized the tit for tat. "Warren's fine." Before Jimmy could ask for details, I disconnected and sat there for a few minutes, watching the crows in the failing light. I decided that the object of their culinary affections was more likely a raccoon than a coatimundi. Coatis ranged further south. Or they used to, anyway. Mostly found in South and Central America, a few had even been spotted north of Tucson. Animals, like people, were changing their migratory patterns. Not me. I was staying right here in Arizona, even though experience had shown me that Arizona cowboys were no more faithful than Hollywood directors.

What now? Back to Los Perdidos? The Lazy M?

After reflecting on Jimmy's information, I decided to pay Reverend Hall a dinner visit, but before I pulled the Jeep back onto the highway, his battered Taurus approached in the direction of town. A passing car's headlights provided enough light for me to see that there was only one person inside the Taurus: Hall, so intent on a cell phone conversation he didn't notice me. Good. Now I could get his wife's take on Nicole's disappearance. I suspected she would tell a totally different story.

Wrong.

When I pulled up to the parsonage, Olivia Hall was standing just inside the open front door, her expression bleak. She snapped out of it when I exited the Jeep and crunched across the gravel.

"What do you want?" Not the most welcoming of questions. Apparently the good reverend had never taught her how to handle the public.

"To talk about Nicole," I said, climbing the steps. "I want to find her for you but to do that I need to know what's really been going on."

She shut the door in my face.

Shocked, I stood there for a moment, then pounded on the door. Nothing. After a few more minutes of pounding, I realized that Olivia's fear of her husband was stronger than her love for her daughter, so I gave up.

While driving to Los Perdidos, I thought about Olivia's behavior. All pretensions to religion aside, the Halls appeared to be just another dysfunctional family. And an investigative dead end.

But perhaps not the Wahabs.

Praying that the Wahabs had reevaluated their belief that I'd kidnapped Aziza, I drove to their place. The house appeared deserted, but when I started up the walk, a curtain twitched at a front window.

Quibilah Wahab answered the door as I lifted my hand to knock. Instead of flinging accusations at me, she said, "I am sorry my husband accused you of such a terrible thing." She wrung her hands so desperately I was amazed the fingers didn't fall off.

"He was just upset," I soothed. "Is he home?" I had expected to find the Wahabs huddled together in their grief, but the house was silent behind her.

"On Fridays Kalil stays late at work. As manager, he must see to the shutting down."

"And your other children? Where are they?"

"With friends."

"Leaving you alone?"

"Yes." Those hands still twisted.

Remembering the Middle Eastern penchant for courtesy, I said, "You know, I was thinking about that wonderful coffee of yours. May I have some? The night's getting chilly."

It was obvious Quibilah preferred me gone, yet she ushered me in and gestured me toward the sofa. She disappeared into the kitchen, returning quickly with a tray containing a carafe and two tiny cups.

"Everyone is working hard to find Aziza," I said, putting my cup down after one sip.

"The people of Los Perdidos are very kind." She had trouble meeting my eyes.

"Mrs. Wahab—Quibilah—is there anything you didn't tell me about Aziza or the girl known as Precious Doe, that you forgot to mention during my last visit?"

"There is nothing."

I took the photo of Precious Doe out of my carry-all and thrust it toward her. "You're certain Aziza didn't know this girl?"

She shook her head, not taking her gaze from her cup, which was pretty, but not pretty enough to deserve such undivided attention.

"Quibilah, you didn't even look at the photograph."

She still didn't look up. "My Aziza does not know that person. Neither of my daughters or my sons know her. No matter how many times you ask, the answer will always be the same."

"Perhaps if you studied the picture more carefully?"

"Ask my husband these questions. Kalil will be home around nine."

I tried another way around her evasions. "A mother always knows more about her daughter's acquaintances than the father."

At this, she finally met my eyes. "That is not true of Egyptian fathers." Then she resumed staring at her pretty cup.

"Did you ever hear Aziza speak of a school friend, someone she'd grown close to?"

"It is as my husband told you, neither Aziza nor Shalimar have friends we do not know."

Such certainty might be possible in Egypt, where a parent could more easily control a child's environment, but not in America. Here children brushed up against one another at school, in the library, on the street, or shopping at Wal-Mart. And they weren't usually accompanied by their parents.

Keeping my tone as gentle as possible, I asked, "Did Aziza ever point to anyone while you were shopping and say something like, 'Oh, look, there's Nicole.' "

"*Nicole*? Who is this *Nicole*? Neither of my daughters knows anyone by that name."

Peggy Binder claimed the opposite, so something was wrong here. "Are you certain?"

"All of our children's acquaintances are known to us."

I tried again. "There may be something you noticed and forgot. Think hard."

Her hands were red from all that wringing. "As I said, Kalil will tell you there is nothing. Now, if you do not wish more coffee, please forgive me, but I have much cleaning to do before he comes home." She gestured at her immaculate house. However politely, she had given me my walking papers.

Outside in my Jeep, I checked my messages one more time before heading back to the Lazy M. During my interview with Quibilah, Victor Friedman had called. His message said it was urgent that he talk with me right away.

Friedman must have recognized my cell number from his Caller I.D., because he didn't even bother saying hello when I rang him back.

"Nicole's here," he said. "And she's not alone."

Chapter Eighteen

Nicole no longer resembled the photograph Sheriff Avery had released to the media. As we sat in the Friedman's den, I saw a face thin to the point of hollowness, hair hacked into a porcupine bristle. A voluminous dress covered her from neck to ankle, as if attempting to make the pretty teen inside disappear into its folds.

By contrast, Aziza Wahab's snug *hijab* accented her Mediterranean beauty. Even at seven, it was easy to see the breath-taking woman she would become. But now terror distorted her features and she clung to the teen in desperation.

Evelyn tried to coax her away. "Dear, everything will be all right, didn't I promise? So why don't you go join the other girls while we talk to Lena in private?"

"I will not leave this room without her!" Aziza's diction was formal but unaccented. It puzzled me until I remembered that she had lived in Los Perdidos since infancy.

"But there are *personal* things Nicole needs to discuss," Evelyn said, as gently as she could.

Aziza buried her head against Nicole's narrow chest. "No!"

Nicole stroked her hair. "Hey, kid, it's all right. These people aren't gonna make you do anything you don't want. But I gotta talk to Miss Jones." The maternal sweetness in her voice reminded me that although Nicole's baby had been given away, she was still a mother.

Aziza twisted around until I saw the corner of one dark eye. "Make the man leave."

Bending close, Nicole whispered, "He already knows, honey. When we first got here and you were in the bathroom, I told them both."

"I said *no men!*"

Without a word, Victor Friedman left the room.

We would be talking about a sex crime, then. As a former police officer, I had been in similar situations before, where women related terrible accounts of molestation and rape, so I steeled myself for what was to come. Aziza's continued presence in the room disturbed me. Why didn't Evelyn just pick her up and take her away? I decided that if Nicole's story became too graphic, I would do that myself.

Holding the child close, Nicole took a deep breath. "They cut me."

I waited for the details, but none were forthcoming, which wasn't uncommon among abused children. Opening up about the pain they endured was difficult for all, impossible for some. Yet no matter how bad their experiences, they usually remained loyal to their parents, their abusers.

To prompt her, I asked as matter-of-factly as possible, "Where did they cut you, Nicole? On your arms?"

The sleeves of the teen's old-fashioned dress extended past her wrists. In this wicked old world, parents cutting or burning a child's arms wasn't uncommon, but they usually targeted their children's backs, where the scars were easier to hide.

Nicole shook her head. "They cut me *down there.*"

Her legs? Not so common a target, but I had seen vicious scarring on children's legs before. "Your calves or your thighs?" I asked, hating whoever had done that to her. My bet was on Reverend Hall, making Nicole pay for getting pregnant, making her pay for not being *his.* What, I wondered, did Olivia Hall's legs look like?

The den grew so quiet that in the next room I heard the polygamy runaways giggling as the channel switched from

CNN to some laugh-tracked sitcom. From the pasture nearest the house, a sleepy horse nickered.

I prompted Nicole again. "You don't have to tell me everything at once, just a little at a time. That'll make it easier." *Until I have enough information to give to the police.* I wouldn't tell her that last part. Even abused children hated to be removed from their homes.

When Nicole spoke, I could hardly hear her. "Not my legs."

"Your back, then? Your torso?"

Evelyn Friedman, that tough, rifle-toting Annie Oakley, sniffled. Nicole flicked a look at her. Seemingly drawing strength from the other woman's sudden weakness, she lifted her chin and said in a voice so flat it gave me shivers, "They cut off my genitals."

Surely I'd heard wrong.

Aziza wailed, "And they were going to do it to me!"

"She's telling the truth, Lena. I saw for myself," Evelyn said, shaking with fury after Nicole had ushered the weeping child out of the den. "Her genitals have been *amputated* and she's as bare down there as a eunuch. The only thing left is her vagina, but even that's mostly sewn shut. She says there's a plastic tube shoved up in there to keep it open enough for her periods but too narrow for intercourse. Which, I guess, was the whole point. My God, the sadistic bastards didn't even bother to anesthetize her."

I stared at her in shock, unable to speak. Then the door opened and Victor came back in, followed by a resolute Nicole. "Aziza's calmed down now," he said. "We gave her some chocolate milk and talked her into staying out there with the other girls. They're watching the *The Brady Bunch*."

"Reruns on TV Land," Evelyn muttered. "The polygamist kids love it."

"They wish their families were like that," Nicole said, sitting down. "Me, too." Then she looked at me. "Okay, what else do you need to know?"

"Who castrated you?" I demanded.

Before she could answer me, Victor said, "They didn't take her ovaries, Lena, so technically, it's not a true castration."

"It might as well be, for what it did to her," I retorted. Then I repeated my question to Nicole. "Who? Your father?"

She shook her head. "The Cutter. I never knew her name and I didn't see her face 'cause I was blindfolded the whole time, but she had some kind of African accent. She musta been the same person who cut those other girls—Tujin Rafik and Sahra Hassan. Except they were lucky. They bled to death." She sounded so forlorn I wanted to cry.

Tujin Rafik, the missing Iraqi girl. Not just missing, then. Dead. And Sahra Hassan? I saw a small black hand protruding from a shallow grave, heard a plea from a nightmare. "Nicole, was Sahra Hassan the child we've been calling 'Precious Doe?' "

"Yeah. She used to live in Los Perdidos, so her parents brought her back to get cut. After I found out she died, I grabbed Aziza and split before the same thing happened to her."

When I was able to speak again, it sounded like I'd been crying for years. Which maybe I had. "How did you find out the girl was dead? I thought your father didn't let you watch television or read the newspapers."

She managed a weak smile. "You think I don't know how to get out of that house? I'm here, aren't I? There's a meeting place by the river where us kids go after our parents are asleep. Even Aziza's sister, Shalimar, hangs out there. Well, used to, anyway."

She was describing the teen encampment I'd found, probably the location where Nicole used to make love with Raymundo. "All right, so you were down at the river and heard what happened to Precious…" I still had trouble not calling her by her correct name, "…what happened to Sahra Hassan. What made you think something like that was about to happen to Aziza? I've met her parents, and they seem like nice, polite people. Surely they wouldn't do anything like that to her."

Nicole's face twisted into a sneer. "*Nice people*? Because they have good *manners*? Don't make me laugh. Tujin's and Sahra's parents acted polite, too, but they still paid the Cutter to do what she did. Eighty-five dollars, bandages extra. My father told me it was my own fault I was getting cut, because I fell into sin, just like my mother. He said once I got cut I'd be numb down there and never get tempted again. Well, guess what? He was right. Now the thought of sex makes me sick."

She stopped, then added, "Those girls that died, they got cut at seven, before they could feel anything for a boy." Then the well-practiced teen sneer fell away, revealing the pain underneath.

Genital amputation to prevent physical pleasure, purity at the risk of death. I could barely speak I was so outraged. "You're telling me Shalimar just *volunteered* the information that Aziza was about to get, ah, cut?"

"Yeah. She was kinda upset, but there wasn't anything she could do about it, was there?"

"She could have called Child Protective Services. Or talked to a teacher." The words were out of my mouth before I realized how foolish they sounded. Shalimar Wahab probably didn't even know what CPS was, let alone how to reach them. As for talking to a teacher, most teens would never consider the idea. Teachers were part of the adult hierarchy, therefore not to be trusted.

Nicole's next words proved me right. "Talk to a *teacher*? Gimme me a break. But what's Child Protective Services? That sounds interesting."

I wanted to scream with frustration. Why weren't kids given this information? "CPS is a government agency designed to help children in trouble."

At that she laughed, but there was no joy in it. "The *government*? Oh, pul-eeze!"

With dread, I asked the next question. "Nicole, has Shalimar been cut?"

She nodded. "About a year ago. Some guy in Egypt, the one her parents are making her marry, insisted on it. That was the only way to make sure she'd be faithful, he said, and he wanted it done here so she'd be healed in time for the wedding. Since his family has tons of money and has already paid the Wahabs for her—Shalimar called it a bride price, but to me it sounds like he's buying her like a slave or something—her parents did what he wanted. Anyway, that's why she doesn't meet us at the river so much anymore. She got sewed up wrong and limps real bad."

Beside me, Evelyn groaned. Victor looked like he wanted to kill someone.

I felt sick. "Shalimar's what, fifteen?"

Nicole nodded. "Yeah, but she's been engaged to that guy since she was five or six. Just like Aziza, who's supposed to marry the creep's brother. It's an Egyptian thing, I guess."

But this was the U.S. We didn't allow arranged marriages here. Then I remembered the polygamy runaways in the next room, who had fled forced marriages to elderly men. "Wait a minute, Nicole. Why didn't your mother put her foot down when Reverend Hall said what he wanted to do?"

That terrible laugh again. "Have you met my mother?"

She was right. That spiritless woman couldn't even protect herself, let alone a child. Nicole wasn't anything like that. Although the teen hadn't been able to save herself, she'd risked everything to save Aziza. If Olivia Hall had managed to muster up a fraction of her daughter's courage, none of us would be here tonight.

But then Aziza…

Nicole turned to Evelyn. "Okay. I did what you wanted. I told her everything, and now I'm done. I'm not going back home, not ever, and I'm not letting them take Aziza back, either. Next week's her seventh birthday, and they've already paid the Cutter."

With that, she stood up and slipped out the door. Before it closed behind her, I heard Marcia Brady say something witty to her mother. The laugh track went wild.

As the evil that had been done to Nicole sank in, I thought of all the terrible things I had seen in my career as a police officer, and later as a private investigator. Yet I had never heard of anything like this: genital amputation on a living child merely to ensure that the genital-less girl would make a faithful wife.

Victor Friedman's face was grim. "You realize this has to be reported to the police."

"Tonight." Once the doctors saw Nicole's genitals, or rather the field of scar tissue where they had been, the Halls would be arrested. But Aziza hadn't yet been harmed, and despite Nicole's claims, there was no way to prove she was in danger of being harmed in the future. Not unless Arizona law allowed a forcible genital exam on Shalimar, which I doubted.

Victor wasn't finished. "Our safe house will be in danger if we're the ones who tip off the authorities. CPS would be out here in a shot, and if they find those other girls, they'll be returned to the polygamy compounds."

It had always been CPS policy to return runaways to their parents, even when the parents were polygamists about to force the girls into sham marriages with men who already had multiple wives. This was why activists like the Friedmans had established a chain of safe houses across Arizona and Utah.

"Nicole won't reveal your location, but Aziza's a different story. She's young, and if the authorities question her hard, which they will, she'll blurt out everything. There's no way around it."

"That might not be an insurmountable problem," Victor said. "Aziza was asleep in the back seat when Nicole drove up. For all she knows, she's right outside Phoenix."

"But she knows your names. How many Victor and Evelyn Friedmans can there be who run cattle ranches in Arizona?"

He gave me a wintry smile. "For security reasons, we never use our real names around the runaways. They know us as Roy and Dale." As in Roy Rogers and Dale Evans. In their television program and movies, the old-time Arizona ranch couple helped the helpless, and now a modern couple was doing the same.

"There might be a solution," Victor continued. "Nicole told us they'd been staying at a homeless camp near the border, about fifteen miles from here. Maybe they can drive back there and you can just happen to find them."

I nodded. "It might work. I'll follow right behind to make sure they're safe, then I'll alert the authorities. But we might have trouble proving that Aziza's in danger."

Evelyn found her voice again. "There's no way Nicole's lying."

Victor interrupted. "Honey, just because such a terrible thing happened to Nicole doesn't guarantee the same thing's about to happen to Aziza. At least that's the way the law will see it. Her parents won't let that older sister hang around long enough to be examined, either. The second this business hits the fan, she'll be on the next flight to Egypt. Hell, she might be gone already. I'm sure CPS will go after Reverend Hall, but they might put Nicole's warning about Aziza down to post traumatic stress. They'd be partially right, too. A kid can't endure that kind of brutality without suffering long-term psychological effects."

He was right. In this situation, emotional problems were all but guaranteed. Nicole would need years of therapy. Both mental *and* physical.

"Two girls dead and two other girls wishing they were," Evelyn mourned. "How many people in Los Perdidos are involved in this?"

Victor grunted. "God only knows. Somebody has to do something. What was it Nicole called the woman who did this to her?"

"The Cutter," I said. "She called her the Cutter."

We had to find her.

And get her client list.

Chapter Nineteen

"How did you learn about this place?" I asked Nicole, as we huddled in the Buick at the edge of the homeless encampment. The border was so close I could see the lights of Naco, Mexico, twinkling in the distance.

"One of the girls at the river told me."

Ah, the infamous teenage grapevine. It always amazed me how teenagers could know so much, yet so little. Like what might happen to them in the future. Nicole had told me that when she'd first helped Aziza out of her bedroom window, she planned to take the girl over the border into Mexico. From here, the crossing would have taken mere minutes. Her plans changed when she remembered the Friedmans' safe house.

I peered through the night toward the forms of the homeless, lit only by the full moon. Most seemed to be harmless families and individuals down on their luck. Several, I suspected, were undocumented aliens, also harmless, trekking northward to obtain minimum-wage jobs. Still, homeless camps were notorious for attracting the criminal element.

A recent roundup at one such encampment near Phoenix had rousted a woman wanted for questioning in the beating death of her toddler, two men fleeing domestic battery warrants, an escapee from the Criminally Insane ward at Phoenix State Hospital, and an accused rapist who had jumped bail. A search of the area, the bank above a dry riverbed, had uncovered several shanks, two machetes, three handguns, and a sawed-off shotgun. Adding liveliness to the hoard were several stashes of crack, crystal meth, and a shopping bag full of stolen prescription drugs. Homeless camps made for dangerous sanctuaries.

In the back seat, Aziza whimpered through a dream. I turned around to make certain she was all right and saw her wrapped cocoon-like in blankets, surrounded by empty fast food containers and crumpled napkins. Tacos appeared to be the girls' food group of choice, and the scent of stale Fire Sauce mingled with nervous perspiration. Through the rear view window, I saw my moon-bathed Jeep parked behind us and longed for its fresher air, but the girls needed the safety of the locked Buick.

"How did you think you were going to support yourself in Mexico?" I asked Nicole, whispering, so we wouldn't wake Aziza.

"I figured we'd hitchhike to Nogales and work as tour guides or something," Nicole whispered back. "Raymundo taught me a little Spanish."

Tour guides or something. I didn't know whether to laugh at Nicole or hug her. Given her meager resources, she'd done pretty well for Aziza. At least she had managed to keep the girl intact.

A half-hour earlier, I had called the sheriff on my cell, and told him where to find us. I'd purposely kept my story vague, confiding just enough about Nicole's condition that he agreed not to contact either set of parents before arranging a medical exam for the teen. I was attempting to come up with a way to explain Aziza's story about "Roy" and Dale" when a movement at the Buick's passenger side window startled me. A man's face, battered from an accident or fight, pressed against it. He was so tall he had to bend almost double to peer in.

"C'mon, girls, let me in the car," he whined. "Don't ya know it's cold out here?"

"Go away!" I yelled. A terrified Nicole shrank against me.

The man tried the door, but it was locked. Frustrated, he pounded on the glass. I hauled out my .38 and made certain he saw it. "I said, go away."

He went.

Glancing toward Aziza, I saw the hump of blankets stir, but she slept on.

As Nicole trembled against me, I assured her I would shoot anyone who tried to hurt either her or Aziza.

When she calmed down, I asked, "How long did you two stay here?"

"Um, that first night, you know, when Aziza and I first took off, we parked on some dirt road between Los Perdidos and Benson and slept there. But being alone was pretty scary—God, there were coyotes and everything."

Which meant she and Aziza had spent two days in the encampment. I wondered if she realized how far they had stretched their luck.

"We stayed near the women," she said, as if reading my thoughts. "So everything was mostly okay."

I didn't miss that *mostly*. "What happened?"

A sleepy voice from the back seat stopped me. "I must use the bathroom." Aziza, finally awake.

Nicole twisted around. "Oh, honey, can't you wait?"

"No!"

Whispering, Nicole asked me, "What if that guy's out there? When we were here before, he was looking at us real funny. He was drunk then, too. Or something."

One drunk against my loaded .38 didn't worry me. Nevertheless, leaving the car was a bad idea. "Aziza, I saw an empty cardboard cup back there. Can you use that?"

"Go in the *car*?" She sounded scandalized. "No!" Scrabbling sounds told me she was gathering Taco Bell napkins. "I must hurry!"

Her urgency suggested there was no time for argument, so I relented. "All right, but I'm standing guard." Once I checked our surroundings to make certain the drunk had fled, I retrieved my carry-all and helped the child out of the car. "You come too," I told Nicole. "We need to stay together." I ushered both girls to the space between the Taurus and the Jeep and directed Aziza to squat down.

She wasn't having it. "People can *see!*"

Ordinarily, her modesty would have been admirable, but not now. "It's safer near the car. If someone else comes along, we can jump in and lock the doors." Then I remembered that she had slept through our drunken visitor's advances and was unaware of the danger.

"I do not care. I must go over there, where it is dark." She motioned toward a thicket of creosote bushes. The front of the creosote was moon-tipped and silvery, the shadow side was nearly black. It could have hidden anything or anyone.

I disliked frightening children, but in this case, it was the lesser of evils. "Better not. Rattlesnakes nest in places like that."

At first it seemed as if my tall tale would work, but after a moment of hopping from leg to leg, Aziza dashed toward a mesquite grove that was even darker than her first choice. I ran after her, Nicole close behind. For such a small girl, Aziza was amazingly fast, and by the time we reached the mesquite, she was already hidden in shadows.

"Aziza!" I hissed. "Hurry back to the car. It's not safe out here."

"I *do* hurry!" A rustle of clothing and Taco Bell napkins.

The shadows were so deep and the child so small we couldn't see her, just hear her. Nicole, her maternal instincts kicked into overdrive, split off from me and ran into the darkest part of the grove, leaving me the only person lit by moonlight. I didn't like this at all.

"There you are!" I heard Nicole call, her relief matching my own.

A final rustle from Aziza's direction, an accompanying giggle.

Then heavy footsteps from the same direction. Not a child's.

Nicole screamed.

I rushed into the dark.

As I became accustomed to the lack of light, I saw Nicole struggling with the same tall man who had attempted to get into the Buick.

"C'mon, Sweetie," he mumbled, groping at her breasts. "Give Ol' Hugh a kiss."

Not bothering to pull my .38 this time—he was beyond threat, and besides, a shot might hit Nicole—I closed the distance between us. When I was near enough to smell the man's rank body odor, I wrapped the straps of the carry-all around my hand and swung.

The carry-all, weighted by my firearm, connected with the side of his head. The blow wasn't hard enough to knock him down, but it did make him release Nicole. She scuttled out of the way and ran to Aziza, who by this time, had emerged from the shadows.

"Take her to the car and lock it!" I yelled, as the man lunged at me.

"Bitch! I'll fix you for that." He sounded more enraged than drunk.

Out of the corner of my eye, I saw Nicole stooping down for a rock. Instead of taking Aziza to safety, she intended to join the battle. In order to avert that particular disaster, I brought my right knee up and cold-cocked Ol' Hugh. As he bent over to clutch his privates, I grabbed him by the hair and slammed my knee into his nose.

With a splatter of blood, he went down.

"Back to the car!" I called to the girls. For once, they obeyed. After retrieving my carry-all, I left Ol' Hugh moaning in the dirt and followed them.

As soon as I locked us inside the Buick again, I began my lecture. "Homeless encampments aren't safe places for girls." I caught myself. "I mean young women. The majority of these folks are good people, but as you've just seen, some pretty rough guys..."

My attempt at lecturing the unlecturable trailed off as a line of flashing blue lights topped the horizon. After making certain Ol' Hugh wasn't hovering nearby to exact his revenge, I opened the car door and waited. Scurrying noises and movements in the brush signaled that several individuals in the encampment were already on the run. Most campers remained where they were, but their faces, lit by approaching headlights, tightened with anxiety.

Sheriff Avery's cruiser arrived first, and when I flashed the Buick's headlights, he braked to a halt next to us. "How are the girls?" he asked, stepping out.

"Fine for now, although you need to arrest some big guy calling himself Ol' Hugh. He attacked Nicole. But he's not the major problem. Did you bring anyone from Child Protective Services?"

He looked past me into the car. "I recognize Nicole, but is that Aziza Wahab in the back seat?"

"Yes. Did you hear me, Sheriff? Is anyone from CPS here?" All I could see were uniformed deputies, no civilians.

Avery waved a dismissive hand. "There's plenty of time for that. I promised Aziza's parents I'd bring her straight home."

"You called them? After I told you not to?"

"I don't take orders from you, Ms. Jones. In fact, I'm mighty curious how you managed to track down these girls when the combined resources of the sheriff's department and Department of Public Safety couldn't do it."

"You can't take Aziza home!"

Ignoring me, he tried to open the car door, but Nicole, who must have heard our conversation, sprang forward and locked it.

"*Open that door, Miss Hall!*" Avery shouted.

The teenager shook her head furiously, and for added emphasis, put her hands on the steering wheel and switched on the ignition.

Frightened that she was about to bolt again, I seized the sheriff by the sleeve, a risky thing to do, cops' reflexes being what they are. "You need to listen to me. Aziza's in danger."

He tried to brush my hand away, but I hung on.

Glaring, he reached onto his belt and unsnapped the handcuffs. For Nicole's sake, I had hoped to explain the extent of her injuries privately, but the sight of those handcuffs made me realize that if I didn't speak up now, it would be too late. So I blurted out everything.

The Cutter. The amputations. The two dead girls.

I told him Aziza was next on the Cutter's list.

When I was through, the sheriff stared at me like I'd lost my mind.

But he put away the handcuffs.

An hour later, we pulled up in front of the Wahab's house. The porch light was on, and Dr. Wahab, fully dressed in sweater and slacks, answered the door on the first knock. His face beamed delight when the sheriff informed him Aziza was safe.

"Quibilah!" he called to his wife, adding something in Arabic. Then, in English, "She is safe, Quibilah! I see her in the car!"

Within seconds Aziza's mother, wrapped in an elegant brocade robe, joined her husband on the porch. Behind her were the Wahab sons, also in robes, but no Shalimar.

"We are most grateful to you and your men," Dr. Wahab said. "Such excellent work!"

Sheriff Avery corrected him. "Thank Ms. Jones, sir. She's the one who found the girls."

Wahab sounded puzzled "*Girls*, did you say?"

Impatient with all this, Mrs. Wahab pushed past us. "Aziza! Aziza! Come in the house!"

What with the shouting and the idling cruisers, we made quite a commotion, and lights winked on all over the neighborhood. Front doors opened and curious faces appeared at windows. Both Wahabs were oblivious, focused only on their daughter.

Aziza's mother was halfway down the walk to the cruiser when the sheriff caught her. "Not yet, ma'am!" he said, arming her back to the porch. "I need to speak to Aziza's older sister."

Dr. Wahab's face assumed a cautious expression. "What does Shalimar have to do with this? Surely you understand that we are eager to see Aziza, to comfort her. Why, she has been gone from her family for three entire days! This is unsupportable."

To my relief, the sheriff didn't budge. "There have been certain allegations made against your family. Shalimar can tell me whether they're true or false, which is why I need to see her."

Sounding frightened, Quibilah Wahab spoke to her husband in excited Arabic. When Dr. Wahab replied in a sharp tone, she fell silent.

After pushing Quibilah roughly behind him, Aziza's father addressed the sheriff again. "I fail to see why the whereabouts of Shalimar concerns you, but since you are so forward as to insist, I inform you that yesterday we put her on a plane to Egypt. She is to be married tomorrow."

"What?" I could no longer contain myself. "She's only fifteen!"

Dr. Wahab didn't bother looking at me, a mere woman. "Our customs are different," he said, dismissively. Then, to the sheriff, "Hand Aziza over. I insist."

It was Avery's call. Without Shalimar to confirm the Wahab's plans to have Aziza cut, he would have a tough time convincing CPS to take the young girl into protective custody. Not only that, the political fallout, if Nicole's concerns turned out to be groundless, would be tremendous. The sheriff might find himself out of a job.

Avery shook his head. "Aziza will spend the night with Child Protective Services, sir. Your attorney can contact me in the morning."

With that, he turned on his heel and left the porch.

I jumped into my Jeep to follow the sheriff's cruiser to his office, but before turning on the ignition, threw a glance over my shoulder. The Wahabs remained on the porch, staring at the police car. Then the sound of a slammed door captured my attention. Terrycloth robe clutched around her, an elderly woman exited the house next door and walked toward the Wahabs. I recognized her as Asenath Nour, manager of the Nile Restaurant.

Dr. Wahab growled something at her in Arabic.

The old woman hesitated, then moved forward again, her eyes riveted on Quibilah Wahab.

When Dr. Wahab raised his voice to a near-shriek and punctuated his words with a shaken fist, she paled and started back to her house.

But not before giving Mrs. Wahab a look that would have frozen the desert.

Chapter Twenty

"Nicole's injuries are consistent with her story," Dr. Lanphear told the sheriff the next morning, when he emerged from the examination room at Los Perdidos General Hospital. "Her external genitalia have been amputated, and the vagina will require major reconstructive surgery. That plastic tube…" He cleared his throat. "Now if you'll excuse me, I have a patient to see."

Without looking either the sheriff or myself in the eye, he began walking down the hall, as if to get away from us as quickly as possible.

And that confirmed my hunch.

"Hey, Doctor!" I yelled. "I'm not finished with you."

He walked faster.

"Lena?" Sheriff Avery said, shocked. "Have you lost your mind?"

"I just found it." I chased after Lanphear, catching up as he was about to board the elevator. I moved in front of him, blocking his access.

"*You knew!*" Of course he did. No doctor with access to the Internet could have failed to recognize the meaning of Precious Doe's wounds.

Lanphear showed no emotion. "I'm a busy man, Ms. Jones, and I really do have to see another patient. If you're unhappy with my actions or the lack thereof, take it up with the Medical Review Board, but don't be surprised if they back me up. What do you think would have happened to this town if I'd said anything? Remember what happened to Polk. We'd have had ten, maybe twenty Floyd Polks."

"You were just going to leave it like that?"

He shook his head. "The minute Precious Doe was identified I planned to call CPS and have her family investigated." With that, he boarded the elevator and closed the doors in my face.

Sheriff Avery, who had followed my sprint down the hall, said, "He's right, you know. There would have been mass lynchings in this town."

I glared at him. "Were you part of the cover-up, too?"

"Give me more credit than that, Lena." His face was so pained I believed him.

"So what are you going to do now, Sheriff? Surely you're not going to return Aziza Wahab to her parents. The girl's in terrible danger."

"I have to follow the law."

"Like Dr. Lanphear?"

He ignored that. "As soon as Nicole gets dressed, she's headed to a group home. Then I'm bringing the Halls in for questioning. Speaking of questioning, how did you find those girls."

Before I attempted more misdirection, the door to the examining room opened and Nicole emerged, the CPS caseworker at her side. The woman's jaw clenched in rage, but her words were clear. "Sheriff, I'm taking Miss Hall to the group home now." She slipped a protective arm around the girl.

Nicole's eyes plead with mine. "I want to be with Aziza."

I made certain that my voice was as gentle as the social worker's. "Go with the social worker, Nicole. Thanks to you, Aziza is safe." *At least for now.* The sheriff, firmly aboard his own guilt trip, had promised to keep me in the loop.

When the two disappeared into the elevator, I asked him, "What about those kidnapping charges against Nicole?"

"Pending."

"How pending?"

He wiggled his fingers in a "we'll see" gesture. Although the teen had broken the law, she had done it for unselfish reasons, endangering her own welfare to save a child. Whether that would cut any ice with the county attorney was anybody's guess. We lived in strange times.

"What's going to happen to the Wahabs?"

Avery's frown deepened. "With their older daughter in Egypt and out of our jurisdiction, we have no proof of anything illegal. I'll bring them in for questioning, but unless something new emerges, we'll have to let them go."

"And CPS will return Aziza to their custody. Right?"

He didn't answer. He didn't have to.

The law was good at punishing crime, but not so good at preventing it. The thought of Aziza being cut up like Precious Doe—whose name we now knew was Sahra Hassan—chilled me.

"Sheriff, you said that the Phoenix police are searching for Sahra Hassan's parents. If they find them and their other daughters have been cut, that'll help, won't it?"

"Maybe." He didn't sound optimistic.

I remembered a ruined cabin smoking in the early morning air, the odor of burned meat. "This means Floyd Polk never harmed Sahra."

He nodded. "When people take the law into their own hands, they seldom get it right. When I find whoever lit that fire, they'll be facing a murder charge."

Duane had been victimized by the self-appointed posse, too, but at least he and his mother made it out of town alive. Blocking the image of their gutted trailer from my mind, I said, "We need to find the woman Nicole called 'the Cutter' and lock her up so she can't maim any more little girls."

"What do you want me to do, Ms. Jones? Arrest every North African immigrant in Los Perdidos? The ACLU would have plenty to say about that."

He was right. Given the cultural makeup of the town, the list of suspects would run pretty high, which meant that we'd have to wait for one of the girls' parents to name the woman. There wasn't much chance of that.

But the memory of Olivia Hall's weak face gave me hope. "Can I go with you when you arrest the Halls? I might be able to get Nicole's mother to talk, one woman to another."

He gave me an odd look. "Arrest? I'm afraid you're getting ahead of yourself, Ms. Jones. I'll talk to them first and see what they have to say. Reverend Hall will probably claim to know nothing about her injuries. It's the word of a 'man of God' against that of an obviously distraught teenage runaway. And as for the one-woman-to-another thing, you think I don't have female deputies?" His tone was dry.

"You mean you're not going to arrest them?" I asked, disgusted. "After hearing what the doctor just told you?"

"Every move of this office is under intense scrutiny, both by the county attorney's office and the media, not to mention the ACLU. While you've been of some help in this investigation, you're going to have to butt out now." With that, he turned on his heel and headed for the elevators.

So much for keeping me in the loop.

Since it was still a free country, more or less, the sheriff couldn't keep me from sitting in my Jeep in Freedom Temple's parking lot while he and his deputies picked up the Halls. Reverend Hall, unencumbered by handcuffs, slid into the patrol car looking as self-righteous as ever, but his wife's hand trembled as she tucked back a stray wisp of hair. Women that frightened tend to follow their husband's orders, and Hall would have certainly commanded her to keep silent.

As the line of cruisers crawled past me, I picked up my cell and called my partner for the third time that morning. My own voice on the office answering machine asked if I wanted to leave a message, so I tried Jimmy's cell. On the second ring, he picked up. Background noises of children's yells and slamming doors revealed that he was out in the field.

"You at the Hassan's place already?" I asked. He'd told me earlier he was going to check on the Somali couple suspected of being Precious Doe's parents.

"Parked right across the street from their house," he answered. "Both parents were led out in handcuffs a couple of minutes ago, and as we speak, CPS is taking custody of the kids. You can probably hear the screams."

"How many kids?"

"I counted six. Three boys, two girls, one baby. Couldn't tell the sex of that one. Blanket was pink, though."

"Ball park the girls' ages for me," I said.

"One's in her teens. The other, it's hard to say. Nine, ten?"

In other words, both girls were old enough to have already suffered the same genital amputations that killed their younger sister. Or rather, their *supposed* sister, since nothing had yet been proven. U.S. immigration records would reveal how many children the Somali family had entered the country with, and DNA findings on Precious Doe would prove whether or not the dead girl was a Hassan.

What would happen to the Hassans after that was a matter for the Arizona legal system. While we had no law forbidding genital amputation—few states had even heard of the practice, let alone legislated against it—Arizona did have numerous statutes against child abuse. The parents faced prison or deportation, probably both. At least the baby would be saved from similar butchery.

This wasn't over. The Hassans' attorney would counsel them to make no statements, not even if those statements might save another child's life. Or her genitals. As long as the Cutter remained free, other young girls in Los Perdidos were in danger.

Jimmy interrupted my gruesome thoughts. "You headed back to Scottsdale now?"

"Not yet. But keep me posted, okay?"

"Roger that." He rang off, leaving me staring at the rear of a sheriff's cruiser as it eased onto the highway.

In Los Perdidos, all hell had broken loose. Bernice Broussard, publisher of the *Cochise County Observer*, stood outside the sheriff's office amid a herd of reporters and photographers. It was just a matter of time before the TV satellite trucks arrived. Speaking to one reporter was a representative of the Los Perdidos Good Neighbor Society. Could the ACLU be far behind? From the questions being asked, it was plain that someone had leaked the genital amputation story. My bet was on Herschel Berklee, Dr. Lanphear's assistant.

I listened as the reporter, a pimply young man with unstylish horn rim glasses, interviewed the Good Neighbor lady, a kindly-looking matron.

"The Los Perdidos Good Neighbor Society stands behind its Egyptian and Somali friends. We are certain that these charges of child abuse are nothing but racial and religious stereotyping." Her voice, as soft as her face, held a steely edge.

"But what about the Halls?" the reporter countered. "They're white, native-born American citizens, and they're facing the same charges. Care to comment on that?" Drawing closer, I noticed his press I.D. hanging from a lanyard around his neck. MAX BROUSSARD. Son of Bernice. His tough mama had taught him to ask tough questions.

The Good Neighbor lady frowned. "In this country, freedom of religion is sacrosanct. While I am no apologist for the Halls' religious beliefs—whatever they are—they do have a right to practice them."

"Even if those beliefs damage children?" Good for Max Broussard. He wasn't letting her weasel out with the usual tired excuses.

She was ready for him. "Some American religious groups let their children bleed to death rather than undergo blood transfusions. Others allow their children to die from cancer without treatment. So who are we to judge the Wahabs or the Halls? If what you say is true, I'm sure they were only acting out of love for their daughters when they had them circumcised."

Circumcised? Hardly an accurate word for total amputation, but somehow I managed to keep from screaming "Jackass!" at her. The woman meant well, but apparently didn't mention that the government always stepped in when a parent's religious beliefs threatened a child's welfare. She also didn't mention that the denominations she referred to never intentionally harmed their children, and certainly didn't slice off their daughters' genitals in order to keep them chaste or to fetch a higher price on the marriage market.

Unwilling to listen to any more misguided P.C. crap, I muscled through the throng and into the sheriff's office, where I found my way blocked by a deputy.

"Turn around and go right back out that door, Ms. Jones," he snarled.

"I need to talk to the sheriff."

"So does everyone else. Give Sheriff Avery a break and leave him alone. He'll talk to you when things calm down." Then he stepped so close that our bellies bumped. While I didn't feel particularly threatened—this particular deputy had always been polite enough—I decided not to stretch my luck.

When I reached the sidewalk, the Good Neighbor lady was still surrounded by reporters, still repeating the P.C. mantra she had inflicted upon Max Broussard. As I reached my Jeep, the first big satellite truck eased up to the curb, the logo on its side announcing, CNN in foot-high letters. When I pulled out, another satellite truck, this one from MSNBC, slipped into my parking spot.

Titillated by the sexual connotations of the case, the national media had finally decided to pay some attention to Los Perdidos' lost daughters.

At the end of the day, the Wahabs were released with no charges filed. Same with the Halls. Lawyers began to arrive in numbers equal to the media, and as I exited the sheriff's office I noticed that one enterprising businesswoman had set up a catering truck in the parking lot. It was swarmed by attorneys and reporters chowing down on tacos, falafel, and chicken fingers.

Appalled by the growing media circus, I headed for the Wahab's, only to find them barricaded inside their house. My knocks at the door went unanswered, prompting a few told-you-so's from the assembled reporters.

I didn't expect any more success from the Halls, but I had forgotten how much the good reverend loved the sound of his own voice. Pulling up to Freedom Temple, I saw him preening on the church's front steps as he brayed his poisonous gospel to a congregation of microphones. His flock had turned out in full force, a gaggle of unloved women clustered around the only man who took notice of them. They were either oblivious to the fact that he was a monster or they didn't care, just as long as he was *their* monster.

Hall was enjoying his day in the spotlight, but as he spoke to the reporters, I noticed that he stopped short of saying anything that might cause him a problem in court. He might be crazy, but he was careful: the most dangerous type of lunatic.

When I slipped around to the parsonage, I saw Olivia Hall's white face staring out the window. Seeing me, she jerked the curtain closed, but she forgot to lock the door.

"Why did you allow it?" I asked, slipping inside.

Her blurred face revealed she had been crying, but probably for herself, not her daughter. "I don't know what you're talking about."

"The hell you don't. Why did you let that man cut up Nicole?"

"Daniel didn't do anything to her."

Was she stupid as well as spiritless? "Let me rephrase my question, then. Who did he *hire*? What's the Cutter's name?"

"Cutter? What's a cutter?"

I wanted to slap her. "Olivia, give me her name. She needs to be stopped before she kills someone else."

"That was an accident!" Then she gasped and covered her mouth with her hands.

So she knew all about Sahra Hassan, a.k.a. Precious Doe, and probably knew about Tujin Rafik, as well. Yet she had done nothing. Cowardice was just another form of evil, wasn't it?

Since she only understood fear, I grabbed her by the arm and squeezed hard enough to make her wince. "Tell me her name!"

Terrified, she shook her head.

Behind us, the door opened and Reverend Hall, having abandoned his adoring throng, walked through. Seeing me, he smiled without sincerity. "Ah, Miss Jones. I'd say it's nice seeing your lovely self again, but then I'd be lying, wouldn't I?"

Olivia cringed away from him. "I didn't say anything, Daniel!"

What kind of hold did the man have on her? Then I remembered an earlier observation. He was *her* monster, and as such, she was loyal to him. Feeling a twinge of pity, I said, "Your wife kept her mouth shut, Reverend. She followed your orders, so I'll direct the question at you. Who's the Cutter?"

He gave me the same eyebrow-lifted expression I'd seen on O.J. Simpson, the usual ham actor's portrayal of innocence. "'Cutter?' Well, if you're looking for a good butcher, I might recommend Gravelli's Meats, on Dragoon Street. Wonderful sirloin. Just turn left on Apache Avenue, then…"

"Stuff it."

That insincere smile again. "No need to be rude. I was just trying to help."

My gun hand itched. But he wasn't worth doing time over, so instead of shooting him, I left.

Chapter Twenty-one

As I drove into town, my rumbling stomach complained that it hadn't been fed since I'd bought some fry bread off the catering cart outside the sheriff's office, so I stopped at the Nile Restaurant for an early dinner. The place was already crowded, but several stools were available at the counter, where I found myself waited upon by Asenath Nour, the restaurant's manager. She looked as tired as I felt.

"The Special," I said, giving back the menu. "Shish kabob and pilaf with pine nuts."

"Beef, mutton, or goat?"

Sheep were too cuddly and goats were, well, too goaty. "Beef."

Instead of carrying my order to the kitchen, she leaned closer and said, "You are a detective, I hear, but not with the police. Is that correct?"

This wasn't simple curiosity. "What do you want to tell me?"

She gave me a searching look, then appeared to come to a decision. "Perhaps before you eat, you would like to see the back of my restaurant?"

I stood up. "Sounds fascinating."

She handed off her order pad to a much younger waitress who bore a strong family resemblance. "Table five has not yet been waited upon. They need water. This lady's order, the Special, do not bring it until you see us return."

With a resigned expression, the younger woman nodded. She was already balancing two plates on each arm.

"The back" turned out to be an unpaved alleyway behind the restaurant. It was heaped with empty crates that once held produce. A fat calico cat sat on one, eyeing us expectantly.

"Go away, Farouk," Mrs. Nour told it.

The cat ignored her.

"I fed him one time and now he thinks he owns me."

"Cats are like that."

"Farouk is not my pet, you understand. I am too busy to care for pets." Although Mrs. Nour tried to hide the affection in her voice, she didn't fool me. She was crazy about that cat.

I once had a pet I'd loved like that, but it was long ago, in a time best forgotten. "Mrs. Nour, do you have some information for me?"

Farouk began washing himself. She watched as if fascinated. "I hear you are investigating the dead girls."

Girls, plural. "You think the Iraqi girl who disappeared six years ago is dead, too?"

"She was a Kurd, but yes, almost certainly. But Tujin Rafik and the little Precious Doe remain *pure*, do they not?" The sarcastic stress on the word revealed her true feelings. And, possibly, knowledge.

I needed to be careful here. "That's one way to put it."

"Last spring, when Aziza's mother and I were talking over the fence, she said that when it came to the marriage market, an impure girl was a worthless girl."

"Mrs. Wahab actually used the term *marriage market?*"

With a sudden motion, the cat leaped off the crate and ran down the alleyway. Mrs. Nour watched as he ducked under a parked pickup truck. With Farouk gone, she turned her whole attention to me again. "Do not let the Wahabs fool you with their nice college degrees and nice house and nice cars. Inside, where no one can see, they are no different than ignorant Nile Valley tribesmen who cut their daughters with tin can lids. Do you understand what I am speaking of?"

"Yes. I do."

"Shalimar, the Wahab's oldest girl, she was sick once."

I thought about that. "Before or after your conversation with Mrs. Wahab?"

"After. My granddaughter, who was in her class, says Shalimar missed a week of school. When she returned she was very different and spoke to no one. Afterward, when I saw her watering the flowers in her garden, she limped. That particular kind of limp, it is common in Egypt. The scar tissue, you see, it sometimes pulls at the leg. Many girls who are cut do not walk well ever again. I was more fortunate. I do not limp."

When I realized what she was telling me, that she herself had been cut, I shuddered. I tried to say something, but failed.

Dismissing remembered pain, Mrs. Nour waved her hand. "In Cairo, these things are usually done by midwives or barbers, women who are experts with straight razors. For Shalimar, well, American barbers do not perform such procedures. Neither do American doctors. So the Wahabs went to the woman known as the Cutter."

Further along the alley, a dog barked. Farouk scampered out from under the pickup and resumed his perch on the empty crate. Mrs. Nour smiled at him, he purred back.

I hated to break up the love fest, but an obvious question needed to be asked. "Mrs. Nour, if you suspected what was going on, why didn't you report it?"

An expression of shame crossed her face. "Because I am a widow with no man to protect me, and after 9/11, I have been afraid. After all, what proof did I have to claim bad things about another Muslim when we are all so disliked now? Not that the Wahabs are true Muslims. Like the terrorists, they only practice the sections of the Koran that suit them."

Terrorists?

She must have noticed my alarm. "No, no. I have not made myself clear. Dr. Wahab is no terrorist. He is happy here in America, he likes it very much, especially the money! In Egypt, despite his education, he was considered to be from a low family. The same with his wife. In the Middle East, family is everything. This is why they so desired that particular marriage for Shalimar. You know about the marriage?" At my nod, she continued. "That family is a good one, very respected. But the groom is the youngest son."

This information begged another question. "Then what did this 'good' family want with Shalimar, if her family was, um, *low*?"

A bitter smile. "To strengthen a connection to America. Like her parents, Shalimar is a citizen now. Her new husband and two of his brothers wish to immigrate to make their own fortunes. Having an American in the family eases that process, correct?"

"I don't know anything about immigration law, Mrs. Nour." My anger, formerly under control, surged again. "Let's see if I have this right. In anticipation of making a 'good' marriage for Shalimar, the Wahabs had her genitals cut off." I refused to use that inaccurate word, *circumcised.*

"Of course. And now she is gone. To Egypt, to marry a man she has never met, a man who already has one wife. When he emigrates, he will probably leave First Wife behind in Egypt, that is the usual way of things. Or he might bring her here, too. The first wife would act as maid—how do the young people say it here?—a maid 'with privileges'? This is sometimes done."

At my shocked expression, she said, "Ah, I see that you disapprove. Well, Shalimar did not want this marriage, either. As you must have noticed, our houses are close to each other, and the night before she left, I heard her crying."

So much sorrow hardly bore thinking about. "That's terrible," was all I could find to say.

"It is *wicked*, and someone should stop it. But no one ever does. It is as if little girls do not matter. Not even here, in America."

I'd often thought the same thing myself. For all our so-called concern about human rights, when the world's victims were women and girls, America turned a blind eye. Churches and charitable groups, for instance, made so much fuss about the Lost Boys of the Sudan, yet never spared a though for the Sudan's lost girls.

Weren't girls human, too?

No time to worry about American hypocrisy now. "Mrs. Nour, do you have any idea who the Cutter is?"

Her dark eyes burned into mine. "If I did, she would no longer breathe."

The sun had almost set when I arrived at the ranch, where I saw Selma in the corral with a mare and a brand new foal. She waved. I would have walked over to talk to her, but she looked every bit as exhausted as had Mrs. Nour. Ah, the joys of owning your own business. Up before the sun, to bed with the moon—if even then.

My work wasn't finished yet, either. While the sun cast a buttery glow through the window, I plucked my cell phone out of my carry-all, and started returning messages.

"The Hassans are in real trouble," Jimmy told me, when I reached him at Desert Investigations. Half-owner of the business, he was still working and probably would be for a couple more hours. "A little bird in Phoenix PD told me that the Hassans entered the U.S. with one more daughter than they can presently account for, and she'd be around seven years old right now. They claimed they sent her back to Somalia last week, but INS says that's the first they heard of it, and they would know. Both parents just had their mouths swabbed, too."

For a DNA test. "Already?" Getting that kind of court order usually took longer.

"CPS doesn't like the condition the two girls were in. Little Bird says they were missing essential parts."

In other words, the girls' genitals had been amputated.

"Did Little Bird have anything else to say?"

"Nope. I guess he figured that was enough. Lena, I want to drive down there and help. You don't need to be by yourself in an investigation like this. Those poor children." His voice broke on the last word.

To give him time to recover, I stressed how much I needed him to remain in Scottsdale, then filled him in on my search for the Cutter. "She's a menace, Jimmy, and needs to be deported. At the very least."

"*Deported?*" Fury replaced sorrow. "I'm thinking serious jail time! Life without parole! In a windowless cell! With rats!" This, from Desert Investigations' gentler partner.

"I'm working on it." I could not keep a picture of the Cutter from forming in my mind. Big, well-muscled—she would have to be to hold a struggling girl down—lips curled in sadistic pleasure as she sliced through tender flesh. I was certain I would recognize this handmaiden of evil if I ran into her on the street. And then I would...

Jimmy snapped me out of my own revenge fantasy. "All right. I'll mind the store up here as long as you need me to, but call me the second you need help, promise?"

"I promise."

"Good. Now promise something else."

Sighing, I said, "What?"

"That you won't go anywhere without your service revolver. People who would do such rotten things to children wouldn't hesitate to hurt an adult."

"I promise. Again."

"You sure?"

Sometimes my partner's over-protective tendencies became irritating, but I didn't let my impatience show. "Yes, Jimmy, I'm sure. The .38 goes wherever I go. Listen, I have a few more calls to return, so I'll talk to you tomorrow."

He grumbled a good-bye and hung up.

Several phone calls later to clients anxious to know how their cases were progressing, I was ready to return the message I'd been putting off.

"It sure took you long enough," Warren said, picking up.

Sometimes I hate Caller I.D. It makes first words so abrupt.

"I had places to go, people to see," I told him.

He caught the mockery. "Too bad I wasn't one of them. Listen, we really need to start working on our…"

"Relationship?"

"Exactly. And that'll be easier once I move to Scottsdale. Speaking of, have you done any house-hunting?"

What gall. "No, I haven't. I've been working a case."

"Oh. That's right." His embarrassment bounced off the satellite all the way from California. "Don't tell me that what I've been hearing on the news is true. Female circumcision? In America?"

I disabused him of the "circumcision" part, insisting on the proper terminology by describing the procedure. "It's *amputation*, Warren, not circumcision. You're circumcised, and it sure hasn't kept you out of action. But these people, they slice *everything* off the little girls, right down to the root, without anesthesia. Now let's change the subject. When I was in L.A. Friday, I drove over to your house."

"At about what, ah, time?" He sounded wary now.

"At about, *ah*, the same time you and the blonde were leaving on what looked like an out-of-town trip. You two still together, or are you tired of her already? I've noticed that you Hollywood types seem to have a short attention span." A *real* short attention span.

After a moment's silence, he said, "Lena, didn't you recognize her?"

His question kept me from hanging up. Come to think of it, there *had* been something familiar about the woman, but in my shock, her face hadn't truly registered. "What do you mean, did I 'recognize her'? And what difference would it make, anyway?"

"That blonde was Delphi Forrester. I was taking her to Promises, the rehab facility."

Delphi Forrester. As the blonde's face came into focus, I remembered reading a tabloid story while waiting in line at Safeway. A former child star whose film career had been side-tracked by heavy partying and even heavier drugs, Delphi's friends had been trying to get her into rehab for months. "You know Delphi Forrester?"

"She's been my next-door neighbor since she was a kid. And that kiss you saw? I didn't initiate it and I certainly didn't respond to it. That's just the way Delphi is, gloms onto people all the time, especially older men. There were problems with her father when she was younger. I'm sure you can guess what kind."

Another scandal the tabloid had hinted at. Supposedly, Forrester Senior had his own drug problems, not that drugs excused his treatment of his daughter. He was currently doing time in some medium security facility, and if it were up to me, he'd never get out.

Warren was still talking. "When Delphi finally made the decision to check into Promises, I happened to be the only person nearby that she really trusted, so what was I supposed to do? Tell the poor kid to call a cab?"

No, he couldn't. He wasn't that kind of man.

Before I had time to respond, he said, "Look, I know you've got trust issues, Lena. What with your childhood and all, it would be a miracle if you didn't. I can deal with them, but you need to meet me halfway. Don't go running off half-cocked when you see or hear something you don't understand. Talk to me first. And as long as we're having this heart-to-heart, I should probably tell you that regardless of our arrangement, I haven't been with another woman since we got together. I haven't wanted to. You're the only woman I want. Will ever want."

At that, I couldn't say anything.

"Lena? Are you crying?"

"Of course not," I lied.

"Oh, lord, I can't stand this. I'm flying out there. Tonight. No, on the next plane leaving LAX."

That promise or threat, whichever it was, reminded me of the business at hand. "No! There's too much going on."

"I don't care. We need to be with each other before this whole long-distance relationship thing goes south for good."

He was right, but at the wrong time. I filled him in on what had been happening in Los Perdidos, the two runaway girls, their defiant parents, the possible Phoenix connection to

Precious Doe, the still-unknown identity of the Cutter. "It's a real mess, and I can't...I can't..." I searched for a tactful word, couldn't find one, so I just blurted out the rude truth. "I can't be distracted."

He didn't say anything.

"Warren?"

Finally, a sigh. "I understand." He didn't sound angry, just disappointed.

"I want you with me, I do. But those children..."

I could almost hear his smile. "I wasn't just using the word, Lena. I *do* understand. You could no more turn away from a child who needs you than you could forget to breathe."

Tears stung my eyes again, but I refused to let them distract me. "Thank you," I just said.

We talked for another few minutes, and the last thing he told me before hanging up was, "I love you, Lena."

For the next fifteen minutes, I tried to recoup my sanity through a frenzy of activity. I fussed around the cottage, closing the drapes against the late afternoon glare, straightening a pile of magazines on the coffee table, and rearranging my toiletries in the order I would use them in the morning. But the more I fussed, the more disoriented I felt.

Giving up, I fled the room, seeking solace in the Arizona twilight. Refusing to think about anything, especially my rocky relationship with Warren, I headed up the trail toward the San Pedro River and its cocooning silence. As the sun sank lower, tipping the leaves with gold, I walked the bank and listened to the rush of the river, the cheeps of sleepy songbirds. Step by step, my tension slipped away.

By the time I reached the teen camp, I was almost back to normal, or at least what passed for normal with me. To my relief, the camp was deserted, although strewn with even more refuse than before. Deciding to do my part in keeping Arizona beautiful, I grabbed a Circle K bag and started picking up Coke and beer cans, SuzyQ wrappers, and empty trail mix packets. The cigarette butts were the nastiest. Hundreds of them littered the ground, many of them lipstick-stained. Hadn't anyone told these kids about lung cancer?

Three full Circle K bags later, with the light fading into dusk, I was almost finished picking up butts. As I stuffed two pink-smeared Salem Lights into the bag, a spray of dirt kicked up into my face.

Simultaneously, my ears registered a gunshot.

"Hey!" I yelled. Did some idiot think I was a deer? Another gunshot. This time, I felt the heat of the bullet as it just missed my head.

Dropping the Circle K bag, I dove into the underbrush and landed on my stomach underneath a creosote bush, a cholla cactus bristling dangerously near my face. Better a poke in the eye than a bullet in my brain.

Another shot.

A pistol, but what kind? A .38 revolver like mine? Or a semi-automatic with a fully-loaded clip?

Dirt kicked up again ten feet to my right. Either the shooter had lost his fix on me, or was attempting to lull me into a false sense of security. Already frozen in place, I now stilled even my breath. Around me, Nature did the same. No sound emerged from the crickets or nightbirds, just uncaring chuckles of water from the San Pedro River.

The shooter made no noise, either. He planned to wait me out.

I saw two choices of action. Stay hidden under the creosote bush in hopes he would eventually give up and go away, or find a more defensive position. I remembered seeing a tumble of granite boulders a few yards to my left, and wondered if it was possible to reach them without alerting my attacker to my position. I certainly couldn't defend myself from here. Although I'd taken care to strap on my holster before leaving the cottage, the snap as I freed my .38 might betray me in such silence.

Since action comes more easily to me than inaction, I began to crawl. Praying that the dim light hid my movements, I slid on my belly until reaching the spot where the boulders hunched against me and the surrounding tall weeds helped obscure my form.

Then I heard twigs snapping.

Footsteps.

Were they coming closer? Or moving away?

As I breathed in dust and dirt, nearby crickets began to chirp again, which meant that the shooter was moving in the wrong direction. I waited a while longer, then as quietly as possible, unsnapped my holster.

The snap sounded to my ears every bit as loud as a gunshot. Then, taking even more care, I flipped out the .38 and cocked the hammer back.

Another gunshot, not mine.

This time my attacker's bullet zinged through the underbrush only inches from my face. Yes, the shooter almost achieved his end, a dead Lena Jones, but I'd seen a flash from between two cottonwoods. I raised myself up over the weeds and fired two quick shots in that direction.

A gasp.

Fright? Or had a bullet found its mark?

Footsteps charging away through the underbrush answered the question. The shooter, thinking his quarry was unarmed, had acted boldly. Things changed when his quarry returned fire.

Coward.

Chapter Twenty-two

I was in the sheriff's office signing off on my report about the shooting, when Raymundo Mendoza shoved his way through the door.

"Where's Nicole?" he cried.

The deputies rushed forward. One of them, the stone-faced mountain of a man who'd taken my report, said, "Calm down, son."

Raymundo turned a fierce face on him and clenched his fists. "Don't you tell me to calm down! Where's Sheriff Avery? I need to talk to him!"

Deputy Mountain—his badge said KENNY SMALL—didn't answer, just pushed at him somewhat less than gently. Raymundo didn't like that, and raised a fist. Before he could throw a punch, I stepped between the two. "Nicole's not here, Raymundo. CPS has her. She's safe."

The boy noticed me for the first time. "Safe? Are you crazy?" The usual teenage contempt for authority raged in his eyes, but he lowered his fists. "You brought her back here, didn't you? I should never have told you where she was!"

The door to the sheriff's office opened and Avery walked out. "Raymundo, go home."

"Not without my girl!"

To Deputy Mountain, the sheriff said, "Got any more room in the cells tonight?"

Deputy Mountain reflected. "Well, considering everything, it's been relatively quiet for a Saturday night, so we have a few vacancies."

Seeing which way this was headed, I took Raymundo by the arm. "Let's talk outside."

At first it seemed as if the boy would continue ranting, but he thought better of it. Throwing one more growl behind him, he stalked to the door.

Outside, a few people still milled around, but most of the satellite trucks were gone to wherever satellite trucks go at night. I spotted a few familiar faces: Clive Berklee and his nephew Herschel, both looking like they'd downed too many Molson's; a few faces from the Geronimo's Rest Trailer Park, including Foo Fighter Man, father of the foul-mouthed Ladonna. I also saw Lee Casey, CEO of Apache Chemical, speaking quietly to a group of men near the parking lot. When I caught his eye, he moved into the shadows.

I gave Raymundo a sympathetic pat on the shoulder. "Let's get some coffee."

Geronimo Espresso, just down the street from the sheriff's office, was open, so we found ourselves a corner booth underneath yet another photograph of a peaceful-appearing Geronimo. This time the old Apache was chatting with two derby-wearing white men at what appeared to be a county fair. I remembered Selma Mann telling me that during his long captivity, he had appeared at several, an odd ending for a man who had avenged the murders of his children by murdering other children.

Toward the front of the coffee bar, a grouping of Los Perdidos teenagers sipped their frothy confections while text-messaging. Fairly quiet as teenagers go, their chatter still made the place less private than I would have liked. At least the coffee shop was darker than McDonald's, but not quite dark enough to hide the pain on Raymundo's face. His obvious anguish made me forget my own troubles and the fact that someone had just tried to kill me.

After ordering our drinks—an espresso for me, a Caramel Frappuccino for him—I checked the time. Almost ten. "We brought Nicole and Aziza in last night. Don't tell me you just found out."

That expression of contempt again. "Of course not. But nobody said anything about her being hurt! When I turned on the local news tonight…" The contempt changed to bewilderment. "The newscaster said something I didn't understand, about something called *FGM?* What the fu…what the heck's that?"

Ah, the media was at it again, cleaning up the grisly facts. Now they'd switched their euphemisms to FGM—female genital mutilation—a vague term to disguise complete amputation. Why bother telling the ugly truth?

"The story's been on TV all day, Raymundo," I told him.

Teen contempt returned. "I've been at work all day, since before nine. And the store stays open late on Saturdays. The tourists eat dinner, start talking about all the pretty pots they saw around town, then decide to buy some for their New York apartments. Half the time they're hammered when they arrive, so they buy more high-end stuff than normal. After we ran the last guy out at nine, I helped clean up. When I got home and turned on the TV, I heard them talking about this *FGM* thing. What's that mean? Did that Hall jerk-off do something to her? If he did, I'll *kill* him!"

One of the teenagers at the other end of the coffee shop glanced our way.

Not wanting to make a scene, especially one involving death threats, I said, "Calm down, Raymundo. Did you talk to anyone outside the sheriff's office tonight?"

He shook his head. "Nah. I just barged straight in. Why?"

It seemed impossible the boy didn't yet know what had been done to Nicole, since everyone else in town did, but maybe he was telling the truth. "Raymundo, did Nicole ever say how Reverend Hall punished her for getting pregnant?"

"Punished? He gave our baby away, that's what he did! What could be worse than that?"

"There is something else."

He glowered. "Worse than giving away our baby? He beat her, I'll bet, but she swore he didn't. He never cared anything for her, on account of he's not her real father." At the expression on my face, he nodded. "Yeah, she told me about that. He never let her forget it, always calling her 'the child of sin.' She said he was getting worse, too. When she snuck out to the river, I tried to get her to tell me what was going on, but she cringed away every time I came near her. Jesus, she never used to be like that. She loved it when I..."

He blushed. "Anyway, I never saw any bruises, but I know Hall must have done something terrible to her. Nicole sometimes looked at me with this really *sick* expression that's hard to describe, and she told me once that if I didn't leave her alone, she'd stop hanging with us and stay home. So what could I do? I figured that seeing her, even if she wouldn't let me touch her, was better than nothing. So I did what she wanted. I shut up."

He looked down at his Frappuccino, his face bereft. "Nicole's my whole world."

His sincerity reminded me that young love can be true love. Sometimes. But how would this healthy young man react when he found out the truth about his beloved's injuries and just how life-changing they were? And he would find out, of that I had no doubt. The media might still tippy-toe around the issue, using the standard, truth-obscuring euphemisms, but Ramondo had access to the Internet. It was probably just a matter of hours before Raymundo learned what those euphemisms really meant.

Of course, I could tell him myself and cushion the blow as much as possible, but would that be wise?

As I was pondering my choices, his hand clamped down on my wrist. "I want to see her! You've got to tell me where she is! I can help her!"

I stared at him until he loosened his grip. "I told you. She's in a group home and I have no idea where. In Tucson, probably, because CPS will have wanted to get her as far away from her parents as possible. I imagine she'll call you soon." If the group home operators allowed her near a phone, that was. Poor Nicole. She was the victim in all this, yet the most punished.

Trying for threatening, Ramondo narrowed his eyes. "I said, I need to see her! *Now!* You can find out where she's at!"

When his voice rose, one of the teen boys at the other end of the coffee shop stood up and walked toward us. He was even taller than Raymundo. "Everything okay over there, Miss?"

Great. Now I was about to get involved in a coffee shop brawl, only one step above a bar fight. I smiled at my would-be rescuer. "I'm fine, thanks."

To my relief, the boy rejoined his friends.

Raymundo flushed, realizing how his behavior must appear to others. Placing both hands on the table where they would be visible to my teen protector, he leaned toward me and whispered, "Can't you see that I'm worried sick over Nicole, Ms. Jones? First her parents adopt out our baby, then she won't talk to me, and now she's been taken away! Not knowing what's going on is driving me crazy!"

His pleas accomplished what his threats couldn't. He was right. Not knowing always was the worst thing.

I put my hand on his shoulder. "Let's go for a drive, Raymundo. There's something I need to tell you."

Chapter Twenty-three

When Reverend Hall's flock arrived at Freedom Temple the next morning, they found him lying near the altar with a bullet in his face.

In a live feed from in front of the church, a brunette newscaster related the bare facts. "We have few details about the killing yet, but Sheriff Bill Avery has scheduled a news conference for noon. We do know that there have been no arrests, although he is reportedly interviewing several persons of interest."

Looking away from the tiny counter-top television set, Selma stared at me across the breakfast table. "Several? Hell, who *didn't* want to kill him?"

Who, indeed?

The newscaster struggled to keep her face neutral when she recapped the mutilation murder of "a girl identified only as Precious Doe," the arson death of a convicted child molester, and the mysterious child disappearances in Los Perdidos.

She almost succeeded. "Two of the missing children turned up safe Friday night and are now in protective custody, but sources in Los Perdidos tell us there have been rumors about unusual unlicenced medical procedures being performed on at least one of them, a teenaged girl. These procedures may be connected, the same sources tell us, to the dead minister's church. In an interesting development, we also hear that Child Protective Services is joining with the Cochise County Sheriff's Department in this investigation, and that the county attorney has cut short her participation in a week-long conference in Washington D.C. to fly back here. As we learn more, we will keep you posted."

First circumcision. Then FGM. Now *unlicenced medical procedures*. Media folks sure have trouble calling a spade a spade, don't they?

Mirroring my disgust, Selma rose from the table and turned off the TV. "So much for a quiet morning."

No longer hungry, I pushed my plate away. Was Reverend Hall's death my fault? If so, did I care? Last night, after telling Raymundo about Nicole's mutilations, I hadn't left until he calmed down. But perhaps the mood I'd judged to be acceptance was, in fact, determination. He probably had access to a gun; almost everyone in Arizona did. Despite our modern trappings, we remained a frontier state, as proved by the vigilante killing of Floyd Polk.

"Something wrong with your omelet? Too many chilies?" I looked up to find Selma studying me with a worried expression.

"It's delicious. I just had a late night." Not wanting to worry her, I hadn't told her about my experience at the river.

She gave me a small smile. "Hangover?"

"I don't drink."

"Maybe you should. If a horse turned up looking like you this morning, I'd shoot it."

Come to think of it, how many guns did Selma have? I had counted six in the living room alone. Granted, most were museum pieces, but I'd seen some relatively new ones, too.

Dismayed by my suspicions, I stood up. "I'm going into town."

"Good luck if it's to see the sheriff. He's probably hip deep in interview requests."

She turned out to be right. When I arrived at the sheriff's office, satellite trucks were lined up all the way down the street, fronted by a gaggle of talking heads yapping into microphones. After pushing my way through the crowd and into the office itself, I found myself blocked as effectively as Raymundo had been blocked the night before, and by the same huge deputy.

"I need to talk to the sheriff," I said, uncomfortably aware that I echoed the boy's words.

"Take a number," Deputy Mountain grumped. He glanced at the clock. "Sheriff Avery should be able to get to you, oh, some time in December."

"We're working on the same case, for Pete's sake! So what's the…"

He didn't let me finish. "Ms. Jones, would you please go away? We have enough on our plates without having to deal with you, too."

"Tell me one thing. Has the sheriff…" I stopped myself just in time. I had been about to ask, *Has the sheriff interviewed Raymundo Mendoza yet?*

Deputy Mountain raised his eyebrows. "What?"

"Nothing," I muttered, and left.

The minute I emerged from the sheriff's office, the newscaster I had seen on the morning news ran over and stuck a microphone under my nose. "Ma'am, are you with the Cochise County Sheriff's Department?"

"No." I tried to duck away, but she followed me.

"Child Protective Services?"

"No."

"But you live in Los Perdidos, right?"

"No."

Her expression grew strained, but she didn't pull the mike away. "Do you have anything to say about the murder?"

"No."

"My sources tell me there was another shooting last night, but that no one was hurt. Have you heard anything about that?"

"Another shooting? News to me." Hey, if you can't lie to the media, who can you lie to?

She wouldn't give up. As I hurried to my Jeep, she trotted right along, the satellite truck rolling along with her. "Those rumors of medical procedures being carried out by unlicenced medical practitioners. What have you heard about them?"

I almost repeated my "no comment" comment, but then had a better idea. I stopped, leaned into her mike and said, "Why don't you go talk to Kalil and Quibilah Wahab? They might be able to tell you a great deal about those so-called unlicenced medical procedures. Which, by the way, are complete genital amputations carried out on living little girls, without anesthesia."

Then I climbed into my Jeep and left for Freedom Temple.

A satellite truck was just exiting the church's driveway when I pulled in. Passing several more, I drove around to the back and parked by the parsonage. Instead of knocking, I walked right in.

Olivia Hall was seated on one of the sofas, surrounded by a dozen women wearing white robes. The Women For Freedom. Olivia alone was dry-eyed, but that meant nothing. I'd known people who remained stoic when confronted with the news of the death of a loved one, but committed suicide as soon as the funeral was over.

When Olivia raised her head and met my eyes, I feared for her, too. There was a vast emptiness in her expression, as if only her body sat in the room. Her soul, if she'd ever had one, was gone.

Sitting down in the chair directly across from her, I spoke gently. "Mrs. Hall? I'm very sorry about your loss, but there are a few things I'd like to ask."

She spread her hands in an "I don't care" gesture.

"Do you have to?" snapped a harsh-faced woman of around fifty. "She's in mourning."

I ignored the woman. "Olivia, what time did you last see your husband alive?" Knowing the estimated time of death would help my own investigation.

She looked at the photograph display on the wall. Her attention seemed riveted on the picture taken in Africa. Was that where it all began?

"He left the parsonage around midnight," she finally said. "I figured he was going over to the church to finish up some work."

"He never came back?"

She shook her head. "I don't know."

"You didn't notice that he didn't come to bed?" She might have been a deep sleeper, although considering the hell she'd allowed her husband to inflict on her daughter, I didn't understand how she could sleep at all.

Staring at the photograph, she answered, "Daniel and I haven't shared a bedroom in many years."

The room became so quiet I heard the deputy coughing on the other side of the church, traffic passing on the highway. "Was it usual for him to leave the parsonage at night?"

"To go to the church, yes."

"If you didn't share the same bedroom, how do you know he always went to the church? Perhaps some of those times, he went elsewhere."

Hearing a quick intake of breath, I looked over at the young woman whose cowled, white robe couldn't hide her flame-haired attractiveness. Seeing her guilty expression, I knew that the good reverend wasn't as pure as his beaten-down wife believed.

I directed my next question to the redhead. "Were you having an affair with Reverend Hall?"

The redhead gasped again, then stood up and shouted, "You dirty-minded bitch! Someone should cut *you*!" With that, she fled out the door.

Olivia watched her go. "Elaine used to embrace sin, but now she is pure. She made that sacrifice for him."

Several white-veiled heads nodded. With that chorus of gestures, a terrible suspicion formed in my mind.

The temperature in the room was pleasant enough, but I shivered anyway. "Just what kind of sacrifice are you talking about?"

Olivia's voice became a mere whisper. "The foregoing of pleasure."

I had to be wrong. No one would willingly let themselves be butchered like that. But I had to ask the question. "Have you all been *cut*?"

Several women smiled with empty-headed pride. Others looked away. But no one denied it.

The harsh-faced woman broke the silence. "We are all pure here. Except for you."

I realized, then, that I was surrounded by female eunuchs.

McDonald's go-cup in hand, I sat in the park near the library listening to my police scanner, watching Mass-goers leave the Los Perdidos Catholic Church down the hill. It was a pretty day, with a sky dimmed only by a few scuttling clouds, so the church's congregants wore summery clothes topped by the lightest of jackets. They appeared happy, as well they should. Their priest had absolved their sins with no cutting involved.

Self-mutilation is legal in the U.S. As long as you are of legal age and can pass a sanity test, you can do any crazy thing you want to your own body. Still, most people stopped short of amputating body parts.

There are exceptions.

When the members of the Heaven's Gate cult committed mass suicide in 1997, the autopsies found that six of the males had been castrated. Some of them had even performed the procedure on themselves to ensure that they were pure enough to be taken on board the spaceship that trailed Comet Hale-Bopp.

Religion was an odd thing. Believers represented both the best and the worst of the human condition. Religious leaders used their particular faith's message to soothe grief, to cause grief; to council peace, to incite terrorism.

And in some cases, to make their flocks feel ashamed for just being normal.

Snippets of John Lennon's *Imagine* drifted through my troubled mind, especially the line where he suggested that without religion, there would be no war, no terror. I'd never bought into that philosophy, having noticed that religion-free regimes—such as those headed by Stalin, Hitler, Pol Pot, and Chairman Mao—had no trouble waging war or committing atrocities. Then again, those leaders had made gods of themselves, hadn't they?

Just like Marshall Applewhite, the addled-brained prophet of Heaven's Gate.

Just like Reverend Daniel Hall.

Hall had not acted alone. And unlike Marshall Applewhite, he had not confined his barbarous beliefs to willing adult believers. After Nicole's pregnancy proved she was no longer 'pure,' Hall ordered her cut. Nicole told me that the Cutter, the woman who actually carried out the procedures, spoke with an African accent. An old African acquaintance of the Reverend's who'd immigrated to Los Perdidos?

Before leaving the parsonage, I had attempted to make the white-robed women of Freedom Temple tell me the Cutter's name, but they maintained their silence. Overwhelmed by a mixture of pity and disgust, I'd given up and left, but now that I examined the ramifications of the situation, I knew I had to speak to Sheriff Avery right away.

In case the Women For Freedom had daughters.

If anything, the media frenzy had built since my last visit, but this time I didn't let Deputy Mountain turn me away.

"Want to find more children's bodies?" I asked, as he approached. "I have an idea who's been cutting them up." A stretch of the truth, but Avery needed to be alerted to the continuing danger posed by Freedom Temple and any other group that believed that a dead girl was preferable to an impure girl.

Deputy Mountain thought about that for a moment, then said, "The sheriff's at the hospital, where they're doing the autopsy on Hall. Don't tell him I told you."

"My lips are sealed."

Ten minutes later I stood waiting by the hospital service elevator, from which the duty nurse had told me the sheriff would emerge. Thirty minutes passed. An hour. Just before noon, the elevator doors opened and Avery walked out. His face held a greenish cast, not completely attributed to the hospital hallway's flourescent lighting. Having attended a few autopsies myself, I knew how he felt.

"What now, Ms. Jones?" he said, upon seeing me.

I filled him in on my conversation with the ladies of Freedom Temple.

He shook his head. "It just gets crazier and crazier." Then, to my great relief, he barked orders into his radio. The ladies of Freedom Temple would soon greet uniformed visitors.

"Anything else?" he asked.

"Same thing I told you before. Find the Cutter before another little girl winds up mutilated or dead."

"And I have the same problem I had before, something called the U.S. Constitution. My deputies can't go around grabbing every African female off the streets of Los Perdidos."

My answer came in the form of another question. "What are the chances that every woman in Freedom Temple will be able to keep her mouth shut? Especially if she's been cut. There's a chance at least one of them might regret her decision." I remembered the redhead's distress, her rush from the room.

He frowned. "And when my deputies bring 'em all in, which they will, what do you expect me to do? Have them lift their pretty white robes for a show-and-tell?"

An angry flush chased the green tint from his face. "Even if their attorneys let it happen, which they won't, so what? Do you expect them to all of a sudden burst into tears and blurt out the Cutter's name? Come on, Ms. Jones, you've been a cop! You know better than that. If what you're telling me is true, and it probably is, since Hall was as charismatic as he was crazy, those women will play the martyr and keep their mouths shut. At least for now. In a few months, when the bastard's been dead awhile and his influence fades, maybe then they'll see the error of their ways and start talking. But for now, they're not gonna say shit!"

He took a deep breath and recovered himself. "As I see it, the immediate problem is the safety of their kids, so excuse me while I get on the phone to CPS. Oh, God, by the time this is all over, those folks are gonna be so sick of me."

After he made the call, I asked one more question. "When did Hall die?"

"Why should I tell you?"

"Because you're about to hold a press conference and tell everybody else. Since I've shared all my information with you, don't you think you owe me something? Even if it's only a thirty-minute jump on the media?"

He grunted assent. "Hall died early this morning, somewhere between one and four. While running for the door, he took two bullets in the back. Neither hit any major organs, they just knocked him down. The killer finished him off with a shot in the face."

"Handgun?"

"A .38. Probably a revolver, since there are damned few .38 automatics around and no casings on the floor. By the way, you carry a .38 revolver, don't you?"

I didn't like where this conversation seemed to be headed. "Need to see it?"

"If you don't mind."

Knowing better than to haul my revolver out of my carry-all, I handed over the whole thing; billfold, cell phone, comb, sun screen, medicated lip gloss, fliers of Precious Doe.

The carry-all was so heavy he almost dropped it. Throwing me a dirty look, he rummaged inside for a moment, then extricated my gun. He sniffed at the barrel. "It's been fired recently."

"If you remember, someone shot at me yesterday evening and I returned fire. I filed the report this morning, dotted all my I's, crossed all my T's."

"Sure makes a handy explanation as to why your gun smells like an ammunition factory, doesn't it? You realize I need to take this into evidence and see if the bullets in Hall match up."

Somehow I managed not to grind my teeth. "They won't. Just make sure you return it. Carrying a handgun is part of my job description."

He snorted. "My, my. Ain't we tough? By the way, do you have a concealed-carry permit?"

"It's in my billfold. Which you have." Since he already knew I carried a .38, I had no doubt he'd already run a computer search and found the record of my permit. This was pure harassment.

He took his time rummaging through my carry-all again, finally found my billfold, and after flipping through several credit cards and pictures of Warren, drew out the permit. He studied it for a while, acting like he'd never seen one before. Then, after dropping the wallet into the carry-all, he slid my .38 into its holster and looped it around his arm.

"Can't say how long ballistics will take," he said, handing the carry-all back to me.

As long as he wanted, probably, which could be a long, long time. "Sheriff, you know damned well I didn't shoot Reverend Hall."

"Denial noted."

We parted in the hospital parking lot, and I watched him drive off in the direction of Freedom Temple. Maybe he would have better luck with Olivia Hall. He was, after all, male, and she was more likely to obey a man than a woman.

An odd thought occurred to me then. Maybe I was wrong about the redhead. Once I'd settled into the Jeep, I pulled out my cell and called Herschel Berklee, the M.E.'s assistant. From the background noises when he picked up, I could tell he was at the hospital and not at all happy to hear from me.

"I can't get caught talking to you," he whispered.

I ignored his fears. "Have you seen Hall's body?"

"Yeah. I'm hanging up now."

"Hold on. I need to know one thing, Herschel. Did the good reverend still have all his equipment, if you get my drift?" Given Hall's strong beliefs about the necessity for sexual purity, I wouldn't be surprised to discover he was as neutered as those Heaven's Gate fools. Or his own just-as-foolish followers.

"I get your drift all right. But his corpse is still in possession of the family jewels." With that, Herschel hung up.

So much for my new theory. Hall had been crazy, but not that crazy.

Another conversation with Raymundo Mendoza seemed necessary. Yes, it was Sunday, but since the Mexican pottery business was chiefly a tourist business, the store might be open.

I was right. When I pulled into the parking lot, Raymundo was just turning the CLOSED sign around so that it read OPEN.

He didn't appear nervous when I approached, just sad. "What do you want, Ms. Jones? Can't you see I'm busy here?"

Gee, everyone was so happy to see me today. "Been watching the news, Raymundo?"

His face hardened. "You expect me to say I'm sorry or something? Fat chance. Too bad it didn't happen a long time ago. Then Nicole and I would have our baby and she'd still be…" The smile vanished and he lowered his head. "And things would be different." He sounded ready to cry.

I followed him inside the store. "Is there anything you want to tell me?"

"Such as what?" He started rolling some of the larger pots onto the front patio.

I kept pace with him. "Where were you between one and two last night?"

"Sleeping."

"Not hanging out by the river?"

"Don't I wish. But I had to attend Mass with my family this morning, then come to work. The only time I can make it to the river is on Friday nights. If at all. And there's no reason to now, is there? Nicole's gone." It's hard to read someone's body language when they're rolling a heavy terra cotta pot, but something about the rigid set of his head hinted not only at sorrow but at barely-contained rage.

"So there's no one who can vouch for you?"

"Give me an alibi, you mean?"

I nodded.

"No one in the world." With that, he went inside the store, letting the door slam in my face.

Our conversation hadn't eased my concerns, merely heightened them. Raymundo could easily have killed Reverend Hall.

He had motive, opportunity, and probable access to a gun. The same might be said of Nicole. For the first time it occurred to me that she was lucky to be in CPS custody, far from Los Perdidos and a murder she had every reason to commit. *If* she remained in CPS custody. That girl was expert at vanishing acts.

With that less-than-comforting reminder, I drove over to Geronimo Espresso, ordered a Latte Grande, and put together a time line of the major events in the case.

FIRST FRIDAY: Warren and I find Precious Doe. Autopsy results reveal she's been dead only hours.

MONDAY: I return to Los Perdidos.

WEDNESDAY: Nicole rescues Aziza Wahab. Vigilantes torch Floyd Polk's shack, he dies in the flames.

SECOND FRIDAY: While I'm in L.A., Nicole and Aziza arrive at the Friedmans' safe house. The girls are turned over to CPS.

SATURDAY EVENING: Someone shoots at me.

SATURDAY NIGHT/SUNDAY MORNING: Reverend Hall shot and killed.

As I studied the time line, something nudged at the edge of my consciousness, but I couldn't identify it. I tried again, this time counting only the deaths. First Friday, Precious Doe. Wednesday, Floyd Polk. Saturday night, Reverend Hall.

No. That wasn't it.

I slurped my way through the Latte Grande and ordered another. Then I tried another version of the list, noting the exact times and days I had interviewed certain people. This version took longer, but nothing clicked. What connection was I missing?

Halfway through my second latté, the caffeine caught up with me. As I began writing yet another version of the list, my trembling hand knocked over my cup, spilling milky foam across my notebook, soaking it several pages deep. I grabbed a napkin and began mopping up the mess.

When I blotted my way back to the first version, I noticed that the coffee had pooled across SATURDAY EVENING: *Someone shoots at me* and SATURDAY NIGHT/SUNDAY MORNING: *Reverend Hall shot and killed.*

My unease returned as I stared at the lines.

Saturday. Who had I talked to and exactly when? I cross-referenced my second list. Saturday I had talked to Nicole before CPS took her away; to Dr. Lanphear; to Sheriff Avery; to Jimmy; last of all, I'd talked to Mrs. Nour, the manager of the Nile Restaurant. Then I'd returned to the ranch, returned phone calls, and taken my ill-fated walk.

Several hours later, Reverend Hall was dead.

I was about to move to the other list when the source of my unease emerged. Why was I so certain there was only one shooter? Why couldn't there be *two*?

While rereading the other list, I noted that while three deaths—Precious Doe's, Floyd Polk's, and Reverend Hall's—had occurred in the vicinity of Los Perdidos, the cause of death was different in each case. In Precious Doe's case, blood loss. In Polk's, fire. In Hall's, gunshot.

Three killers? Three motives?

Such a theory seemed outlandish—how could such a town the size of Los Perdidos harbor three different murderers—but not beyond the realm of possibility. Some towns were rougher than others, and Los Perdidos, with its frontier past and unusual ethnic mix, was a likely enough place.

Under scrutiny, though, the theory was improbable. Precious Doe's autopsy proved she had died of blood loss due to the botched amputation: ergo, the Cutter killed her. Polk, a convicted child molester, died the victim of vigilante justice. The vigilantes might not even have meant to kill him, just run him out of town as they had the more fortunate Duane. Something else occurred to me then. What if vigilantes hadn't killed Polk after all? What if Polk had been killed by a single killer who torched his place to cover up his crime? Again, improbable but possible.

Hall had taken three bullets, not necessarily from the same person who'd tried to kill me.

Where was the connection?

There was only one way to find out if my shooter was the same person who shot Hall; go back to the shooting scene near the river. Revolvers didn't eject casings, but automatics did. If I found any, I would know two shooters were operating, not one. Once I presented the casings to the sheriff, he could run a ballistics test on them at the same time he tested my own handgun. And maybe, just maybe, we would find out the name of the shooter.

The thought of a return visit to the river didn't thrill me, because thanks to Avery, I was now weaponless, so I had to ask myself—did I really care who killed Reverend Hall enough to risk my own safety?

The answer came quickly.

Yes, I cared.

As long as the murderer wasn't Nicole. Or Raymundo.

Soon I was hip-deep in brush by the San Pedro River, searching for bullet casings. If the shooter returned, I wouldn't be able to defend myself, but since my earlier visits to the river had taken place in the early evening, not during this time of day, I felt safe enough. For now, at least.

With my foot, I started to roll aside a Diet Coke can to look under it, then froze.

There was only one person who knew I liked to walk by the river in the evening. Selma Mann, the well-armed owner of the Lazy M Guest Ranch.

With that unsettling realization, I rolled the can over and resumed my search.

Chapter Twenty-four

An hour later, I had found no bullet casings, which probably meant the shooter used a revolver. Given the speed of his retreat, he certainly hadn't lingered to pick anything up. He might have returned earlier this morning to retrieve them, but I doubted it. Abandoning my fruitless search, I walked back along the river toward the Lazy M. It was time for a heart-to-heart with Selma Mann.

She was crossing from the house to the barn when I arrived, several bridles slung over her arm. The smell of saddle-soaped leather wafted toward me on the breeze.

I caught up to her as she was returning the bridles to their hooks.

"Ready to go for a ride?" she asked, gesturing toward a big bay gelding. "I've been trying to lure you onto a horse ever since you arrived. Tecumseh there rides like a Cadillac."

He sounded wonderful, but I wasn't here for recreation. "Sorry, I just want to talk. Can we go in the house?"

After giving the bridles a final tug to even out their reins, she nodded. "I need to take a break, anyway. How about some coffee? About this time of day, I switch to decaf."

It was not yet noon. Back in Scottsdale, I would still be hitting the high octane stuff, or even a Tab, which contained enough caffeine to give an elephant the jitters. But considering the conversation we were about to have, decaf sounded good. I didn't want any more adrenaline pumping around that kitchen than necessary, especially not with all those guns in the house.

I followed Selma into the kitchen, where she fetched two mugs from the kitchen cupboard. Mine said, WELCOME TO LOS PERDIDOS; hers said, GERONIMO—FIGHTING DOMESTIC TERRORISM SINCE 1851. When she'd poured big mugs of black brew for the both of us, I decided to just come out with it. "Someone took a shot at me yesterday evening."

Selma sat her mug down so quickly that coffee splashed onto the table. "Where?"

"Down by the river, near the old settlers' graveyard."

She looked stricken, but maybe she was just a good actress. "Why didn't you tell me before? I heard some shots but took it for granted a hunter was jack-lighting deer."

"I wanted time to think about it. Besides, the shooter was no poacher. After I yelled, whoever it was kept firing. I was going to bring it up this morning, but then we heard the news about Hall."

She walked over to the counter, pulled a dish rag out of a drawer and wiped up the spilled coffee, then sat down. "I don't know what to say, other than I'm sorry. It's usually perfectly safe around here."

Not for little girls, it isn't. "I just came back from searching for casings, but there weren't any, which leads me to believe that the shooter used a revolver. You own a couple, don't you?"

Her gaze didn't waver. "A Colt and a Smith and Wesson. Along with various rifles and shotguns. Over the years, any rancher collects a small arsenal, and my grandfather and father were no exceptions. What's this all about, anyway? Do you suspect me? Because if you do, be advised that I wouldn't have missed."

At that, I smiled.

She wasn't finished. "I doubt if the shooter was one of my ranch hands, either. I have strict rules for the bunk house: no drugs, no booze, no guns."

"And you are She-Who-Must-Be-Obeyed?"

Relaxed now, she laughed. "Touché. Granted, I can't control their every movement, but they're all decent, hard-working men. Hell, I even went to grade school with some of them. Los Perdidos is a small community, Lena. If any of those guys had a tendency toward violence, I'd know it."

We sipped our coffee as companionably as possible when you've just accused your sipping partner of trying to kill you. But afterward, as I walked to the cottage, I realized something. Selma had adroitly deflected my suspicions of her onto her ranch hands, the same way she had once offered up the CEO of Apache Chemical.

The question remained. Why would Selma Mann try to kill me? I changed directions, and found Selma washing the mugs we had just used. This time I didn't go in, just stood inside the door. "Lee Casey says you two used to date."

She paused with her hand in the air, a mug dangling from her finger. "Why, yes, we did. But I'm astonished he brought that up."

"Really?"

She set the cup on the drainer. "Our breakup was pretty ugly."

"That's what he said."

A frown creased her forehead. "He admitted it?"

An odd choice of words, *admitted*. "Yes. He said you took it pretty hard."

"*I* took it hard?" She picked up the mug again, flicked it with a dishtowel, then put it in the cupboard.

I began to get it. "Selma, who broke up with who?"

"*Whom*," she said absently, frowning at the mug. It was now cracked, but hadn't been when I drank from it earlier.

"Whatever. Mind answering the question?"

She took the mug back out of the cupboard and tossed it in the wastebasket. "So much for that. Anyway, I broke up with Lee, but I get the impression he told you the opposite."

"He's lied?"

She nodded. And waited.

"May I ask what broke you two up?"

Selma stared at me for so long I thought she wasn't going to answer, but she did. "I broke up with Lee Casey because I suspected he murdered his wife."

With that, she disappeared down the hall, leaving me standing there open-mouthed.

At the guest cottage, I sat down at the desk and called Jimmy on his cell. When he answered, he sounded like he was suffering from a cold.

"Did you ever find that accident report on Lee Casey's wife?" I asked.

A thick-voiced, "Nope."

"Hey, you getting enough vitamin C? You sound awful."

He cleared his throat. "Thanks for caring. About that car wreck. I was able to get in touch with one of those insurance types who worked on the case, and he told me that the accident investigator felt uncomfortable about the whole thing, especially since Mrs. Casey had no known record of drug use."

"Drug use? I don't understand."

"The autopsy revealed that when her car went off the mountain, she was stoned on Quaaludes," he rasped.

I took a deep breath. "Mountain?"

"Yeah. For some reason, Mrs. Casey popped a few pills, then took a sunset drive in the Dragoons. When her car went off the road, she broke her neck."

The whole thing smelled fishier than an anchovy cannery. "Was Mrs. Casey under treatment for stress, or any other type of emotional problem?"

"At the time, her friends said no. Anyway, because of the Quaalude factor, the insurance company refused to pay up. The investigation was brief, but you know how these things can go. Since no one found anything overtly suspicious, the case eventually faded away."

"Were you able to find out who prescribed the drug for her?"

"Nope. There was a half-empty vial of the stuff in her purse, but no label. It was assumed she bought the stuff in Mexico. Or from a local dealer."

Selma had told me she'd broken up with Lee Casey because she suspected he'd killed his wife. Now I wondered, too. The site of the accident wasn't all that far from Los Perdidos, so it was within the realm of possibility that Casey drugged his wife, staged the accident, then hiked back to town. I saw another scenario. He could have paid an accomplice to make the kill for him. "Okay, so no insurance payoff. How much did he lose?"

"One point five mill."

"Casey inherited his wife's estate, didn't he?"

"A flat twenty."

I whistled. "Twenty *million*?"

"What else?" He cleared his throat again. "She was an only child, and her father, who predeceased her, owned timberland outside Flagstaff. He logged, then he developed. We're talking hundreds of acres of housing tracts and strip malls."

Yep, that could accumulate twenty mill pretty fast. "Any rumors of trouble between Casey and his wife?"

"Early in the marriage there was one report of a domestic, but the wife refused to press charges. Other than that, the guy's clean, except for a few traffic tickets. Talk about a need for speed."

I was silent for so long that Jimmy asked, "Lena? You there?"

"Yeah, yeah. So in the beginning, the marriage wasn't perfect, but things quieted down. Maybe Casey learned to control himself. Or maybe she learned not to call the cops. Then a few years later she dies in a suspicious accident and he inherits everything. You thinking the same thing I'm thinking?"

"I'm way ahead of you, kemo sabe."

"Of course, accidents sometimes happen."

"Sometimes." His voice sounded even huskier than at the beginning of our conversation.

"Try some throat spray, Jimmy. You're throat's so rough I can hardly hear you. And do me another favor. First thing in the

morning, run a check on one Selma Mann. She owns the guest
ranch I'm staying at outside Los Perdidos."

"Sorry, I'm gonna be in late tomorrow."

Even though I lived in an apartment above Desert Investigations,
Jimmy usually beat me to work. "Doctor's appointment?"

His turn for silence. He finally broke it by saying, "No,
because Enterprise says they can't pick me up until ten."

"The car rental place? You having trouble with your truck?"
Jimmy's Toyota pickup was almost new, and like most Toyotas,
its problems were few and far between.

After a short silence, he said, "Truck's gone."

"*Gone?* What do you mean, gone?"

His mumbled answer was so low he needed to repeat it.
"Lydianna took it."

Lydianna. The woman Jimmy had been dating. "Took? As
in borrowed?"

"*Stole!*" he said, his voice breaking. "*Stole!* She told me she
had to move some stuff, so I loaned it to her and she never came
back. I called and called but she never answered her phone, so
my cousin drove me over there, and her landlord said she cleared
out in the middle of the night. She'd stripped the place bare,
even stole his furniture *right down to the lamps!* Satisfied now,
Miss I-Told-You-So?"

I didn't know what to say, other than I was sorry.

After another bout of throat-clearing, he said, "Thanks for
the sympathy."

"Did you file a police report?" My betting was that he hadn't.

"No. And I'm not going to, either."

I sighed. "We sure have our troubles, don't we, partner?"

"Does that 'we' mean you lied about things going great with
Warren?"

I told him the truth, that my love life was as screwed up as his.

After showering off the grime I'd collected while searching for
bullet casings, I slipped into fresh jeans and tee shirt, then picked

up Precious Doe's picture from the night stand. I looked at it for a long while, thinking about her suffering, remembering my own.

The foster homes. The beatings. The rapes.

But I had survived.

Why me, and not her?

I studied her face again. Her eyes were forever shut against the world, but I knew they would have been a warm mahogany, gentle and trusting.

Superimposed on them, the Cutter's malicious eyes glinted like a freshly-sharpened knife.

Because of civil rights laws, Sheriff Avery couldn't go house to house interviewing every African immigrant in town, but I could. Before we'd hung up, Jimmy had given me a list of every African tribe that practiced female genital amputation. I flipped through the phone book, but quickly gave up on that form of inquiry, since I had no idea what surname belonged to what African tribe. On the off-chance that a reporter might be hanging around the *Cochise County Observer* on a Sunday, I called the newsroom, where Bernice Broussard answered.

She listened while I made my request, then with obvious disapproval, said, "You want a list of just the *African* families and their tribal associations? You're treading on delicate ground here, aren't you, Ms. Jones? The very white, very American Reverend Hall has apparently been perpetrating the same tribal practice, so why pick on the Africans?"

"Because Nicole Hall said the Cutter had an African accent, that's why." I reminded her of Precious Doe's injuries and the very real possibility they might soon be inflicted on another child. "Bernice, we have to get that woman off the streets."

She grunted. "Point taken. The best person to give you that info would be the president of the Good Neighbor Society, who could tell you everything you need to know, but I doubt she'll talk to you. She's pretty protective of them." I heard a rustling of papers. "Give me an hour. I'll go through our files and see what feature stories we've written in the past few years which identified the tribal groupings of some of our newer citizens. That'll at least give you a place to start."

I remembered our earlier conversation, when she had sent me over to the Los Perdidos Library to look up the story on Tujin Rafik. "I thought your morgue files only went back a year?"

"We keep our computer backups forever." With that, she hung up.

She was as good as her word. Fifty minutes later, while I lay stretched out on the bed reading the Dean Koontz paperback I'd picked up at the Tucson airport, my cell rang. It was Bernice, with a long list of names and tribal associations.

"You find her, I get an exclusive, right?"

"Right." If it were possible. Given the swarm of media in town, she could easily get scooped.

On that note, we rang off and I headed to my Jeep. Selma was in the corral again, working another horse. When she saw me, she waved gaily, as if no hostility had passed between us. I waved back.

The first name on my list of African immigrants was Abdul Jokabi, who had moved to Los Perdidos with his family ten years earlier. The newspaper had written a feature on him when he became the town's first African immigrant to buy a house. It was located in a small tract not far from the main drag, and as I parked on the pleasant, well-manicured street, I spotted a new Dodge minivan and an almost-as-new Honda Civic in the driveway. Happy children's voices greeted me as Jokabi himself opened the door. A handsome man clad in the standard Arizona uniform of artfully-torn jeans and Arizona Diamondbacks tee shirt, he seemed friendly enough until I told him who I was looking for.

"You crazy?" he yelled, his accent faint. "We do not associate with animals like that! Why you think we move here in the first place?"

He slammed the door in my face.

Chapter Twenty-five

Giving up on the hostile Jokabi, I next tried the Maranji family. They lived in a peeled-paint duplex where the front yard was littered with broken children's toys, and the only vehicle in evidence was a rusty Chevy Cutlass that had once been blue. In the neighboring yard, a pit bull growled from a chain attached to a laundry pole.

A young woman wearing a bright dashiki and carrying a pink-wrapped baby answered the Maranji's door. "Yes?"

Keeping my nose out of door-slam reach, I started my spiel.

Halfway through, she interrupted me. "These are things we do not talk about. We are Americans now."

"I understand, but the girl they call Precious Doe died because of this procedure. Perhaps other girls in town have, too. If you've heard anything at all, please tell me."

She studied my face, then nodded. "I saw you on the television this morning when you told that reporter woman about Dr. Wahab. When you walked away, that woman went over to his house and asked ugly things. Other television people did, too. I watched it all, right here from my living room."

For the first time, a smile touched her lips. "It made me laugh. You wonder why I am so happy at that? My husband works for Dr. Wahab. He is a bad man, that one." She glanced up and down the street, taking in the boys shooting hoops next door, the girls riding their bicycles along the sidewalk. She shifted the baby on her shoulder and stood aside. "You come in. We talk."

Encouraged, I entered the house. In a small but tidy living room decorated with African carvings and masks, twin boys wearing matching jeans and shirts played with a Game Boy.

Their mother reached over and turned the game off. "Go to your room."

"Aw, Mom!"

"You heard what I said."

"As soon as we finish this game." A wheedling whine.

"Now!"

Grumbling, the boys stalked off.

"Good-looking kids," I offered.

She sat down and motioned for me to do the same. "They are not respectful. In some ways, the old customs are best."

"But not all?"

She kissed the top of her baby's head. "This cutting of which you speak, that is a wicked custom I was happy to leave behind. To perform such evil on a little girl, it is a great sin." She kissed the baby again. "Such a thing will never happen to my Caroline. My husband has given his word. Unlike Dr. Wahab, he is a good man."

I studied my notes. "You came here, what, ten years ago?"

"When I was twenty, yes. I did not have my boys yet." At my expression, she smiled. "They are only eight."

"Big for their age."

Her smile grew broader. "Children do not starve to death in America or die so much from AIDS. And your wars, you fight them other places."

Goody for us.

I wasn't here to discuss the benefits of living in America as opposed to anywhere else, so I brought her back to the subject at hand. "Mrs. Maranji, do you know anything about the woman called the Cutter?"

She caressed her daughter's black, silken hair. "That thing, it always happened to the girls in my tribe. There is a ceremony and when the cutting is finished, the grandmothers who guarded us all night so that we would not run away, sing that we are now women." Gazing at her child's innocent face, she added, "My good friend, Esiankiki, she died beside me on the cutting mat. So did Chanya and Na'Zyia."

I realized, then, what she was saying. "You lived through it."

Before she answered, she kissed her baby again. "Yes. But many mothers cried that night."

Then why did they have their daughters butchered in the first place, I wanted to yell, but I already knew the answer. An impure girl was a worthless girl.

"This Cutter, the one who lives in Los Perdidos. Do you know her name?"

To my disappointment, she shook her head. "Her name is never spoken. She is just called the Cutter."

"If I wanted to contact her, how would I begin?"

The baby made a gurgling noise and spewed some foam. Her mother smiled. "My pretty," she cooed, kissing the tiny forehead. "My so very, very pretty girl."

"Mrs. Maranji? Where can I find this woman?"

"There is a place where some of our people meet in what they call a discussion group, but I do not know if that woman attends. Someone will know, perhaps one of those who do not care for the customs here. These people, they plan to return to Africa once they are rich."

At my exclamation, she said, "American money goes far in Africa. On what my husband makes at the chemical plant, they will live like kings, and in Kenya, where I was born, the men can have as many wives as they want." She scowled. "These people who meet at this place I tell you about, many of them think it shameful that an American man is allowed only one wife."

The people she was talking about didn't know about Arizona's polygamists and their ten-wife families. If they ever found out, it could save them plane fare.

Following Mrs. Maranji's directions, I soon found Los Perdidos Unitarian Church. After wading through a crowd of well-dressed parishioners, an elderly man directed me to the church secretary. "Barbara knows everything that goes on around here."

Somehow I doubted that.

A few minutes later, after most of the parishioners drifted away, Barbara, a middle-aged woman with a comforting voice and just-as-comforting waistline, showed me the outbuilding where the Middle Eastern Discussion Group met.

"They won't get together again until next Friday, after prayers," she said. "Our book club's meeting there tonight, though, if you're interested. Seven o'clock, drop-ins welcome. They're discussing *Snow Flower and the Secret Fan*, by Lisa See. It's about foot-binding in old China."

Great. More horrors perpetrated against little girls. I thanked her anyway, explaining that my choice of reading seldom made the book club list. "Actually, I'm looking for an African group, not a Middle Eastern group."

"One and the same, frequently. Muslims of all different colors and cultures, united by faith. It would be nice if we Christians could say the same thing about ourselves, wouldn't it?"

This wasn't the time for a debate on the relative merits of ecumenism, so I simply asked, "Do you know who leads the discussion group?"

"That would be Dr. Moustafa Abdou."

Another Egyptian with a PhD. Didn't that country have any dropouts? "Don't tell me. He works at the chemical plant, right?"

She nodded. "Head of research. A nice man, if a bit, well, old-fashioned about women's place in the world." She smiled as if it didn't matter.

After a few more moments of chat, she gave me his address, adding that if he couldn't help me, to try his wife. "Mrs. Abdou knows what's going on in town, more so than her husband."

The Abdou's house was right down the street from the Wahab's house where a lone media truck was still camped in front, the brunette reporter who'd attempted to interview me, standing on their doorstep. At first glance, the Wahabs didn't appear to be home.

The reporter didn't let the silence deter her. "Dr. Wahab!" she yelled, waving her mike while the cameraman zeroed in on the house. "Is it true that CPS has taken custody of your daughter?"

A face flashed in front of the window, then disappeared.

Encouraged, the reporter moved forward with the cameraman. "Did they take custody because you were about to have your daughter circumcised?"

There was that damned inaccurate word again, *circumcised*. Wouldn't the media ever get it right?

With all the fuss on the street, I figured my visit with Dr. Moustafa Abdou was doomed, so with no hope of success, I rang the doorbell. To my surprise, the door opened immediately and a stern face resembling a particularly handsome pharaoh peered out.

"Enter. Quickly. Before that television creature sees."

I scuttled inside.

Dr. Abdou's house was larger than the Wahab's, and sported a collection of silk Persian carpets that would put most museums to shame. Their vivid reds, blues, and golds blazed up from the underlying marble tile, while more carpet pieces in the form of plush toss pillows accented matching white sofas. Above the tall fireplace, a life-sized, full-body painting of Dr. Abdou frowned down on the room. This was a humorless man, and proud of it.

"So you think you will now make trouble for the Abdou family as you did for the Wahabs?" he growled.

Since it was always a mistake to back down from serious men, I replied, "Only if you deserve it. Do you?"

He fell silent for a moment, then clapped his hands three times and shouted something in Arabic. Immediately, as if they had been lurking around the corner, a woman of around Dr. Abdou's age appeared, wearing a long *abayah* with a matching *hijab* that covered her hair. Behind her trailed five girls ranging from around six years old to a gum-chewing pre-teen. They wore jeans, but like their mother, their heads were covered by *hijabs*. All were giggling.

The sternness left Dr. Abdou's face, but after a brief internal struggle, he regained it. "Girls, comport yourselves with dignity."

The giggling ceased. The grins did not.

Feeling in control now, Abdou pointed to me and said, "This person, to her great shame, is interested in your health. Tell her all is well so that she may go annoy someone else."

The eldest snickered, then cracked her gum. "Yeah, yeah, we're fine."

"Kyra!" her mother admonished. "Apologize to your father for your poor manners."

Kyra tucked her gum into her cheek and ducked her head toward her father the tiniest bit. "I apologize, Poppi." To me, she said, "My parents wish me to tell you that all of the Abdou females are fine, with all body parts present and accounted for."

"Kyra!" Dr. Abdou sounded outraged.

The girl shrugged. "We've been watching the news, Poppi, and besides, we already know about those awful Wahabs and what they did to Shalimar."

Aghast, their mother ordered, "Kyra, go to your room. And take your sisters!"

Off they went in a flurry of giggles, *hijabs* flapping.

Their mother remained. Her scowl made Dr. Abdou look downright cheerful.

Ignoring her, Dr. Abdou said, "Is your husband aware that you are carrying on like this? Approaching strangers, asking unseemly questions?"

Without realizing it, he had just described the life of every private investigator. "I have no husband."

"And probably never will!"

The barest of smiles flickered across Mrs. Abdou's face.

"Thank you for that prediction, Dr. Abdou. Since you already know why I'm here, we might as well cut to the chase. Do you know who the Cutter is?"

He hissed, as if I had said a filthy word.

Mrs. Abdou walked up to her husband, put her hand, on his arm and said something in rapid Arabic. He answered in kind. She shook her head and said something else, this time in a tone as stern as his.

"I forbid it!" he yelled, in English.

Another spate of Arabic from her, and whatever she said made him gasp. He fled in the same direction as his daughters.

Her face calm, Mrs. Abdou watched him go. "Good. Now we can speak freely. But before we begin, would you like coffee?"

When I declined on the premise that I had already surpassed my caffeine allotment for the day, she gestured me to a seat. "First, you must understand I *know* nothing."

I'd played this game before, and was comfortable with it. "Then just tell me what you suspect."

Parameters drawn, Mrs. Abdou said, "There has been talk of a woman, an African, who clings to the old ways. We Abdous, of course, have contempt for such barbarism, but people like the Wahabs, who believe they can make money off their daughters, they are dirt. In our country, this *cutting*, as they call it, is said to benefit young women because it focuses their minds on Allah, not the pleasures of the flesh."

I didn't challenge this monstrous philosophy, since it was not hers. Out of cultural solidarity, she had felt it necessary to mount a token defense.

Her next words confirmed my suspicions. "As you know, the procedure is now illegal in Egypt, which is as it should be. However…" She paused, searching again.

I waited. She wanted to be frank, but hadn't yet figured out how.

Her hands clasped so tightly that her knuckles whitened, she resumed. "However, few are in agreement with the new law, which is never enforced, anyway. Parents believe that without the procedure, their daughters will become wild and bring disgrace to the family. Also, they worry that an uncut girl cannot make a good marriage. You realize that the Middle Eastern attitude toward marriage is different than the West's?" She made it a question.

I nodded. "In America we marry for love." And divorce as soon as the glow wears off.

Her smile matched my cynicism. "To Muslims, marriage is an arrangement that benefits both families, the bride's and the groom's, not simply the young people themselves. This is an entirely different philosophy from yours."

I drummed my fingers on the sofa's arm rest. "I understand all that and am sympathetic to cultural differences unless it involves butchering little girls. Now, could you please tell me about the Cutter?"

"Very well. Since you are in such a hurry—another problem with America, if you will allow me to say—I tell you that this African woman does not attend prayers or our woman's discussion group. Perhaps she does not feel comfortable with us. As I have said, I do not know her, just *of* her. They say she lives near the Safeway, with her brother, his wife, and their children. Her first name is something like Deeke or Seike. I forget. When she is spoken of, which is not often, she is merely called the Cutter."

My disappointment grew. "You don't know her last name?"

"Sorry." Now it was her turn to fidget. She plucked at her *hijab*, drawing it closer around her face. For the first time I realized how uncomfortable she was with our conversation.

"How can I find her, then?"

"Los Perdidos is no crowded Cairo, so why should the search be difficult? I hear that the wife is tall and fat, but the husband short and skinny like his sister. There have been many jokes about this. There are four children, all boys. A good thing, do you not agree?"

I certainly did.

Now all Sheriff Avery had to do was figure out how to talk a judge into giving him a search warrant for any house near the Safeway resided in by an unnamed thin woman, an unnamed thin man, an unnamed fat woman, and four unnamed young boys. The judge might enjoy the laugh, but probably not enough to issue the warrant. I, however, was not hampered by such legal sensitivities. If I had to crawl through windows or dig my way into cellars to find Precious Doe's killer, I would.

"One more thing, Miss Jones. I hear that the Cutter's sister-in-law is with child again and will give birth soon. So you see? How many families can there be like that?"

Not many.

Before I left, I asked one final question. "You have been very helpful. Why?"

"Because it is terrible what has been done to those girls. And also because Mrs. Wahab once called my youngest daughter a bad name."

Vengeance, thy name is Mother.

We talked for a while longer, but when further questioning elicited no more information, I rose to go.

"Wait!"

I sat back down.

"I must say one more thing. My husband did not want to speak to you, and therefore he made unkind statements, hoping to discourage you. Pay no attention. Men speak for effect, not to state the truth. That is part of what is wrong with this world."

I suspected she might be right.

For the next hour, the Jeep's police scanner kept me apprized of Los Perdidos' petty crimes. While listening to accounts of purse-snatching and break-ins, I orbited the Safeway in ever-expanding circles searching for likely candidates for the Cutter's family, or even the Cutter herself.

For a Sunday, front yards appeared oddly deserted and, in keeping with Arizona's love of motor vehicles, few pedestrians strolled the sidewalks. Around two, my growling stomach reminded me that I hadn't yet eaten lunch, so I parked in the Safeway lot and headed for the deli section. The pre-wrapped sandwiches had already been pretty much picked over, but the smiling African woman behind the counter offered to make me a fresh one.

"Special today is salami, mozzarella, smoked ham, sweet Italian peppers, tomatoes, onions, fresh greens, and hot mustard on a six-inch submarine role. Medium soda included. You like?"

Oh, yeah. I liked.

After paying for the sandwich, I looked for a place to sit, but the deli's few tables were filled. Knowing that Los Perdidos City Park was only a couple blocks away, I decided it would be more pleasant to dine there under a tree in the front seat of my Jeep, so I headed there.

That turned out to be crowded, too, which explained the neighborhood's relatively deserted streets. Children screamed with laughter from swing sets, teens kicked soccer balls across jewel-green grass, lovers cuddled on wood-and-iron benches. For a town its size, the park was amazingly well appointed, and would not have been out of place in Scottsdale. Then I remember seeing, as I walked by the park's main entrance, a small sign bearing the words, PARK LAND AND EQUIPMENT DONATED BY APACHE CHEMICAL.

Ah, the largess of insecticide.

I spotted an empty bench near a family huddled around a picnic table, and the aroma of charcoal-broiled hot dogs and hamburgers made my stomach growl even louder. But before I reached the bench, a soccer ball slammed into the back of my knees, almost knocking me down.

"Sorry, miss!" piped a small, bright-eyed boy, as he snatched the ball away.

"Herman!" yelled a thin, middle-aged man I took to be his father. "Did I not tell you to stop playing and eat? You could have hurt that lady! Tell her you are sorry." An African accent.

Clutching the soccer ball to his chest, the little boy ducked his head. "Sorry."

I winked at this budding Beckham and said, "I'll live."

With an expression of relief, he ran to his family.

I reached the shaded bench without further incident, and was soon munching happily. The sandwich was every bit as good as the deli woman promised, but probably twice as fattening. If

I didn't watch myself, I could conceivably wind up as obese as the young soccer player's jolly mother, who was laughing with the father.

Oops. Not merely obese. Pregnant, too, and already with a handful of children, all boys. At least the wizened woman with them was helping out, shoveling beans onto the children's plates, even though her tiny hands trembled with Parkinson's.

Parkinson's, a bad disease. A slow decline, if its sufferers were lucky, then death. However, medical science created small miracles every day, and a cure loomed on the horizon. If the old woman could hold on long enough, she might live to see her great-grandchildren. As I watched, I wondered if her family would work her to death first. A real possibility, since the thin man treated her like a servant, not allowing her to sit down and eat with the others. He just kept snapping orders for her to do this, do that, and stop making such a mess.

The poor old thing's manner toward the pregnant woman— she even bowed when she handed the smug-faced bitch a heaped plate—smacked of servility.

Frowning at this injustice toward an ailing grandmother, I started to take another bite of my sandwich, then stopped with it halfway to my mouth.

I studied the family again and counted heads.

A short, thin father. A tall, obese mother in the late stages of pregnancy. Four boys. A tiny, thin woman, who, because of the ravages of illness, I had assumed was a grandmother. As I watched them, I considered the way the man treated her. He exhibited none of the deference Africans usually accorded their elders, just a surly impatience with her Parkinson's-induced clumsiness.

Because she wasn't the children's grandmother.

She was their *aunt*.

The Cutter.

Chapter Twenty-six

This time Sheriff Avery not only listened, he acted.

Within minutes of my arrival at his office, he dispatched a cruiser to pick up the Cutter, whose family I had followed from the park to their house. Ten minutes later, two deputies ushered in a frail old woman whose fear was so marked I actually felt compassion for her. Parkinson's made the woman's hands tremble so badly she could hardly hold the cup of water a deputy handed her, and sloshed the liquid over the rim onto the floor. To think those hands had cut into little girls!

But they had, and the inevitable finally happened. One slip of the knife and it was all over for my beautiful Precious Doe. And for Tujin Rafik, probably, although we would never find her body.

Sunday or not, the sheriff soon obtained his search warrant. As the deputies left to search the home of Dekah Ellyas Daahir, who, as it turned out, was the *wife* of Ellyas Dalmar Gulleet, not his sister. The pregnant woman was the man's second wife, and no, there had been no divorce. When Dekah had been found unable to bear a living child—a frequent complication of the genital amputation she herself had undergone—he took another wife, keeping the first as his maid. So Avery brought in Dekah on suspicion of child abuse and her husband on suspicion of bigamy, a fine irony in a state which seldom prosecuted its many polygamists.

"Is this a pile of shit or what?" Sheriff Avery asked, after his deputies led Dekah and her husband into separate interrogation rooms.

"Steaming," I said. "But aren't you forgetting something?"

"All right, I'll bite."

"We still don't know who killed Reverend Hall."

He gave me a stupefied look. "*She* did. Dekah."

"Motive?"

"The usual reason felons fall out, to protect her own ass. She was afraid that Hall—who loved the sound of his own voice, remember—would eventually implicate her in his scheme to 'purify' Los Perdidos' female population. Hell, by the time we wrap up our investigation, we'll probably find a trail of dead girls leading to her place."

He was right, not that it mattered. "Sheriff, Hall wasn't dumb. I listened to his rant on his church steps just before he was killed and noticed how carefully he couched his words. Not once did he come right out and say that he actually ordered genital amputations, just that his right to practice his religion was being compromised by a fascist government. He knew perfectly well that a person can't be prosecuted for *believing* in criminal behavior, that the criminal action has to actually take place in order for any kind of prosecution. He was a careful man, and a smart one."

"Yeah, well, we've got our 'criminal action' now. Her name's Nicole. What's left of her."

I shook my head. "Nicole told me she never saw the Cutter's face, that she only heard her speak. So I ask you again, why would Hall implicate the Cutter when to do so would implicate himself?"

"Maybe Hall wasn't as smart as you believe and the Cutter knew it. So, zip." He made a cutting motion across his throat.

It would have been poetic justice, Hall dying of a slit throat, perhaps by the same knife that had sliced up so many little girls. But he died of gunshot wounds.

The sheriff gave me a condescending smile. "You've been a big help, Ms. Jones, but we'll handle it from here. I'm needed in the interrogation room." He held out his hand.

I shook it, but hung onto it for a moment, loathe to let him get away before I said my piece. "While you're in there, make sure Dekah gets another glass of water."

He tugged his hand away. "In Los Perdidos, we always see to our prisoners' comfort. No rubber hoses, no water-boarding. All the Diet Coke and water they can drink."

"Water will work fine. And watch her drink it. After she does, or tries to, ask yourself how someone in her condition could shoot Hall three times. Twice while he was a moving target."

With that, I let him go.

Outside, the media was waiting. The brunette newscaster, apparently tired of harassing Dr. Wahab, pounced as soon as I stepped onto the sidewalk. "Is it true that the sheriff arrested a Somali refugee?"

At her use of the word *refugee*, I froze. The hardships of Africa's refugees had justly become an international concern, and there was a chance the Cutter might be awarded automatic victim status right along with them.

I hadn't planned on speaking to the media again, but their continued inaccuracies about Dekah's crimes worried me. Cautiously, I said, "Arrested, no. However, a woman has been brought in for questioning in the case of Precious Doe. She is also being questioned about another child's disappearance."

"But isn't the woman in flight from terrorism?" The reporter had focused on Dekah's possible victimhood, and why not? Victimhood made for great stories, regardless of the truth.

My anger made me throw verbal caution to the wind. "Dekah Ellyas Daahir is the chief suspect in the death of two innocent, seven-year-old children. She is also suspected of mutilating that teenager you acted so outraged about the other day, so save your pity for the real victims here, not that child-butchering bitch!"

Slander lawsuit all but guaranteed, I hurried to my Jeep with the ladies and gentlemen of the press baying at my heels.

I tore out of the parking lot without regard for the speed limit, but the cops were too busy controlling the media to worry about me. By the time I reached the edge of town, somehow miraculously avoiding a collision, I realized I needed a quiet place in which to cool down. The guest cottage at the Lazy M came to mind, followed quickly by an image of all those guns on Selma's living room wall. The river held no attraction for me, either, and the Los Perdidos Library was closed.

Which is why I wound up in the McDonald's hilltop parking lot again with a cup of high-octane coffee. Here I was literally above it all.

Below, I saw the herd of satellite trucks mooing around the sheriff's office. A block away, customers filed into the Nile Restaurant for an early dinner. On another hill sat Los Perdidos General Hospital, where Precious Doe's body cooled in a locker. South, along SR80, sprawled Apache Chemical. A more attractive sight was Mendoza's Mexican Pottery, with its crowded parking lot. Business boomed, even when hearts were broken.

Farther along the highway gleamed the tin roof of Freedom Temple, its own parking lot deserted except for the Halls' ancient Taurus. The sheriff had impounded the Buick Nicole took when she fled with Aziza. Had none of the white-robed ladies stayed to comfort the grieving widow? From here it appeared they'd left her alone with her ugly memories.

Plenty of those to go around.

I shifted in my seat and looked toward the Dragoon Mountains. With the sun slipping toward the Western horizon, they blazed in red and gold. Beautiful, certainly, but how many more little girls lay buried in their canyons?

I closed my eyes, only to confront the face of Precious Doe.

Her lips moved, but I heard no sound.

"What are you trying to tell me?" I whispered.

"*Her hands,*" she whispered back.

Can the dead speak? Or do we, out of our own sorrow, speak for them?

When Precious Doe's image faded, I opened my eyes and looked back down the hill to see several satellite trucks following a cruiser away from the sheriff's office. As I watched, the cruiser turned down a street near the Safeway and drew up in front of a small house, the satellite trucks close behind. The cruiser's door opened and two people emerged. Intrigued, I took my binoculars from my glove box and trained them on the scene.

Even before I found the correct focus I identified the couple: the Cutter and her husband.

That could mean only one thing. The deputies who searched their house had turned up no evidence, so Sheriff Avery couldn't hold them.

The man dashed into the house with the Cutter trailing behind. The cruiser left, but the satellite trucks remained, spilling out a clutch of reporters and cameramen. They ran to the door and pounded, but it never opened. Instead of returning to their trucks, the reporters positioned themselves dramatically in front of the house and began yapping into mikes.

I wanted to ask a few questions, too, but knew that attempting to talk to the Cutter now was useless. Better to wait until the press got bored and left.

Plan formed, I put on my headset, switched on my iPod, and listened to Hank Williams sing about cheating hearts.

Two hours later, when the last reporter left, I cruised down the hill to the Cutter's house, hoping that none of the Gulleets had seen me previously on a news broadcast. Knowing better than to try the front door, I slipped around to the rear. I knocked quietly, the way a family friend would. The door opened and the Cutter's husband peered out.

He frowned, as if he'd been expecting someone else. "Who are you?"

Good. He hadn't recognized me.

"I'm a friend of Reverend Hall's," I lied. "And I need to talk to Dekah. It's about the trouble your family is having. Maybe I can help."

His own whisper proved he bought my story. "Are you a lawyer?"

"I'm in a law-related profession, and I really need to see Dekah or I can't help."

His face relaxed. "Ah, law help. Well, she is not here. Someone telephoned, then she left."

Frowning, I asked, "Do you know who called?"

"She answered the telephone. I was watching soccer on ESPN. To calm down, you understand. The police, they were not good to us."

As if I cared. "Do you know where she went?"

"Maybe on business, who knows what that stupid woman does?" He wasn't interested in her problems, just his. "She is lazy, that one. Good for nothing." He started to close the door.

Risking a bad bruise, I shoved my foot between the door and the jamb. "Did she take the car?" Missing from the driveway was the white minivan I'd seen them drive away from the park earlier.

"I told her not to leave but she defied me and left. So now what do we do about supper?" He seemed to expect me to come in and cook it.

Since I might need to talk to him again, I kept the fury out of my voice when I said, "McDonald's has great fries, and it's a short walk up the hill."

I left him standing in the doorway with a puzzled expression on his face.

While driving the streets for the next hour, I spotted several white minivans, none driven by the Cutter. Although I searched as far beyond the town limits as Mendoza's Mexican Pottery and Freedom Temple, I had no luck. Giving up, I drove back to the Cutter's house.

In my business, stakeouts are the name of the game, so I parked across the street and zipped the Jeep's top closed against the night chill. After switching on my police scanner for entertainment, I settled down to wait.

When the sun rose the next morning, I was still waiting. The Cutter never returned.

I soon found out why.

As I watched the Cutter's house, considering the wisdom of leaving to pick up some coffee, the police scanner informed me that two teens on their way to school had found a woman's body in a white minivan.

Chapter Twenty-seven

Since I was only two blocks away, I beat the cops to the scene.

The minivan was parked in an alley, drawing a crowd. At the front of the pack, two girls spoke excitedly into their cell phones.

"I was, like, really grossed," the blonde yapped. "Her one eye was all bugged out and everything. It was *so* eew!"

The redhead, with a more spiritual turn of mind, sniffled into her cell, "Maybe I should pray for her. But what if she's not, like, into Jesus?"

Careful not to touch anything, I bent down and looked in the van. The Cutter slumped over the steering wheel, blood leaking from the hole in her forehead, a .38 dangling from her left hand. The odds were strong it was the same weapon that had killed Reverend Hall. She didn't look like the handmaiden of evil, just a pathetic old woman.

Behind me, the first cruiser pulled up. Sheriff Avery climbed out, royally pissed.

"What the hell are you doing here, Ms. Jones?"

"The usual," I replied.

"Which is?"

"Investigating." I stepped aside so he could take my place. For a full five seconds he studied the mess in the van.

"Suicide," he pronounced, straightening up.

"If that's a suicide, I'll eat my Jeep."

He snorted. "Get the Tabasco ready."

"Look again, Sheriff. The gun's in her left hand, but the wound's above her right eye. A clumsy way to shoot yourself, don't you think?"

"Perfectly possible."

Was he being obtuse on purpose? Or was he trying to fool me into going away? "But not probable."

Before we could continue our argument, three more cruisers rolled up, and close behind them, a caravan of satellite trucks. Deputies emerged and pushed the crowd back, while others police-taped the alley.

The sheriff asked how I had wound up at the scene of the crime, and fortunately, the two teens stopped yakking into their cell phones long enough to vouch for my story. Listening to them reminded me of another teenager.

"Is Nicole Hall still in that CPS group home, Sheriff?"

He blinked. "As far as I know, yes."

Which meant he didn't know for certain. I decided not to ask him the whereabouts of Raymundo Mendoza. The boy would either be headed for the border with Nicole, or opening up the family store. I hoped it was the latter.

"Nicole knows Reverend Hall is dead, right?"

"One of the social workers told her."

I thought about that. "Did she take it okay?"

He shrugged. "I didn't hear otherwise."

Not much on follow-up, was he? "Unless you need me here, I'm leaving."

"Town, I hope."

"Not without my .38."

He grimaced. "All right, I'll call over and have it released. You can pick it up on your way to Scottsdale."

"Sorry to disappoint you, but I have to take care of something else before I leave town."

Prevent another death.

An hour later, the weather turned ugly. The sky, which had appeared so harmless when the sun rose, darkened as black clouds blew over the horizon. The wind rose, driving the temperature down to the high forties, pneumonia weather for we thin-blooded southern Scottsdale folks. My Phoenix Suns windbreaker provided little comfort against the chill, so by the time I arrived at Freedom Temple, I longed for the sunny streets of home.

Freedom Temple looked deserted, but Olivia Hall's old Taurus was parked in front of the parsonage. I smelled coffee brewing and something baking, oddly normal activities for a woman who had just lost her husband and seen her only child seized by CPS. When I tried the door, I found it locked. She had learned a few things from her earlier run-ins with the press.

I knocked.

Nothing.

I knocked again, called, "Olivia?"

Approaching footsteps, the sound of a deadbolt clicking back. The door finally opened. "Oh. It's you."

Nicole's mother wore another of her shapeless dresses, but instead of her usual bun, her brown-and-gray hair tumbled down around her shoulders. With the lines on her face softened, she appeared almost pretty, perhaps because her husband was no longer around to convince her that she wasn't.

"You were expecting someone else, Olivia?"

She frowned. "The Women For Freedom are coming over to help plan Daniel's funeral. It's tomorrow."

So business would continue as usual at Freedom Temple, just under new management. I had suspected for some time there might be the remnants of a backbone hidden underneath Olivia's cloak of servility. I turned to go, thinking it might be best to leave and return later, when I would have more time with her alone.

Then I changed my mind. Better two minutes now than none. "Five minutes, no more. Then I'll go."

She shook her head. "After the Women leave, I need to pick up some buffet items from Safeway. As I'm certain even you noticed, Daniel was very popular. There'll be a big crowd after the funeral and I don't want anyone to go hungry."

I had attended enough après-funeral functions to know that women always arrived bearing casseroles, so this was just an excuse to get rid of me. Arranging my face into an expression that I hoped passed for sympathy, I said, "A couple of questions, that's all."

Indecision flickered in her pale eyes. Then, deciding that the quickest way to get rid of me was to cooperate, she said, "Oh, come on in, but you have to leave the second the Women arrive."

After I followed her into the parlor, she continued into the kitchen with the explanation that she needed to take some rolls out of the oven, so I just stood there staring around. Something had changed since my last visit. While most photographs of the Halls' earlier church postings remained on the walls, several were gone, among them the one showing Reverend Hall on the steps of Freedom Temple. For some reason, the missing pictures made me uneasy.

As I puzzled at the wall, she called from the kitchen, "You wouldn't like a sticky bun, would you?" Ever the preacher's wife, her hospitality was knee-jerk, if not sincere.

Eager for the chance to extend my visit, I answered, "Sounds wonderful!"

A displeased grunt. She already regretted her offer.

I kept studying the photographs until she returned with an elegant silver coffee server, the kind with a candle underneath to keep the coffee hot. "My mother's," she said, noticing my gaze. "It's the only thing my parents left me. Stu got everything else."

"Stu?"

"My brother." After she lit the candle, she returned to the kitchen and re-emerged with a platter of home-made sticky buns. "You might as well sit down," she said, gracelessly.

As soon as I eased myself onto a faded sofa, I saw the missing photographs laid out on the coffee table, arranged in what appeared to be chronological order.

"For the memorial service," Olivia explained. "A record of Daniel's life and accomplishments."

More like a record of his barbarity. "Nice." I bit into a sticky bun. It was delicious, and so was the steaming coffee, but I didn't take time to savor them. "Mrs. Hall, did your husband have enemies?"

She poured coffee for herself. "Any man who preaches Truth has enemies."

"But which one do you think killed him?" I wondered how long it would take her to accuse her daughter.

She didn't keep me waiting long. "Nicole hated him the most. He wasn't her real father, you understand. Not biologically, anyway."

What a woman, throwing her own daughter to the wolves. "So you think Nicole did it?"

"The girl *is* a sinner, and it's easy to fall from one sin to another." Licking her lips, she helped herself to another sticky bun.

"But Nicole is in CPS custody, nowhere near Los Perdidos. She couldn't have killed him."

"Then maybe that boyfriend of hers did it, Ray something." She didn't sound all that interested.

I decided to shake things up a bit. "Dekah was found dead this morning."

Her face didn't change. "Dekah who?"

"You know exactly who I mean, Olivia."

She smiled. "Oh. You must mean the Cutter. How unfortunate."

Unfortunate? "Don't you want to know how she died?"

She nibbled at her sticky bun. "Death comes to us all in the end. It makes no difference how we meet it."

Was she really that cold, or was she simply parroting her dead husband's beliefs? "You met the Cutter when Reverend Hall was posted to the Somalia-Kenya border, didn't you? That was how long ago, fourteen years? Fifteen?"

"Fifteen."

"And you gave birth to Nicole soon after you returned to the U.S., right?"

She frowned. "In Idaho, yes. What about it? I sinned, I atoned, I sin no more."

Considering what she'd allowed to be done to her daughter, that statement called for debate, but I let it slide. "Who was Nicole's biological father? Another missionary?"

She gathered up the plates. "It doesn't matter. You promised just a couple of questions, and now you've asked them, so leave. The Women will be here any minute, and we have important decisions to make about Freedom Temple's future."

I wasn't finished shaking things up. "Oh, but it does matter. What if Nicole's biological father tracked you here and found out what happened to his daughter? The pregnancy. The adoption. The cutting. Good men have been driven over the edge by less."

She set the plates back down with such force that one of them broke. "Now look what you made me do!"

I heard a car crunch along the gravel outside. Then another. The white-robed nut jobs were only seconds from the door. "Olivia, you didn't answer my question. Who was Nicole's father?"

Her eyes darted back and forth, toward the door, to the picture wall. "Oh, all right. But you're wrong. It *doesn't* matter. He was with that group, Doctors Without Borders, inoculating refugees against malaria. At the time I believed he was a good man, but he turned out to be just another sinner. After he got what he wanted, he went home and left me in Africa with the mud and the flies. Satisfied now?"

Not yet. "Was it just a coincidence that Dekah and her family wound up in Los Perdidos?"

She smiled. "Of course not. Daniel and I sponsored her, helped set her and her husband up. And that other woman, too." The smile faded. Apparently she didn't approve of Second Wife.

One final question, the worst. "Reverend Hall paid Dekah to cut you, right?"

The door opened and several white-robed figures entered. After uttering one word, Olivia rose to greet them.

That word was "Yes."

I drove down the road for about a quarter of a mile, then eased the Jeep into the trees just off the highway. For the next hour and a half, I sat there thinking about what Olivia Hall had told me. Nothing came as a surprise, because with the discovery of the Cutter's body I knew the truth. But I had no proof to give Sheriff Avery, and there was no way he would conduct another search without proof—the lawman's Catch-22.

My wait was made more difficult by a rising wind that rocked the Jeep as if it were no more than a toy. Above, fat clouds raced across the sky, highlighted by the streaks of lightning stabbing through them. Cottonwoods, bent almost double under the onslaught, whipped their leaves, flinging birds off their perches. It hadn't yet begun to rain, but during the increasingly brief silences between thunderclaps, I heard the San Pedro River roaring its swollen way to Mexico. God help any undocumented alien making his way north today.

When enough time passed, I checked my watch. Almost eleven. Surely the meeting wouldn't last much longer.

But it did. A full hour later, as the wind tried to tear off the Jeep's flimsy roof, a small caravan of white-robed women passed me. After a few more minutes, I saw what I had hoped to see, the Hall's Taurus, with Olivia at the wheel, headed down the highway toward Los Perdidos. She hadn't been lying about needing to shop. Satisfied, I turned on the Jeep's ignition and headed to the parsonage.

Since my lock-pick set didn't work on deadbolts, I bypassed the front door and trotted around to the rear. The kitchen door was a snap, with its open-me-with-a-credit-card lock, so within seconds, I stepped inside.

I hurried through the parlor, noting that Olivia had neglected to blow out the candle heating the coffee server. Dangerous. Too rushed to do anything about it, I continued through the house while the wind screamed at the windows as if it wanted in.

The first bedroom I entered turned out to be Reverend Hall's room. Spacious and elegant, it looked like a set from *Out of Africa*. No crosses were anywhere in evidence, but the walls boasted a plethora of tribal spears, shields, and masks that made Selma's little collection appear skimpy. The bed and reading chair were both covered in African fabrics, as were the shades on the matching lamps flanking the bed. Lying across the wooden floor was what appeared to be a cheetah-skin rug. The good reverend was no conservationist. The thought that cheetahs were endangered had probably never crossed his mind. Or it had, and he didn't care.

But I hadn't broken in to do a design make-over, so I began my search, attempting to leave everything the way I found it. Revered Hall's secrets slowly revealed themselves, and they weren't pretty. His Bible was marked up with Sharpies, and not for the usual reasons. The New Testament passages that dealt with forgiveness and mercy were crossed out in thick, black strokes, but in the well-thumbed Book of Revelations, I saw no crossing-out, merely pages and pages of underlining. Of particular note was the passage about the Whore of Babylon, which he'd double-underlined in red.

Olivia, perhaps?

In the bottom drawer of his dresser, I found a whip two feet long, made entirely of black leather, its many tails studded with small metal knobs, some dotted with a dark red substance. Curious, I peeled back Hall's bedspread and checked the sheets. No blood.

The closet revealed what I'd expected: vain clothing for a vain man. Three cassocks, nine suits—three cashmeres for winter, six silks for summer—and more than a dozen pair of shoes, including one pair in alligator. Quite the dandy, the good reverend.

After finding nothing more of interest, I headed for the next room, which turned out to be Nicole's. Except for a small window from which she'd orchestrated her escape, the room was bare as a monk's cell but without benefit of even a crucifix for decoration.

I saw no stuffed animals, no books, no magazines, no TV, no iPod. A ragged quilt covered the bed, but no rug softened the hard wooden floor. Three dresses hung in the closet, all poorly made, all shapeless. I saw only one pair of shoes, cracked brown brogans that could have belonged to a man. My search of the six-drawer dresser turned up nothing more than two tattered bras and three pairs of ragged panties. The other five drawers were empty, which pretty much defined Nicole's life.

As I stood there, enraged by her parents' self-righteous neglect, the wind grew even stronger. From the grove of cottonwoods behind the parsonage, I heard a loud splitting sound, then a crash as a tree sacrificed a branch to the oncoming storm. Thunder clapped again, much nearer this time, reminding me to hurry. When the rain came, it would arrive as a torrent.

I left Nicole's sad bedroom and continued down the hall, where at last I found Olivia Hall's room at the rear of the house. Not quite as bare as her daughter's, Olivia's bed at least had a cheap white chenille coverlet, but when I pulled it away, I found tiny spots of blood on the tattered sheet where her back and shoulders rested.

The Whore of Babylon, getting what she had coming to her.

Piled on the dresser were the books with which she homeschooled her daughter, all outdated. Her own closet mirrored the bareness of Nicole's, except for a long, white robe. I was about to slide the closet door shut when a small draft turned the robe to the side. Embroidered across the bodice was the letter "A."

You didn't have to be a student of American lit to know what that meant. *A for adultery.* But whereas Hester Prynne, in *The Scarlet Letter*, defiantly turned the stigma into decoration by embroidering her dress with an Old English illuminated flourish, Olivia had stitched a plain, sans serif letter.

Had the good reverend made her wear this travesty in church?

I was still studying the scarlet letter when I heard a woman's voice behind me.

"Looking for this?"

I spun around to face Olivia Hall. The wind had been so loud that I hadn't been able to hear her come in, now here she was, holding a butcher knife aloft. The thing was more than a foot long, with a wickedly sharp blade.

Then I noticed the carving on the portion of the ivory handle not covered by her hand: Arabic.

"Like it?" she asked. "It cuts through a girl with ease."

The moment I saw the Cutter's body, I guessed Olivia's guilt. The sheriff had been right about one thing: Dekah had to die, otherwise she would have confessed everything in order to save herself. The confession would have contained the appalling fact that when her own hands became incapable of performing amputations, she had taken on a student.

Olivia Hall.

Overwhelmed by an equal mix of pity and horror, I could only whisper, "Oh, Olivia. How could you?"

She cocked her head. "How could I what?"

"Mutilate those children."

A proud smile. "Because Dekah had to retire! You saw her hands."

Her hands. That was what Precious Doe's ghost had been trying to tell me. She hadn't meant the woman who cut her. She'd meant the woman who *hadn't* done it, the woman whose shaking hands rendered her incapable of maiming children, and so had passed on the job to her apprentice.

"You killed them, Olivia!"

"Them? No, no. You've got it all wrong. Dekah was the one who let Tujin Rafik die. Her hands shook so badly she couldn't cut correctly." She shrugged. "These little mistakes happen. Even the best surgeons slip up once in a while."

Little mistakes? I thought of those trembling hands with a butcher knife…"So Dekah trained you to take her place."

Another proud smile. "We've always been close, like mother and daughter."

Outside, the wind pushed against the house, and I felt it shudder. Maybe the shaking emanated from me, because my next question was truly fearful. "Were you the one who cut Nicole?"

If anything, her smile grew wider. "Of course! By then Dekah could hardly dress herself, let alone carry out a proper cutting, but she helped me by holding the girls down. Numerous times."

I felt sick. Nicole had heard Dekah's accent and, blindfolded, thought the African woman had been her cutter. She'd been wrong. The real butcher was her own mother.

"Your daughter could have died!"

She shrugged again. "It would have been her own fault."

"*Her* fault?" Even the wind outside seemed shocked, pausing for a moment before it resumed its assault on the house.

Annoyed, she repeated, "Yes, *her* fault. Just like that other girl, Sahra Hassan, the stupid child they've been calling Precious Doe. I told that little brat not to move, but no, she had to scream and fight. Damned little precious about *her*, I tell you! Afterward, I spoke quite harshly to her mother for not raising her better. But I got my money anyway. A cutter learns to always get her money up front, just in case. Dekah taught me that. She's always been a good business woman."

Eighty-five dollars plus bandages.

Controlling my disgust, I asked, "If you and Dekah were like mother and daughter, why did you kill her?" But I already knew the answer. I just wanted to keep Olivia talking, to keep that knife away from my throat. Like most killers, she enjoyed parading her brilliance in front of a captive audience.

"When the sheriff picked Dekah up, she was so frightened of him that she almost blurted out everything then, but she managed to hang on. Still, I knew that it was just a matter of time. No one in America understands the good work we cutters do, the harmony we bring to families. If my mother had cared enough for my father or for me, things would have been different."

Her expression went distant, but before I could make a grab for the knife, she recovered herself. "Let's just say the home I grew up in was…what's the word Daniel always used? *Disharmonious.* Yes, that's it. *Disharmonious.* Mother was…"

Her voice faded again, but she recovered herself quickly. "Let's just say Mother was given to temptation. The cutting Dekah and I do, it removes temptation and restores order. *Harmony.* If I'd cut Nicole earlier like Dekah suggested, she wouldn't have fallen for that awful boy. No baby, no adoption, nothing but harmony."

Her logic escaped me, but sane people always have trouble understanding the insane. "Did getting cut bring you harmony, Olivia?"

She considered that, then shook her head. "I was cut too late. By then, the sin of lust had already destroyed my marriage. But Daniel didn't turn me out, as most righteous men would have. He kept me, sheltered me, took care of me."

"*After* you'd consented to the cutting, right?"

"He was compassionate, not stupid. What if I sinned again?"

And disrupted all that lovely harmony in your home? "Speaking of your husband, Olivia, why did you kill him?" I had already figured out the motive, but I needed to hear her say it. That shot to his face revealed immense rage.

Some of that rage now showed in her face. "He told me he'd tried to hold the marriage together, but it wasn't working. He said he needed someone who had never been defiled, a virgin, not an adulteress."

I cast my mind back to the white-clad Women For Freedom and the pretty redhead named Elaine. "He was leaving you for Elaine?"

"After all I'd done for her! I cut her myself, to make certain nothing bad happened."

"*You* cut Elaine?" I had to stop and take a breath before asking the next question. "Olivia, did you cut all those women?"

"Who else? With Dekah sick, I was the best cutter around." Her laughter came in high, excited peals. "The *only* cutter, now!"

Only a couple of pieces left to finish the puzzle. "The gun, the .38. Where did you get it? A local gun shop?"

"Daniel bought it from a farmer in Kenya, saying he needed it to protect us because the border was a very dangerous place."

So was the Hall household. "You tried to kill me, too, didn't you? How did you know I liked to walk by the river?"

A giggle. "I didn't. I was down there searching for Nicole when I heard you stomping around. It was too good an opportunity to miss."

I would have asked her why she carried a handgun while searching for her runaway daughter, but I didn't want to hear the answer. She knew that Nicole, in order to protect Aziza, was ready to tell the sheriff everything. Olivia might have decided that it was better to have a dead daughter than a talkative one.

A tone of self-pity leaked into her voice. "What am I supposed to do now? The way I am..." she looked down, "...no man will want me. No American man, anyway. They expect passion from their wives, not submission."A tear rolled down her cheek.

As she continued to mutter about her ruined future, I saw a chance to escape from the house before she took that obscene knife to me. I wouldn't have time to open Nicole's tiny window, only five feet away, but smashing through it held its own dangers since glass could cut more viciously than a blade. Instead, I would have to try for the front door, even though a knife-wielding madwoman barred the bedroom's only exit.

So I rushed her.

If Olivia had stood an inch more to the left or right, my tactic might have worked, but she was in the middle of the doorway. To get by her, I chanced the knife.

I almost made it.

As I raised my right arm to knock her out of the way, the knife connected. The pain in my forearm slowed my forward progress just enough that she was able to raise the knife and brought it down again.

Instead of trying to run, I feinted right, then grabbed her cutting arm with my good left hand and jerked her forward and down. Once she was off-balance, I brought up my right knee, smashing her in the face. Then I karate-chopped the side of her neck.

The knife fell with her, rolling under the bed.

There was no time to retrieve it. The blow I had given her with my left hand wasn't my strongest, and I was spurting blood, which meant a nicked artery. In the split second that I stood there trying to figure out my next move, she slipped her hand under the bed and scrabbled for the knife.

Holding my slashed right arm tight to stem the blood loss as much as possible, I staggered into the parlor and headed for the front door, only to confront the deadbolt. With only one hand working, and that one slippery with blood, my attempts at turning the lock were clumsy. The lock didn't budge. Behind me I heard footsteps.

Olivia had almost caught up to me.

"I'll kill you for that!"she screamed.

I dared a glance behind and saw her raising the knife again.

Remembering that open kitchen door, I spun away from the lock and ran for my life. But I hadn't noticed the shopping bags in the middle of the floor. At the last moment I tired to veer around them but in my rush hit the corner of the coffee table and knocked the coffee server and photographs to the floor.

"No!" Olivia screamed. "No!"

Barreling through the passageway leading into the kitchen, I glanced over my shoulder. Pursuit forgotten, Olivia fell to her knees and slapped at the candle's flames as they licked at Reverend Hall's photographs.

Then, to my shock, she dropped the knife and picked up a burning picture, the one that showed Hall standing open-armed on the steps of Freedom Temple.

"Oh, Daniel! Why?" she whimpered, ignoring the flames that inched toward her sleeve.

Jesus, she still loved him. In my pity, I called, "Olivia! Drop it! Get away from there!" I didn't want her dead, just in prison.

When I turned toward her to pull her away from the flames, she lifted her head and glared. As her sleeve began to smolder, she picked up the knife again.

As far as I was concerned, that changed everything.

She was crazy, I was bleeding, and I was getting the hell out of there.

Battling through the howling wind to my Jeep, I somehow managed to shift it into gear with my left hand. As soon as I pulled onto the highway, I steered with my knees toward Los Perdidos while I reached over and pulled my cell out of my carry-all. Within seconds I was telling Sheriff Avery what had just happened, was still happening.

A safe distance from Olivia and her knife, I coasted to the side of the road, and using the drawstring of my Phoenix Suns windbreaker, made a tourniquet to wrap around my injured arm. When the rain began, it was every bit the downpour I had expected. An even stronger wind blasted sheets of it through the Jeep's window. The rush of adrenaline that kept me moving was wearing off, and I no longer had the strength to protect myself from rain or madwomen.

Not knowing whether I would live or die, I rested my head on the steering wheel and let the darkness take me.

Chapter Twenty-eight

The ruins of the parsonage and church—despite the rain, the flames had engulfed it, too—no longer smoked when Warren drove me there the next day. He had flown in the night before, even beating Jimmy to the hospital, and had not left my side since. After seeing for himself that I was all right, Jimmy returned to Scottsdale, but Warren stayed on, pointing out that the seventy-six stitches in my arm necessitated a chauffeur.

For once, I didn't argue.

The stench of burned wood and flesh permeated the air, reminding me of another burned building, another predator. As I exited the rental car, Warren remained behind, knowing that I needed to handle this alone.

At the edge of the destruction, Sheriff Avery waited for me. "I wonder why she didn't make it out," he mused. "She could have escaped through the rear door, like you."

"She didn't want to."

He shook his head. "I don't understand any of it."

Neither did I, not really. Why would a woman willingly give up the right to her own body? Why would she, like a lamb led to the killing floor, just lie down and let someone cut her flesh away? Even worse, why would she inflict the same horror on her own daughter?

But she was dead and couldn't answer my questions.

So I asked one of Avery, instead. "Where's that item you called me about?"

The day before, Olivia's burned body had been removed. Since then, the firemen, aided by deputies, had been retrieving as much evidence from the ruins as they could.

Among them was the cutting knife.

Now the knife lay harmless in an evidence bag at the sheriff's office, never again to be used to cripple little girls. But the knife wasn't the reason I'd asked Warren to bring me to the scene of Olivia Hall's crimes.

"Over here," the sheriff said, leading me to a small pile where his deputies had deposited some of the debris. Among the charred material was a color photograph. "Damnedest thing I ever saw, Lena. It's scorched around the edges, but you can see their faces."

Yes, I could see their faces.

A group of people stood beside a white bus. Among them was a smiling couple holding hands with a little girl around four. The camera focus was so crisp you could read the slogan on the bus' license plate: *New Mexico. Land of Enchantment.*

Sheriff Avery sounded bewildered. "The woman looks a lot like you, but the clothes aren't right."

With some difficulty, I kept my voice level. "That's not me. As for the clothes, the picture was taken thirty years ago. Fashions change."

Yes, the woman's resemblance to me ended at her blue eyes. I had inherited my green ones from the red-headed man beside her.

Next to the smiling couple stood a young Daniel Hall, appearing to be no more than twenty. Even then, he looked crazy.

This was why the picture wall at the parsonage had haunted me so. A part of me had recognized this scene, these people, but I had been so intent on finding out what had happened to Precious Doe that the truth of the photograph never registered on my conscious mind. But when Hall first saw me climbing the steps to his parsonage, he knew exactly who I was.

I reached down.

The sheriff's hand shot out, grabbed mine. "You can't touch that picture. It's evidence."

"Yes. It is," I said.

Finally understanding, he released his grip.

I picked up the photograph and pressed it to my heart.

Then I took my parents home.

Chapter Twenty-nine

By Friday I was well enough to attend the regular *Desert Eagle* production meeting in Los Angeles, but because of the traffic, I arrived even later than Hamilton "Ham" Speerstra. The chairs around the conference table were already taken by a gaggle of surgically-altered actors, their rapacious managers, the series director, and a few shame-faced writers, so I was forced to drag in an extra chair and sit beside the obnoxious child actor, Cory Keane. With the outside temperature a balmy seventy-five, he was dressed in his dark Armani suit.

The meeting had already moved on from the silly script to costuming, and the mood in the charcoal-on-charcoal room was testy.

"From now on, the Indians will wear loincloths," Speerstra announced, "and that's all there is to it."

"Cherokees—and I'm playing a half-Cherokee woman, remember—wouldn't be caught dead in a loincloth," Angel pointed out. "I Googled it."

Speerstra shook his head. "Google schmoogle. An Indian's an Indian. Besides, our viewers want to see you in a loincloth."

"Will it never end?" the actress muttered, not quite under her breath. I had never seen her so angry. Continually cast in the early days of her career as the archetypical dumb blonde, she was now struggling to change the public's perception of her. *Desert Eagle* was to be her chance to leave the T&A roles behind for good.

I opened my mouth to explain the evolution in tribal clothing and customs throughout the centuries when Stage Mom, Kelli Keane, proclaimed herself in agreement with Angel.

"I think loincloths are a bad idea, Mr. Speerstra. A *really* bad idea. All that exposed skin. This is a children's show, right? And Miss Grey in a loincloth and bra top would be too revealing for a children's show. I mean, She's *huge*."

As one, we all looked at Angel's chest.

Used to stares, Angel didn't take offense. "Mrs. Keane, having a child in the cast doesn't mean that *Desert Eagle* is a children's show. However, on this one issue you're right. Me flouncing around in a loincloth just isn't appropriate. Same for Cory there." She flashed the boy a smile.

Cory ignored her, but to Speerstra, he whined, "I want the loincloth. Medicine men always wear loincloths." He snuck a quick peek at his mother, whose over-collagened lips pulled into a frown.

Perplexed, Angel said, "You're not a medicine man, you're a medicine *boy*."

Leaning away from his mother, Cory crossed his arms in front of his chest. "I *said*, I *want* the loincloth!"

His mother moved her chair closer to him. Cory moved his further away so that it almost touched mine. "Loincloth or nothing!" he pouted.

With a bump, Stage Mom closed the gap between them. "Behave, Cory." Her hand disappeared under the table.

Cory's eyes suddenly filled with tears.

Then I knew for sure. And I was, oh, so sick of it.

"You bitch." I stood up, detoured around the boy, and hit Stage Mom in the face so hard with my good hand that her chair toppled over with her in it. As blood gushed from her nose, she sprawled on the thick charcoal gray carpet, her silk blouse rucked up to reveal a chartreuse thong and a stretch-marked stomach.

I turned to Angel. "Call Child Protective Services."

Angel, no dummy, whipped out her cell and made the call.

Speerstra rose to his feet. "What the hell?"

Stage Mom stayed on the floor, gazing blankly at the ceiling. Not that she could do anything else, since my foot was on her chest, and pressing down hard.

Gentling my voice, I said to the child, "Cory, take off your suit coat."

He hung his head. "Mom said not to, not ever, except when we're alone in the house."

When his mother started to say something, I increased my foot's pressure on her chest, and she shut her ridiculous mouth again.

"You're mom's not in charge here, Cory. Take off your coat."

His arms were stiff, so Angel, now off the phone, helped him. When the coat peeled away, everyone in the room—except for his mother—gasped. The child's arms were black with bruises from his mother's pinch marks. Red cigarettes burns added color to the wound salad. I had no doubt that the same ugly pattern was repeated on other areas of his body.

Like some other mothers I'd run into lately, Stage Mom had been willing to maim her child to further her own needs. Only in her case, the cruelty hadn't been perpetrated to ensure sexual frigidity, it had been done for the money Cory's stardom would bring.

All the brattiness had disappeared from Cory's face. Now he just looked lost.

"That's why you wanted to wear a loincloth, isn't it?" I said to him. "You wanted someone to see what was happening. You wanted help, but couldn't figure out any other way to get it."

He said nothing, and he was careful not to look in his mother's direction.

My heart ached for him. "It'll be all right now, Cory."

At least I hoped so.

The flight back to Arizona was uneventful, mainly because I knew better than to allow myself to fall asleep. Therefore, no nightmares rose from my past, only memories.

I was seven. I was running away from my, what? My third foster home? Fourth? Bernie and Edna...Landis? No, Lansing. Yes, that was the name. The Lansings weren't bad people, my adult self realized, just bewildered human beings trying their best to create a temporary home for a deeply disturbed child, a child still recovering from the bullet wound that had almost killed her.

But the Lansings weren't my parents, and I didn't belong with them. As badly damaged as I was, I knew that.

For some reason I believed that if I ran east far enough and fast enough, I would finally come to the place where the trees grew thick and tall, where our house sat at the edge of the creek, and the deer came to drink at sunset. East where my mother waited to hold me tight, east where my red-headed father would caress my hair, east where....

East to the place we'd lived before it all went wrong.

I didn't make it, of course.

The Lansings lived in Scottsdale, less than a half mile west of the Salt River Pima/Maricopa Indian Reservation, a rugged tract of land in the scorching Sonoran Desert.

And I had run away in July, when the temperatures sometimes rose to a hundred and twenty degrees.

The plane hit a spot of turbulence and I braced my hands on the armrests.

"I hate this," gasped my seat mate, a woman dressed for a business meeting.

"Turbulence? Or flying, period?" I asked sympathetically, having endured a few rough flights myself.

"Flying, period. It scares the crap out of me."

I wasn't crazy about flying, either, but I'd become used to it. "It gets easier."

Her fingers clenched the armrests. "Really? I'll have you know I've been flying twice a week for three years, and I haven't noticed it getting any better." She was around thirty, attractive. From the severity of her suit I guessed she was some kind of professional, an attorney, perhaps.

"Work requirement?" I asked, more to distract her than from curiosity.

She shook her head. "Long distance marriage. He lives in L.A., I live in Tucson."

I wanted to say something optimistic, but I wasn't in the mood to lie. Instead, I rested my head against the seat and opened myself to memory again.

I had started off early in the morning carrying two cans of Tab filched from the Lansing's refrigerator. The first mile across the desert passed without too much trouble, but when the heat set in, both Tabs disappeared down my parched throat. As the sun burned down, big black birds—vultures—wheeled in the sky.

Yet somehow I kept running for two more hours, always headed east. East toward home, east toward the house by the creek.

By midday, the rising temperature had weakened me. No strength left, I sank to my knees by a rock. At first I was too exhausted to care when one of the big black birds landed near by, even though it seemed the size of a dragon. The fear came when the vulture hopped toward me, slashing its beak like a knife.

"Go away, Bird!" I rasped.

I glanced at the empty Tab can in my hand. Not desert-wise, I'd hoped to find a stream where I could fill it again.

"Bird! I'll hit you!"

The vulture continued its progress.

I threw the can. It bounced without harm off those glossy feathers, but at least halted the bird's advance.

I reached out and snatched the can from where it had rolled almost back to me, then filled it with rocks and dirt. "I'll hurt you bad this time!" I warned.

The vulture paid no attention, just hopped forward again as several of its friends swooped down to join the impending feast.

"I mean it, Bird! I'll hurt you! I'll hurt you all!" I didn't really want to hurt any of them, but I'd seen birds that looked like them doing terrible things to dead animals. I didn't want those things done to me, so I had to make them go away.

The Tab can felt heavier now, more like a weapon. *"I'll break your wing!"* I screamed to the lead bird. *"Then your friends will eat you!"*

The bird kept coming.

I threw the can and struck the bird in the head. With a squawk, it flew away. But the others remained.

The fight had taken a lot out of me, and I slumped against the rock. Sensing weakness, the rest of the vultures closed in. I had no weapon now, just my hands.

I clenched my fists. I would fight them until they ate away my fingers, then I would battle them with my palms.

One bird reared up and…

A gunshot.

In a great flurry of black, the birds flew away.

Through the roaring in my ears, I heard a man's deep voice. *"Well, now, Little Miss. What're you doing way out here on our Rez? Why don't I take you home?"*

I gazed up into a mahogany-colored face, gentle brown eyes, and saw a policeman holstering his gun. His Salt River Tribal Police name tag said…

SGT. JAMES EDWARD SISIWAN.

As the Southwest flight pierced the clouds on its approach to Tucson International Airport, I sat amazed by this new memory.

My rescuer had been my partner's father.

James Edward Sisiwan.

A man who believed in bringing lost children home.

Chapter Thirty

The next day Los Perdidos lay Precious Doe to rest.

Or rather, the town laid *Sahra Hassan* to rest. DNA testing proved that Precious Doe was definitely the child of Jwahir and Fawzia Hassan, formerly of Somalia, Los Perdidos, and Phoenix, now inmates of the Maricopa County Jail.

From the turnout at the cemetery, you would think a governor was being buried, or at least, a congressman. Los Perdidos' entire Muslim community was in attendance, along with Africans of every faith, cowboys, business owners, teachers, students, the sheriff and all his deputies. Writing furiously on their notepads were several reporters, including Max and Bernice Broussard.

Standing next to me was Warren, who had flown in from Beverly Hills. Afterward, we'd decided, he would return with me to Scottsdale where despite our damages, we would attempt to build a life together.

Behind us, Los Perdidos loomed as deserted as a ghost town.

Sahra's parents, the ones who had ordered her cut, then dumped her in the desert when she bled to death, had not been allowed to attend their daughter's funeral. The Phoenix judge refused to release them on bail, arguing that his decision was for their own safety. He might even have been telling the truth, because someone in CPS had leaked the information that each of the Hassans' daughters had been cut, one so badly that she not only walked with a permanent limp, but would never be able to have children. So much for keeping her "pure" for marriage. Now, according to the Hassans' tribal beliefs, she was worthless anyway.

Jimmy, determined to see Sahra Hassan safely delivered to her final home, had driven down to Los Perdidos in his new truck. He looked so much like his dead father that I wanted to reach out and hug him. But I didn't. Pimas are funny about that sort of thing, although they do make exceptions for terrified children they find cowering in the desert.

Sahra's new grave was on a gentle slope, looking east across the Dragoons, where Geronimo and his band of free Apaches once roamed, east toward the land of her birth. I had paid a premium to ensure that she would be shaded by a palo verde tree, forever surrounded by desert wild flowers.

Lee Casey was there, too, along with his employees. He had given them the morning off with pay so they could attend the funeral. I watched him across the small casket, noting his guilt-shaded eyes. Not guilt over Sahra, probably. Casey had no way of knowing what kind of man her father was when he employed him. As a rule, CEOs didn't delve into their employee's personal lives and cultural beliefs, but that might be about to change.

No, Casey felt guilt about something else.

I looked down the hill to the rocky edge of the cemetery where Floyd Polk, burned to ashes by a group of vigilantes, lay in an unmarked grave.

No trees. No flowers. No visitors.

Casey's eyes met mine. He knew that I knew.

Not far from Polk's grave were those of Reverend Daniel and Olivia Hall. Paid for and attended by the Women For Freedom, the fresh mounds were heaped with flowers. How long would the Women's misguided devotion last, especially since CPS had removed some of their daughters from their custody? Maybe someday, freed from the Reverend's influence, the Women could begin to recover from his malignant control and begin the long process of healing. Until then, they would hate themselves as much as he had.

What was it Reverend Hall had whispered as I walked away from our first meeting?

Control women and you control the world.

A martyr to Hall's hatred of all things female, Precious Doe had died. So had Tujin Rafik. And across the world, so had hundreds of thousands of little girls.

But some survived.

As I looked across Precious Doe's grave, I saw Nicole, that gallant heroine whose selflessness had saved a little girl from butchery. She stood in the crowd with Raymundo, and for the first time in her own sad life, fortune smiled on her. While Child Protective Services labored to track down her biological father, she had been removed from the group home and placed in foster care with Selma Mann.

Selma, who had taken that mysterious trip to Africa in order to adopt a child, had failed when the tribal elders decided to cease all foreign adoptions. Maybe fortune would smile on her someday, too, and Nicole would make her an honorary grandmother.

Raymundo, although he knew exactly what had been done to Nicole, held his beloved girl as tenderly as ever.

Sometimes love does conquer all.

In my carry-all was a copy of the photograph I found in the burned-out rubble of the parsonage. After Jimmy had Photoshopped the damaged original, I could now see the optimism in my parents' faces as they stood beside the white bus that was to take them to Phoenix, where I would eventually be shot and left for dead.

But not by my parents.

My parents had loved me.

Loved me enough to die for me.

Some day I would avenge them.

My partner, Jimmy, son of Pima Tribal Police Sergeant James Edward Sisiswan, would some day track down that white bus. It might be in a junkyard in New Mexico or rusting away in the Arizona desert, but wherever it was, he would find it.

Jimmy wasn't a cop's son for nothing.

One day I would travel to that white bus and run my hands across its side. In that moment I would unravel the secret of my life.

Words in Arabic jolted me from the future to the present. A newly-arrived imam was speaking. His words were brief, and quickly translated into English.

A prayer for compassion, a prayer for peace.

With that, the service was over. People moved toward their cars.

There was only one thing left to do. I stepped to the edge of the grave and tossed in a rose—white, for an innocent girl who had not been allowed to become a woman.

With one final look at the child's tombstone, I walked away.

That tombstone, my final gift to her, read SAHRA HASSAN.

But she would always be Precious to me.

Author's Note

On June 23, 1993, Lorena Bobbitt cut off her husband's penis and the media went crazy.

On June 23, 1993, the same thing happened to thousands of children aged two to twelve, but the media ignored the story. What was the difference?

There are three answers to that question: the victims in the second instance were female; they were black or Muslim; and finally, the misleading word used for the genital amputations the children suffered was *circumcision*.

Language is a powerful thing. By using euphemisms and inaccurate wordage, we blunt the facts, allowing us to keep a clean, safe distance from messy truths. Thus we reduce rape to "molestation," the slaughter of civilians in warfare to "collateral damage," and the unanesthetized amputation of a little girl's genitals to "circumcision."

Few of us are disturbed by the idea of circumcision. We all know (and are sometimes married to) circumcised men who are completely healthy and experience no pain or sexual difficulties from the procedure. Furthermore, doctors tell us that male circumcision helps ward off disease in both the male and his sexual partner. So what's the big deal when it's done to girls?

The procedure performed on little girls—approximately 150 million of them world-wide—is not circumcision, although its practitioners call it that. Instead, the procedure is exactly the same as that performed on John Bobbitt—a *complete amputation* of the external genitalia (Bobbitt was luckier than the girls; Lorena left his testicles alone). Some doctors say the procedure is more akin to castration than circumcision *(see Bibliography, Dr. Mohamed Badawi)*. In the very worst, but most common cases, a child's clitoris, as well as her minor and major labia, is completely amputated and her vagina sewn shut *(see Appendix I)*.

As for after care, there is another difference between John Bobbitt and the thousands of little girls whose genitals were amputated the same day he suffered his injuries. Bobbitt was given immediate medical treatment, and his penis successfully reattached.

By contrast, when girls' genitals are amputated, their wounds are left untreated, which causes a reported 20% to 30% of them to die from shock, blood loss, and/or infection. Of the children who survive their initial amputations, a large number die later from septicemia because of inadequate passage of the menstrual flow. Many die years later from childbirth complications as their body attempts to pass a full term infant through a mutilated birth canal; fifty percent of their infants also die *(see Appendix II)*.

Another complication arises when the now-genital-less girls' wounds are sewn up with fishing line or upholstery thread, a standard procedure. The healing process eventually creates large areas of scar tissue which contort the upper thigh muscles, sometimes resulting in permanent lameness.

The horrors don't end there. The genital amputations are often performed on multiple children at once with the same unsterilized cutting object, which ranges from a tin can lid to a butcher knife. These unsterilized conditions spread HIV and other communicable diseases.

Since the genital amputation of little girls has been proven to have such severe consequences, the obvious question is: why perform this procedure at all? The answer is that in many countries, a girl's sexual purity is considered more important than her life.

In an article published by the United Nations Office for the Coordination of Humanitarian Affairs, Nashiru, a cutter among Kenya's 400,000-strong Maasai tribe (where nearly 100% of that tribe's girls undergo the procedure), defended her work. "When you cut a girl, you know she will remain pure until she gets married, and that after marriage, she will be faithful," Nashiru said. "But when you leave a girl uncut, she sleeps with any man and brings disease into the community."

Nashiru does have a point. The procedure, and the damage it inflicts on the vagina and surrounding areas, causes such excruciating pain that the girls experience sexual relations as torture, not pleasure.

Like many other cutters, Nashiru treats the wounds she inflicts with a paste made from cow dung and milk fat, so in addition to the usual complications, many of her patients die from tetanus. This is of little consequence to Nashiru. Like all other cutters, she receives her full cutting fee for services rendered, whether the children live or die.

As so often happens in human history, various myths have sprung up to explain the unexplainable. The Maasai, as in other highly populated Sub-Saharan African tribes (such as the Bantu and Somali) which practice genital amputation, believe that a woman's clitoris will sever a man's penis during intercourse. They also believe that if the clitoris is not amputated, it will pierce an infant's skull during childbirth, killing it.

In light of these bizarre beliefs, it is tempting to think that genital amputation takes place only among the uneducated. However, this is not the case.

When asked by the *Hartford Observer News* on Dec. 10, 1996, about the medical ethics of carrying out genital amputations on little girls, Dr. Munir Mur, a physician and highly-respected professor of gynecology at Cairo's Ain Shams University, answered, "Most of our parents, mothers, aunts, sisters and so on have been doing this for years, and no one was complaining."

Physicians themselves can be responsible for much of the carnage. Egyptian newspapers reported that in one single day in 1996, Ezzat Shehat, M.D., performed three genital amputations in a Nile Valley village. One four-year-old girl died and one three-year-old girl died, which brought that day's death rate to 66%. On the girls' death certificates, Dr. Shehat listed the deaths as due to natural causes, the usual reported reason for these deaths.

In sheer numbers, most genital amputations are performed in Muslim countries such as Egypt and Somalia. With the rise of fundamentalist Islam, the practice appears to be growing, because some fundamentalist religious leaders have begun demanding it, even though the Koran does not advocate the practice.

In 1981, at Cairo's University of The Great Sheikh of Al-Azhar, a religious ruling (fatwa) was issued by the Egyptian Fatwa Committee on FGM (Female Genital Mutilation, another common euphemism for genital amputation). The ruling stated, "Parents must follow the lessons of Mohammed and not listen to medical authorities because the latter often change their minds. Parents must do their duty and have their daughters circumcised."

Mohammed never taught any such thing, a fact the fundamentalist imams (religious leaders) ignored.

In explaining his role in issuing the fatwa, Gad Haq Ali Gad Haq, a senior religious leader at Al-Azhar, said, "Girls who are not circumcised when young have a sharp temperament and bad habits" (*Hartford Observer News*, 1996).

In an article published by the *British Medical Journal*, August 3, 1996, Cairo shop owner Mahmood Hassan was enthusiastic about the fatwa. "A girl must be circumcised, or she will grow up like a man," Hassan said. "Who will marry her if she is this way?"

So pervasive in Egypt is the belief that genital amputation is necessary for little girls a national survey conducted in 2000 revealed that from 75% to 97 %—from *30 to 40 million women* between to ages of 15 and 49—had undergone the procedure. Although the procedure has been outlawed in Egypt, the law is not enforced.

What does any of this have to do with the West, and specifically the U.S.?

Because with the increased migration to the West, female genital amputation is now being practiced here.

In a recent study, the U.S. Department of Health and Human Services estimated that 168,000 girls in the U.S. have undergone the procedure or were at risk of being subjected to it in the future. The plight of one of those girls actually made its way into the nation's newspapers.

In 2005, in Georgia, a man named Khalid Adem, an immigrant from Ethiopia during a U.S. government refugee resettlement program, was convicted of aggravated battery and cruelty to children because he amputated his two-year-old daughter's genitals at his Atlanta apartment. The Adem case was touted by the media as the first documented case of female genital amputation in the U.S., but this is inaccurate. U.S. court cases referring to the practice date back to the early 1970s, but those cases were sanitized under the label of "child abuse" and handled in closed judges' chambers. They received little to no media attention.

In Europe, the genital amputations of young girls has reached epidemic proportions. The practice has now been found in Australia, Canada, Italy, France, Germany, the Netherlands, Sweden, Spain, and Switzerland. In Britain, 200,000 girls are reportedly at risk, and in Norway, three imams were recently prosecuted for demanding the genital amputation of all Norwegian Muslim girls.

France has been particularly hard hit by this scourge. In 1977, the French Family Planning Association protested the problem to the World Health Organization with little result. In 2000, studies found that the number of endangered girls had risen to 25,000 *in the Paris region alone*. With a skyrocketing death rate among female immigrant children who were subjected to the procedure, the French media overcame its squeamishness and began writing about the problem. Lit by the glare of publicity, the first of a string of genital amputation cases arrived in the French courts.

In one of those cases, Hawa Greou, an immigrant from Mali living in Paris, was sentenced to eight years in prison for the genital amputations of forty-eight little girls, some as young as two years old.

She charged $30 to $80 per child.

Appendix I:
WARNING—GRAPHIC

TYPES OF FEMALE GENITAL AMPUTATION:
Type I: Amputation of the clitoris (clitorectomy)
Type II: Amputation of the clitoris and labia minora
Type III: Amputation of the clitoris and all external genitalia, plus sewing up (narrowing) of the vagina, which is called infibulation

These procedures are commonly performed by kitchen knives, glass shards, can lids, razor blades, and sharpened stones; the amputations are also performed by the introduction of corrosive substances such as acids into the targeted areas. Anesthesia is not used.

DESCRIPTION:
The most severe form of genital amputation, yet done on millions of girls ages 2 through 6, is Type III, also called "infibulation." Infibulation cuts away the entire genital area and replaces the vulva with a wall of scar tissue stretching from the pubis to the anus. A pencil-sized opening, sometimes reinforced with a narrow tube such as a plastic drinking straw, is left to allow urine and menstrual blood to pass through. After the procedure, the stumps of the labia are sewn together. They eventually join into a solid mass via the scar-forming process, thus sealing the girl. To facilitate the sealing process, the child's legs are tied

together for approximately two to four weeks to prevent her from opening the wound.

Once the vagina is sealed, intercourse is impossible, which is the reason for performing the procedure in the first place. When the girl is married (usually between ages of 12 and 16), the scar tissue is so tough and pervasive that the husband must reopen the girl's vagina with a knife. Some girls bleed to death at this point, but most live. Because of the vagina's tendency to heal back into the sewn-shut state, the husband frequently must re-cut the vagina open in order for intercourse to take place.

Appendix II

PREVALENCE OF FEMALE GENITAL AMPUTATION:
The World Health Organization estimates that more than 140 million girls have undergone genital amputation, with an average of two million per year currently undergoing the procedure. The practice is common in 28 African countries, as well as Asia and the Middle East (see below). WHO's study found that 83% of girls in the Sudan had undergone the procedure, 73% of women in Ethiopia, 40% in Ghana. In an area stretching from Senegal in West Africa, to Somalia on the East coast, as well as from Egypt in the north to Tanzania in the south, it is estimated that more than 95% of all women and girls have undergone genital amputation.

COUNTRIES INVOLVED:
African countries—Benin, Burkina, Chad, Camaroon, Central African Republic, Cote d'Ivoire, Djibouti, Eritrea, Ethiopia, Gambia, Ghana, Guinea, Guinea-Bissau, Kenya, Liberia, Madeira, Mali, Mozambique, Mauritania, Nigeria, Tanzania, Togo, Uganda, Upper Volta, Senegal, Somalia, Sudan. In Sierra Leone, where the president's wife *personally* sponsored the cutting of 1,500 young girls to win votes for her husband, amputations are on the rise. That country's Minister of Social Welfare, Gender and Women's Affairs—a woman—threatened "to sew up the mouths" of those who preached against the amputations.

Middle Eastern countries—Egypt, western Iran (Kurdistan), northern Iraq, Israel (where Bedouins practice it), Jordan, Oman, Pakistan, Saudi Arabia and the United Arab Emirates; Southern Algeria, Syria, Yemen.

Asian countries—Malaysia, Indonesia, India.

HEALTH CONSEQUENCES:

Shock; blood loss leading to death; septicemia (blood poisoning), gangrene; tetanus; cysts and abscesses; urinary incontinence; necrosis of the vaginal wall; chronic pelvic disease; the complete closure of the vagina during the healing process; infertility; painful intercourse; serious childbirth difficulties; HIV transmission from unsterilized instruments. Mental health issues are also common because the child loses all ability to trust. After giving birth, young women who have been "cut" have trouble bonding with their children—especially the girls.

Bibliography

Books:

Cutting the Rose: Female Genital Mutilation—The Practice and the Prevention, Efua Dorkenoo

Desert Flower, a novel by Wawris Dirie, cut at the age of 5

Do They Hear You When You Cry, Fauziya Kassindja

[The] Excised, Evelyn Accad

[The] Female Circumcision Controversy, Ellen Gruenbaum

Female 'Circumcision' in Africa: Culture, Controversy, and Change, Shell-Duncan and Hernlund

Female Genital Cutting: Cultural Conflict in the Global Community, Elizabeth H. Boyle

Female Genital Mutilation: A Call to Global Action, Nahid Toubia

[The] Hidden Face of Eve: Women in the Arab World, Dr. Nawal El Saadawi, cut as a young girl.

Infidel, Ayaan Hirsi Ali

No Laughter Here, Rita Williams-Garcia (novel)

Possessing the Secret of Joy, Alice Walker (novel)

Prisoners of Ritual, Hanny Lightfoot-Klein

[The] Rape of Innocence—One Woman's Story of Female Genital Mutilation in the USA, Patricia Robinett

The River Between, Ngugi wa Thiong'o (novel)

Taking a Bath, Lynda B. Ukemenam

[The] Years of Rice and Salt, Kim Stanley Robinson (novel)

Films:

"Female Circumcision: Beliefs and Misbeliefs," a documentary showing the procedure being performed in a city street

"Fire Eyes," a documentary directed by Soraya Mire

"Moolaade'," a critically-acclaimed fictionalized account by Fatoumata Coulibaly

"Rites," a documentary by the American Anthropological Association

An episode of "Law and Order" also spotlighted the practice

Articles and papers:

American Academy of Pediatrics, "Female Genital Mutilation —Committee on Bioethics"

Badawi, Mohamed, "Epidemiology of Female Sexual Castration in Cairo, Egypt," presented at the First International Symposium on Circumcision, Anaheim, California, March 1-2, 1989

Baughman, Christopher, "Doctors Testify Surgeon Secretly Circumcised Woman," *The Advocate,* Baton Rouge, LA, Oct. 30, 1996

Burstyn, Linda, "Female Circumcision Comes to America," *The Atlantic Monthly,* 1996

Crossette, Barbara, "Mutilation Seen as Risk for the Girls of Immigrants," *The New York Times*, March 23, 1998

UNICEF Department of Information, "Position of UNICEF on Female Excision"

World Health Organization "Fact Sheet on Female Genital Mutilation," June 2000

For more information, write to:

Atlanta Circumcision Information Center, 2 Putnam Dr., NW, Atlanta, GA 30342

Equality Now, P.O. Box 20646, Columbus Circle Station, New York, NY 10023

FGM Awareness and Education Project, PO Box 6597 Albany, CA 94706

[The] Female Genital Cutting Education and Networking Project, PO Box 46715, Tampa, Fl. 33647-6715

RAINBO (Research, Actions & Information Network for Bodily Integrity of Women), 915 Broadway, Suite 1109, New York, NY 10010-7108

Women's International Network News, 187 Grant St, Lexington, MA 02173

Recommended websites:

The Female Genital Cutting Education and Networking Project www.fgmnetwork.org

The UN Office for the Coordination of Humanitarian Affairs www.irinnews.org/webspecials/FGM/45986.asp

American Society of Pediatrics: Committee on Bioethics http://aappolicy.aappublications.org/cgi/content/full/pediatrics%3b102/1/153

To receive a free catalog of Poisoned Pen Press titles, please contact us in one of the following ways:

Phone: 1-800-421-3976
Facsimile: 1-480-949-1707
Email: info@poisonedpenpress.com
Website: www.poisonedpenpress.com

Poisoned Pen Press
6962 E. First Ave. Ste. 103
Scottsdale, AZ 85251